THE MIRACLE
OF
DELILAH

MEAGAN DUX

First published by Meagan Dux, 2018
Copyright © 2018 Meagan Dux
Cover design by Orlando Media
Edited by Georgina Gregory

National Library of Australia
Cataloguing-in-Publication data:
The Miracle of Delilah/Meagan Dux
ISBN: (sc) 978-0-6482497-0-2
ISBN: (e) 978-0-6482497-1-9
Young adult – fiction

Making Magic Happen Academy books may be ordered through online booksellers or by contacting:
www.makingmagichappenacademy.com/www.meagandux.com

ALSO BY Meagan Dux

THE RISE OF DELILAH

DEDICATION

To my parents and my brothers, for not only being my home but for loving me when I wasn't loveable.

CHAPTERS

CHAPTER ONE
THE FALL

My mind is racing; I can hear people screaming; I can hear people trying to talk to me, but I can't answer. My head hurts, and my body feels weightless. I try to open my eyes, but they won't open. I try to talk, but my mouth won't move. My life is flashing before me. *Is this what it is like to die?* Suddenly, I can't hear anything. Everything has gone quiet and the darkness that has consumed me for the past few days takes me away, *again...*

I slowly open my eyes, and this time I can see. As my eyes open, I'm met by blurriness, which fades away after I blink a few times. I look around the room. There's nothing on the faded white walls except an emergency CPR poster. I'm in a room by myself, and there are no other beds or patients around. I look to the right of the bed I am lying in, and I notice Dakota sitting in the only chair in the room. She's got her head on her hands, and she is fast asleep. I try to move out from the blanket that is covering my lower body, desperate to get some fresh air, when Dakota suddenly wakes up.

"You're awake! Thank God!" she says as she gets up from the chair. "I thought we were going to lose you!" I notice she's starting to cry as she gently hugs me.

"What are – what are you doing here?" I gently say. My throat is burning, but I don't know why. I can't remember anything that has happened. *Why am I even in a hospital bed?* Dakota sits back in the chair and grabs my hand as she explains what happened.

"I had this horrible feeling in my stomach once I got off the phone with you on Friday night. My gut was telling me something was wrong. I tried to ignore it, but on Saturday morning it had gotten worse. I called mum and told her to make sure you went to Declan's. She told me you were going there, but Declan messaged me and said he hadn't heard from you, so I left the shoot I was at and got on the first flight I could. I knew you had gone to see dad, I could feel it, so when I got back to Perth, I raced to the house and ran upstairs, and I found you. Delilah, you were barely breathing." She starts to cry again as I try to remind myself of what happened. Everything is coming back to me, but it's still blurry.

"What happened? I don't remember anything," I mumble to Dakota, suddenly yelling at my mind. Why did I just say that? I don't want to relive it, but for some stupid reason, I want my sister to tell me her version of what happened. She still looks confused, but she answers my question anyway.

"You really don't know?" she asks, with a concerned look on her face.

I'm fighting the memories of that night off as they come flooding back. It hurts too much, and I don't want to think about it. I'm not strong enough to go over it, at least not yet anyway. Yet I want Dakota to tell me. Maybe I do need to relive that night again, maybe that's the only way I can get over it, or at least try to move on from it.

"No, please, tell me." She moves the chair closer to me before taking a deep breath.

"You went to see dad. I assume it didn't go very well. You went home and drank half a bottle of vodka and took some of mum's sleeping pills. I got to you just in time. I called an ambulance, and they raced you here. They pumped your stomach, and then they woke you up. You were only awake for about ten minutes before you fell back asleep. The doctor said you would be okay, but you've been asleep for a while now. They reassured us that it was a usual response, especially after what you've been through, but I was starting to worry. Jesus, Delilah. I know you're hurting, but why would you try to kill yourself?"

What? *Kill myself?* No, I wouldn't do that.

"Dakota, you know I wouldn't ever try to kill myself. I'm sorry I scared everyone, but I was just trying to stop the pain. I wasn't thinking clearly." I'm saying each word slowly as the burning sensation in my throat intensifies. I try to clear my throat before asking my sister another question. "Where's Cam? Has he been in to see me?" Dakota instantly looks down at the bed, avoiding my eyes at all costs. I know in that moment that he hasn't been around, and I feel indescribable pain race throughout my body.

"I called him and told him. He was worried about you, but he decided to stay away. I'm sorry." I try not to let the sadness show on my face.

"Can you get me some water, please?" I ask, wanting to distract myself, and my sister.

3

"Sure. Do you want anything to eat? You must be starving," she says as she gets up and fills a plastic cup with water from the jug sitting next to the bed.

"No, thank you. I'm not hungry, just thirsty." Dakota hands me the cup, and I slowly sip it, appreciating every drop of water that is cooling my burning throat.

"I'll be back in a second. The doctor told me to get him *if* ... I mean *when* ... you woke up." She walks out of the room, closing the door behind her. I sit up and look for my phone, desperately wanting to contact Cam. I need to see him. I want him to be here for me, and I *need* to tell him that.

I try to get up from the bed when Dakota comes back in with the doctor. He has black hair and thick black glasses resting on his nose. When he sees me trying to get up, he stops me.

"Whoa, Delilah, you've got to rest." He helps me get back into the bed. Once I'm resting back on the pillows, he smiles.

"Hi, I'm Doctor Reynolds. You've had quite an eventful 48 hours." He shakes my hand. "I'm just going to do a routine check. Can you tell me your full name, the month we're in, and the year we're in?" I follow the light from his small torch while answering the questions.

"Delilah Jade Walker, it's late May, and it's 2013."

"Good job. There's no damage to your eyes, and you got those answers right. That's a great sign. Delilah, I do need to talk to you about the seriousness of what has happened though."

I sigh, preparing to hear a lecture about the mistakes I have made. I know they are wrong, but I just don't think I am in the right frame of mind to have this kind of conversation right now.

"Dakota, do you mind waiting outside while I talk to your sister? You might want to call your family so they know Delilah's awake. I know they've been worried about her. They're welcome to come and see her when they're ready."

Dakota nods her head and, after grabbing her phone, she leaves the room. Doctor Reynolds looks back at me as he sits in the chair next to the bed.

"I know this may be hard for you, but can you tell me why you mixed alcohol and prescription medication together? Is this something you've done before?" He has a serious tone that almost scares me. I look over at him and he watches me closely.

"I know what I did was stupid. If you're trying to ask me if I have a drug and alcohol problem, I don't. I've just been going through a lot over the last few weeks and I was in a lot of pain, mentally and emotionally, and I guess physically too. I just wanted to take the edge off, and I thought that might help. Obviously it didn't."

I watch Doctor Reynolds as he writes in his notepad. I wonder why he's doing that, but I guess it's part of his job. Once he's finished writing his notes, he looks up at me, takes his glasses off and rubs his eyes.

"Delilah, sometimes life can overwhelm us and we struggle to find ways to cope. I know you don't have an issue with drugs, or alcohol. I've spoken to your family and they mentioned you don't drink very often, so I'm not worried about any form of substance abuse. I do worry that you may see alcohol and drugs as ways to escape the pain you feel, but they are not. In fact, they're a deadly combination. You were incredibly lucky to survive. If your sister hadn't gotten to you when she did, I'm afraid you wouldn't be here right now."

I try to listen to the words he's saying, but the more he talks, the more I remember things that happened before that night. Suddenly, the severity of what I've done hits me. I shake my head and try to focus on Doctor Reynolds, who's watching me carefully.

"Delilah, are you okay?" he asks as I meet his eyes. I nod my head and he continues.

"We run an excellent support program here. It's designed for people your age, and it's a safe place for you to talk about anything that's going on. It's a way to connect with other individuals who are struggling, and an excellent place to find people to lean on when you feel you can't turn to your family and friends. I'd really like you to check it out." He hands me a brochure, and I look through it, not bothering to read it.

"Please consider it. I'm not going to force you to go, but from experience, this group has helped young adults cope with stressful situations." I flash a fake smile at him as he gets up to leave.

"We're going to keep you in here for another day or two, and then we will re-evaluate you and make sure you're clear from any damage. If you are, you'll be able to go home. If there's anything I can do for you, don't be afraid to ask. I'm here until 7.00 p.m. tonight, and I'll be in again tomorrow morning." I thank him as he leaves the room.

Dakota comes in when the doctor is gone. "How'd you go?" she asks, sitting on the bed with me. I hand her the brochure.

"He wants me to go to a support group. He thinks it will help to talk about everything, although I don't see the point since mum and I both see Mandy."

Dakota reads the brochure before handing it back to me. "It looks good. I mean, it would probably be beneficial for you to talk to other people your age."

I consider her thoughts before deciding I'll look at it closely once I'm released and back in the comfort of my own home.

~

The next two days seem to drag on. My family and friends are in and out of my room at the hospital over the next 48 hours, and my mum makes sure there isn't a time that I am alone, other than when the visiting hours are over. I've watched the sunflowers my sister brought for me slowly die over my time here, and it has made me feel incredibly uncomfortable. On my final night in hospital, I can't sleep. I have finally been cleared, and I was told I'll be going home in the morning, but that doesn't change my sleep pattern. Which has become non-existent since I woke up two days ago. I lie awake, looking at the roof, trying to fight the things I am feeling. I feel intense pain throughout my whole body. It has become so intense that I can no longer ignore it, and it is virtually indescribable. I don't want to worry anyone. I figure it's just easier to keep it to myself. I just hope it will start to fade away once I leave the hospital.

~

My last day in hospital finally arrives. It is Tuesday morning, and at 9:00 a.m. my mum is in my temporary room, helping me get ready to leave. She hands me a bag full of clothes so I can get changed, which I appreciate since I've been in the same long,

7

uncomfortable, itchy, blue hospital gown for the past three days. I head into the bathroom and put my loose-fitting grey shorts, a white singlet, and an oversized hoodie on. I slip my feet into my Nikes and head back into the room, where Doctor Reynolds is talking to my mum.

"Hi, Delilah. How are you feeling?"

"Good, thank you. Happy to be going home," I say, with a slight laugh.

"I bet. I was just telling your mum about the support group. We don't want to force it onto you, but please consider it. If you decide it's what you want to do, just call me and let me know. I will schedule a time for you to go there. Take care of yourself, and if there's anything we can do to help you, you know where to find us."

He smiles and shakes my hand again, leaving the room. My mum looks at me and hugs me.

"I'm so glad you're okay. We will talk about everything when you're ready. Let's go home." I nod and follow her to the car, where I snuggle up in the passenger seat.

My mum and I barely talk on the way home, but I often catch her looking over at me, making sure I'm okay. I know she's worried about me, and I know I have put her through a lot over the last few days. I just hope she doesn't blame herself for suggesting I see my father. When we get home, she helps me inside before taking me into the lounge room.

"I've set up the couches here to accommodate you. I know these couches are comfier than the other ones in the front room, so you'll sleep better here. I'm going to stay down here too, just to keep you company." I look at her.

"Mum, please. I'm fine. I don't want to sleep down here. I want to sleep in my own bed, in my own room." She slumps into the couch.

"I'm sorry. I'm just worried about you. Come on, let me help you upstairs." She gets back up, grabs my pillows and blanket, and I follow her up the stairs. She opens my door and goes in, throwing my pillows and blanket on the bed before going over to the window and quickly opening it.

"Sorry, honey. I tried to get the smell out of your room, but it's so potent. I'll get some spray. That should help." She goes into the foyer and heads into the bathroom, searching for some air freshener.

I sit on my bed and smell the vodka still floating through the air. I shiver, thinking about the memories of that night. My mum comes back into my room a few minutes later holding a can of lavender air freshener. She sprays it through my room and sits next to me.

"Why did you do it, honey? Did you want to die because your relationship ended?" I look over at my mum, stunned by her question, but then I process it before I honestly answer her.

"No, mum. I didn't try to kill myself over Cam breaking up with me. I didn't even try to kill myself. I promise you, that wasn't my intention." Her eyes instantly glass over.

"Then what was it? I've been trying to understand it, but I just can't. I was so worried I was going to lose you."

I try my best to explain things. I know I should tell her about seeing my dad, but I'm worried she won't react well to the truth, but I don't have a choice.

"Mum, I'm going to tell you the truth, but you need to let me tell you everything before you react. I promise you I wasn't trying to kill myself. I was trying to numb the pain that I have felt since dad left. Yes, it intensified when Cam ended our relationship, but I was in pain long before that. I've been having dreams for years now. I remember certain things about dad, and they got more vivid as I started to look for him. I also didn't tell you the truth about where I was going that day. I went to dad's after you told me to see him. I thought it would help. I thought once he saw me, he'd want to fix things, but he didn't. He pushed me away, again. He kicked me out of his house, and he told me never to contact him again. Not only had I lost Cam, but I'd lost all hope of fixing things with dad. I felt incredibly insignificant. I felt like I didn't have anything to fight for and the mental, emotional and physical pain I was in wouldn't go away, so I tried to numb it. I didn't think about it being fatal. I made a mistake, and I know it almost cost me my life, and I'm so sorry I scared everyone. I just, I don't know, I just wanted a night where I didn't feel that level of pain."

I feel the familiar sensation of tears welling up in my eyes before they drop and run down my cheeks. My mum holds me while I cry.

"I'm so sorry he did this to you. He was always such a great father before everything changed, and I don't know why he won't forgive himself. I think it's time to make peace with the fact that he's not going to come back to us. As much as it hurts, we need to heal and move on. Otherwise, it's going to consume our lives forever, and honey, you deserve so much more."

Deep down I know she is right, but I need time to myself, to process everything that life has thrown at me. I need to find my own way to heal, so I can move on and live my life, for me.

"I know you're scared, but I think you should go to the support group. You can talk to people your own age, and you can see a therapist there. As much as Mandy helps, I think you need someone you can talk to without me there. Please, just think about it." I notice the fearful look that has taken over my mum's face.

"I'll think about it, I promise," I say.

"Try to get some sleep. I'll check on you soon."

She kisses my forehead before heading downstairs. I remake my bed and snuggle up, not bothering to change my clothes. I find my phone in my bag and pull it out. I have a few messages from Ryan and my other friends, but my heart sinks when Cam's name isn't on the screen. I read the messages and reply to Ryan.

Hey, sorry I haven't replied. I've been in hospital - it's a long story. I'll tell you all about it soon. Thanks for being concerned. I'm fine though. Speak soon.

~

The week slowly progresses. I have spoken to Melody, and we have decided that we want to release a statement. Since my covers started going viral, I have gathered a pretty impressive fan base and my album is becoming highly anticipated, which means more pressure on me to deliver something that people will connect with and love. I received quite a lot of support when news spread about my hospitalisation. Melody and my uncle have been getting calls and emails asking about it, and I am getting asked questions about it myself, but from it all, I've received worldwide support. People I don't know who have seen my videos have been sending me positive messages, wishing me well, and sending their love, and that means the world to me. These people don't know me personally, yet they took time from their day to wish me well, and nothing I can say or do will ever show how appreciative I am of that. I'm in a world of my own when I hear my email alert beep. I grab my phone and open my inbox. Melody has sent me a copy of the press release so I can read it before it goes out into the world. I open the attachment and read through it.

"One of our singer-songwriters, Delilah Walker, was involved in a recent event that caused her to be admitted to hospital. Delilah is currently facing a personal battle that we are helping her deal with. We have taken appropriate steps to help Delilah in the recovery process. The decision to continue working towards the release date of her debut album has been made, as per the request of Delilah herself. We will give Delilah all the support and time she needs, and we will go over future plans when she is ready. At this time, we ask you to please respect her and her family's privacy. Delilah has urged me to make everyone aware that she is appreciative of all the thoughts, messages, and support she has received throughout this difficult period.

Thank you,
Melody Cooper
Talent Scout and Manager, BrookeHouse Entertainment."

I immediately email Melody back, telling her I'm happy with everything she has written. I know it will be released later that day, and I acknowledge more attention will come my way. I just have to find a way to cope with it. I know deep down that the support group my family wants me to go to might be the answer to all my problems, or at least it might help to kick start my healing process.

I am sitting in my bed, watching my covers on *MusicNow* when Evan walks into my room, holding a cup of tea and a sandwich.

"Your mum thought you might be hungry," he says as he hands me the food. He gently places the cup on my bedside table, and goes to leave the room. I haven't seen or spoken to him much since I've been home; I feel like he is avoiding me. So, I try to clear the air, even though I don't know why things feel so tense.

"Evan?" He turns around and meets my gaze, and I notice the sad look on his face. "Would you mind staying with me? I don't like being alone." He smiles slightly and sits at the end of my bed. I start to eat my sandwich, and Evan looks up at me.

"I'm sorry if you think I've been avoiding you. To be honest, this week has been very confronting for me. My sister, Ashley, killed herself three years ago. She was my best friend, we were only a few years apart, and she was my only sibling. We had the same bond you have with your siblings, so learning to live without her has been difficult, to say the least. When your mum was told about you, it was like déjà vu. She was inconsolable, and she didn't know what to do; she just kept praying for you to wake up and be okay."

I put my food back onto the plate and place it next to the tea, moving closer to Evan, sensing his pain.

"I know we're not very close, not yet anyway, but we started to bond before everything happened,

13

and then you were in hospital, and I thought we might lose you too. The thought of having to go through another grieving process was almost unbearable. I found myself wanting to take your place. I desperately wished I could just take the pain from you, so you didn't have to hurt anymore, but I knew I couldn't do that. I know it's going to be hard, for all of us, but I'm going to be here to help you as much as I can. Please don't leave us."

I see the tears form in Evan's eyes, even though he tries to fight them off. I know that feeling all too well and at that moment, I know he is everything our family needs: he really is the missing piece of the puzzle.

"Evan, it's no secret that I've been searching for my father. I've been on this unstoppable mission to bring him home, but I didn't stop to consider that maybe he didn't want to be found. Perhaps he left for a reason, and maybe he's better off without us. I'm sorry your sister isn't here anymore; I can't even imagine what it would be like to lose a sibling."

Evan grabs my hands and looks at me. "Please know, I'm not trying to replace your father or the void he left, but if you give me a chance, we can have a relationship that we can be proud of. If I can be a father figure to you and your siblings, then I would be honoured to. I know I won't ever be *your* father, but if you give me a chance I, promise I'll try my best to be there for you 24/7."

I embrace him, deciding to let him know that I accept him: something I should have done a long time ago.

"I'm so sorry for not welcoming you earlier. I was scared that you and mum were trying to replace my father. He doesn't want me, he doesn't want us. I've always wanted a father, and he can't be that for me, so if we can work at getting to that place, then I'd like that."

He releases me and smiles. "I'd like that. I know it won't happen overnight, but we can make this transition together, and we can work on being a family."

After my conversation with Evan, I feel better, but I feel exhausted. I try my best to get some much-needed sleep, although after the last week it seems like I'll never be able to sleep properly again. My mind keeps racing, and I keep thinking about the buzz surrounding the snippets of the songs from my album that are now being released. There is a sense of excitement for my debut album. It is nearly completed, and the world has started to get to know me. My uncle, Melody and I have all agreed on moving forward with the album, and I am due to go back into the studio tomorrow, which I'm extremely nervous and excited about.

I am getting offers left, right and centre. For a singer, this is precisely where they want their life to be; it is a dream come true. But, there is a massive part of me that no longer cares. I want to push on with the album, just to get it done, but as far as touring or succeeding is concerned, it feels like none of that matters anymore. I have lost two people I love and need, and I am questioning how I can ever come back from that. I start to worry that I'll never be the same again. But, I have to keep reminding myself that for every new ending there is a new beginning, and my new beginning is about to start. Regardless of whether I am ready for it or not, my fallout is about to hit. I have no choice but to face it head on.

CHAPTER TWO
THE FALLOUT

Nine days after being released from hospital May comes to an end, and I find the strength I need to go back into the studio. Writing songs has been the one constant positive in my life, and it has continued to get me through the tough days. I know it is time to face the fallout of all the things that have happened recently, but I don't know how much life is going to throw at me.

It's the last Friday of May, and I feel strong enough to get back into the swing of things so I can finish my album. I won't lie, I have thought about quitting, but I know I have to do this for myself. Deep down I want to keep going. It is something I can focus on, something I can use to help me recover from everything; after all, music is the one thing that never lets me down. Even when I feel at my lowest, it always pulls me back up.

After telling my mum my plan, I get into my car and head over to the recording studio. During my first week at home, my uncle came over to see me. I told him about my dad, but we didn't talk about what I'd done. I was exhausted from going over it so many times, and he knew that, so he didn't push me into reliving it again. I know that when I'm ready I can tell him what happened. When the time comes I'll do just that, but for now, I want to focus on doing what I was born to do: singing the songs I've written.

When I get to the studio, I hug my uncle and go into the recording booth, where I warm up and put my headphones on. When I'm ready, I start singing my new song, which I have called *Lost Love*. It focuses on dealing with a broken heart and losing people you love. To say it's difficult to face so soon is an understatement, particularly as it is inspired by two people I had loved unconditionally until they both left my life. Although it poses a challenge, I find it therapeutic. It reminds me of what has happened, but it also reminds me to keep moving forward.

I sing the song a few times, then walk out of the recording booth and sit next to my uncle, who is wiping tears from his eyes.

"There's so much emotion in that song; you can hear it in your voice, and see it in your face. How are you feeling?"

If I told him the truth, I'd tell him that I don't feel anything, I feel emotionless and numb, but I don't want to worry my family any more than I already have, so I lie.

"It feels good to be back in the studio, and I'm okay. I'm just trying to take each day as it comes." I crack a smile, trying my best to reassure him.

"Good. I'm glad to hear that. I've spoken to Melody, and while we love the song you wrote about Cam, we wanted to make sure you were still happy to have it on the album? If not, that's perfectly fine. We can take it off, no questions asked."

I think about what he is asking. I haven't even thought about that song since everything has happened. As much as it is a painful reminder of what I've lost, I know it wouldn't be fair to take off a song that came from the greatest love I have ever known.

"It's fine, leave it." I offer another reassuring smile to my uncle, then grab my stuff and get ready to go. I want to talk to him, but I suddenly feel overcome with emotions: ones that I am desperately trying to ignore. So, I decide to leave.

"I'll see you tomorrow. Thanks for letting me get into the studio today."

I push the door open, but my uncle is chasing after me.

"Delilah, stop. I know you're hurt, but please don't try to do anything like what you did that night. We can't lose you."

I look at my feet, feeling the tears building up. "I promise you; I didn't try to kill myself. I just tried to numb the pain. I made a mistake, and I know that. I'm sorry I scared you. I'll be fine; it's just going to take time."

I feel like I am saying the same thing repeatedly, but I know everyone in my family needs to hear it so they can understand why I did what I did. He steps towards me and hugs me tightly.

"I know, and I know you'll be okay. You're incredibly brave and strong. Let's just try to focus on your music. It will help you get through this and I'll be here to guide you, too. I'm not going to let you suffer in silence by yourself."

I smile and kiss his cheek. "Thank you. I'm lucky to have you in my life."

"Let me know if there's anything I can do, I'm here for you, kiddo."

"I will, thanks. See you tomorrow." I wave at him as he stands by the studio door, watching me leave.

When I get home, my mum's in the kitchen with Dakota, who's helping her with dinner. She was due to go back to Sydney a few days after I was discharged from the hospital, but she decided to take some personal leave so she could be with us. She made it very clear that it wasn't just because of what had happened to me, but because she has been missing home – and our family – so she wants to spend some quality time here. Plus, she has a new contract with her modelling agency, and they are sending her to New York at the end of June, so she'll be away for a while.

I sit down at the table; mum looks up at me and smiles.

"Hi, honey. How did your recording session go?"

I smile back. "It was good. It feels great to be back recording songs."

"That's great! I think that'll be good for you."

I nod my head and look at the table: the brochure for the support group is sitting neatly in the middle. I pick it up, open it, and reread the information. I look up as Dakota joins me at the table.

"Are you going to go?" She curiously asks.

"I haven't thought about it too much. I guess I can go and check it out and see if it's something that will help me cope with things better."

Despite being stubborn I know that I should go; I just feel scared to take the first steps in facing everything that has been haunting me. As I'm processing everything Dakota reaches over and grabs my hands.

"Why don't we go and check it out tomorrow? We could go in the morning. Then I'll take you out for lunch? We can spend some time together, like we used to when I lived here."

I feel like Dakota is still worried about me. I mean, I know my whole family is, but I don't want them to treat me like I am going to break. Sure, I feel fragile, I'm aware that I've made a mistake and I am working towards correcting it. I just need time.

"Dakota, you know you don't have to treat me like I'm a little kid. I know you're worried about me, but I really am fine. I'll work through this, but I need you to respect the fact that it's going to take time for me to heal."

She looks at me, and I see tears in her eyes. She's cried a lot since being back in Perth, and I always feel guilty when I see her looking this sad.

"I know you'll get through this, and I'm sorry that I'm treating you like a little kid. It's just this whole experience has scared the life out of me, and the thought of losing you sucks. Delilah, you're my big sister and my best friend. I don't ever want to face the world without you in it."

The tears fall and she puts her head between her hands, letting all her emotions out. I lean over and hug her, trying to comfort her.

"Hey, I'm not going anywhere. I promise."

I sit with her while she cries, knowing it's all I can do. When she's ready, she looks up at me.

"Please go and look at this place. It'll help you heal, and I know everyone in the family will feel a sense of peace knowing you're getting professional help to deal with everything."

Mum is watching us closely; she nods her head, agreeing with my sister. I sigh deeply before speaking.

"Okay, I'll go."

~

As the sun rises on Saturday morning, I reluctantly get up and get changed. When I'm ready I find Dakota, who is determined to take me to the clinic, whether I like it or not.

At the hospital, Dakota looks at me. "I'm going to go park. I'll come and find you soon." I nod my head and get out of the car.

I look at the doors that lead to the reception area; I take a deep breath, desperate to fill my lungs with much needed air and step through them. I approach the reception desk, where I ask where to go. The lady sitting behind the desk calls Doctor Reynolds, who comes down from his office to collect me.

"Hi, Delilah, it's good to see you. I'm glad you're here. Follow me."

I shake his hand and follow behind him. We go into one of the lifts, and it takes us up to the third floor. We walk down the long corridor until we reach a room that is separated by two glass doors. Doctor Reynolds scans a card, and when the doors open, he turns to me and offers me a comforting smile before we walk into the room. I look around, observing the large space. There are a few offices on the left side of the room, which I notice have names of therapists on them, and there are spare office rooms on the right side. There's a kitchen and a table; young adults are making tea and coffee, sitting down, flipping through magazines and reading books.

Doctor Reynolds shows me around the clinic and tells me about the support centre.

"This part of the building is relatively new. Doctor Stein, who had a daughter who wasn't coping with her depression, introduced it in 2010. She wanted a safe place for her daughter to go, a place where she could communicate with people the same age who were going through a similar thing as her; a place where she could talk to professionals in a comfortable environment. The centre is open to all 17 to 25-year-olds, and it's open 24/7. There are always staff members here too, so even if you come in at two o'clock in the morning, there will be someone available to talk to. Each person is given a card so they can access the room after hours. After 7:00 p.m. a security guard stands at the door, so only people who have cards can get in. There are a few beds here too, so if you need a safe place to sleep, we have that option."

I try to take in everything he is telling me, but I am overwhelmed. I've never seen anything like this; I didn't even know places like this existed.

"Doctor Reynolds, do you think I have depression? Is that why you invited me here?" I suddenly blurt out.

I've been wondering if my family thinks I am suffering from depression, but I have researched it and I don't feel like I am. I clearly have depressive thoughts, but I don't believe I'm depressed.

"No, Delilah. I don't think you have depression. I do believe that you're overwhelmed by what you're trying to cope with, and that's okay, but I feel that it is in your best interest to get some support outside of your family. My advice is that you need to be around people who are in pain too. It's good to talk to people your own age who understand the things you may be feeling. Sometimes it's difficult to open up to family and friends, so we try to offer a different kind of support system here. You can deal with things in your own way, but in a healthy way. I want you to talk to one of our therapists here, and you have the chance to communicate with other young people. Sometimes having a friend who understands these things helps you to take productive steps to recovery."

I take in what he says. I haven't ever thought about that side of things. I've always been too scared to open up to anyone other than Cam. I've always been too afraid, to be honest; I always worry my feelings will push people away.

"There's a group session that's about to start. If you want to join in, you can. You don't have to contribute; you can just watch and observe how things work. That way you can decide if it's something you'd like to do."

I consider the idea, and although I am scared, I know I won't know what a support session is like until I experience one for myself. "I'd like that, thank you."

He grins and signals to follow him down to a room at the end of the building. He gently pushes the door open, and I walk in to see a raven-haired woman setting up chairs in a circle.

"Angie, this is Delilah. She's going to sit in on today's session. She doesn't know what to expect, so she might not contribute, but I'd like her to see what happens in these sessions. Then she can decide if she'd like to join in permanently."

Angie smiles at me and shakes my hand. "Hi, Delilah, pleased to meet you. You're more than welcome to sit in on the session."

I thank her. Doctor Reynolds turns to me. "I'll let you be. I'll come back in an hour to see how you are going. I know it seems scary, but allow yourself to open up to the possibilities."

"I will, thank you. My sister, Dakota, is downstairs. Is she allowed to come in here too?"

"I'll go down and get her. She can sit in the common room, have a coffee and wait for you," he says before leaving me with Angie.

I offer to help set up the chairs, and Angie politely accepts. As we move chairs, she tells me about herself.

"I'm 26. I had severe depression when I was 15. It ruled my life until I was 23, which is when I tried to take my own life. I was admitted to this hospital, and that's when I met Doctor Stein. I talked everything through with her, and she looked after me while I recovered. She introduced me to her daughter, Kate, who I became best friends with. She works here too, but she's on holidays at the moment. Doctor Stein had the idea to set this place up, and ever since then we've been working to help teens and young adults who suffer from mental illnesses. I was studying to be a psychologist, but with my issues, I gave it up when I had a year and a half to go. Doctor Stein and Kate helped me go back and finish the degree, and now we can offer therapy to people too. We started these support sessions about a year ago. We provide a safe place to talk about issues, and everything is confidential. We trust everyone enough to know they won't repeat anything that's said in this room. We also respect that not everyone wants to open up straight away, so we don't ever push you to talk before you're ready."

After I set up the final chair Angie sits down near the door.

"Come and sit next to me. I know it's daunting when you're here for the first time."

She's reassuring, and I instantly trust her. I don't hesitate to sit down next to her.

"We don't start for another twenty minutes. We could talk one-on-one if you feel comfortable?"

I nervously agree. "Um, sure. I don't really know where to start." I feel the heat rising to my cheeks: an all too familiar feeling that I hate.

"Start with the basics. What brought you here?"

"It's kind of a long story. Sorry, but I don't think I'm ready to go into it."

"That's perfectly fine. You don't have to do it until you're ready. When that time comes, I'm happy to set up a one-on-one session if that's something you're interested in. Is there anything you're aspiring to be?"

She tries to change the subject, which I appreciate.

"Well, I'm trying to be a singer. I'm actually working on an album at the moment. I have a few covers out already, and I'm just trying to work on my confidence."

"I thought I recognised you. Delilah Walker, right?"

I fidget in my chair. "Yep, that's me. How did you know?"

I instantly feel stupid; she has clearly seen my covers. How else would she know me?

"I've seen your covers. You have a beautiful voice."

"Thank you, that means a lot."

We spend another five minutes talking before people start coming into the room.

"Deep breaths, there's nothing to worry about," Angie says.

25

I look down at my hands, and she starts chatting with everyone as they enter the room. The room begins to fill up with people. When I feel confident enough, I look up. When I do, I get the surprise of my life. Ryan is walking through the door, and when he spots me, he freezes.

"Ryan?" I notice that people have stopped talking and they're looking between Ryan and me.

"Oh, hey Delilah." He approaches me and sits in the chair next to me.

"What are, um, what are you doing here?" He looks as nervous as I am feeling.

"It's a long story. What are you doing here?"

"Um, I, I just come here for my sister. She's got depression, but she hates being around people, so I come here to get support so I can help her."

I sense he's holding back the truth, but I don't want to push him into telling me, so I sit back in my chair.

"I'm sorry to hear that."

"Thanks."

I notice he's avoiding eye contact with pretty much everyone, including me. A few minutes later Angie starts talking. She welcomes everyone and asks if anyone has anything they want to discuss. She looks at Ryan, but he just shakes his head. She moves onto the next person, and I sit and listen as people take it in turns, telling the group how their week has been and how they are coping with the challenges they are facing. Everyone is incredibly supportive and friendly. No one is rude or laughs inappropriately at anything anyone says. It makes me see what this kind of thing can offer people who want to talk but feel too scared to do so. I know that this is a place I can be my true self and talk to strangers. I can get advice and talk to a professional therapist, and I can be around people who know what it is like to be in pain.

After the session ends, Angie hands me her business card and tells me to contact her. I thank her then chase after Ryan, who is trying to get out of the centre as fast as he can.

"Ryan, wait!"

I run after him. He stops in his tracks, drops his head, and turns to face me.

"Please, sit down with me," I say.

"Okay, but not out here."

I look over at Dakota, who's watching me. I put my finger up, signalling I need a moment; she nods at me and goes back to the magazine she is reading. I follow Ryan into one of the empty office spaces. He closes the door behind him, and we sit down in the two chairs that are next to each other.

"I need to tell you the truth. I don't have a sister with depression. In fact, I don't have a sister at all. Six months ago, I had a brother, Jed; he was 22. He was driving home from work one night when a guy ran through a red light. He smashed into Jed's car. The driver survived but Jed wasn't so lucky. He died three days later. After he passed away, my parents split up. I moved in with my dad, who tried to look after me, but I was incredibly close to Jed, and I didn't know how to grieve. I pushed everyone away, and then I was diagnosed with depression. My parents tried to help me but they didn't know how to deal with it. They were still trying to grieve themselves, so I knew it was too overwhelming for them. I felt guilty, and I felt like a burden, so I moved out of home. I stopped talking to my parents, and I've pushed almost all my friends away. Do you remember the guys I was with when we first met? They tried to help me, but I felt like an idiot, and I was embarrassed, so I stopped answering the phone when they rang. The wouldn't give up, so I selfishly changed my number. I just wanted to be alone, but now that loneliness is suffocating me."

I look at him, finally seeing the pain he is feeling. For the first time in the few months I have known him, he has let me in. I wonder just how hard he has worked to keep this hidden from me for so long, but then I realise it wasn't him, but me, I've always been too consumed by my own problems to understand he has been dealing with a lot, too. I know in that moment that I must be there for him; to help him get through his battle.

"I'm so sorry you've been going through this alone. I'm sorry I didn't notice that you were in pain. I wish I saw it earlier. In the time that I've known you, I've never actually gotten to know you. Maybe that's something we can do, together. You were always there for me. Please let me be there for you."

I can see the sadness he is trying so desperately to hide from the world. I see first-hand how it has slowly destroyed him. I want make all his pain go away, but I know I can't do that, so I promise myself that I'll be there for him, as a friend, to help him recover in any way I can.

"Thank you. When the doctor diagnosed me, I felt sick. When he told me I had depression, I felt numb, cold and scared. Since then I've found it practically impossible to be truthful, but I want you to know something. You came into my life when I was at my lowest, you needed me, you actually wanted to be my friend, and you confided in me. You pretty much saved my life. I mean I was a lost cause before I met you. I'd given up on my life and myself, but you changed all of that. You've been through so much, especially lately, and your journey has motivated and inspired me. It has shown me that maybe I can turn all of this around and face everything I've been running from. I just want you to know that."

I feel tears stinging my eyes as I lean over and hug him.

"We will face this together," I say, trying to reassure us both. Then I tell him all about Cam and my dad, and we promise to go to the support sessions together, as well as seeing Angie. We are going to help each other get through all of this. For the first time in weeks, I feel like everything will finally change for the better.

Dakota and I have lunch with Ryan, then drop him off at his car. After waving goodbye to him, we head home, where I tell my mum and Evan about the tour and the support group.

"I spoke to Doctor Reynolds on the way out, and I told him I'd be going back. He got me my own access card."

My mum smiles and looks at the card.

"Oh, I'm so happy to hear that. This is a step in the right direction. I'm so proud of you."

My family sits down at the table, and mum puts the kettle on. As we sip our tea I tell them about something important I learned during the group session.

"Angie, the lady who runs the sessions, talked about purpose. She said that no one other than ourselves has the answers that will set us free and make us truly happy. She also said that purpose is something every person has and it's our job to find what that is. I'd never thought about what *my* purpose is until I heard her talking about it. I started asking myself, and I honestly believe my purpose is to help people through my music. I find writing songs incredibly easy and freeing. It comes so naturally to me, and I think that's an amazing gift to have."

Mum reaches for my hand, and I continue.

"Music has taught me so much, especially about myself, and when I've struggled it has helped me get through the rough patches. It has pulled me through some of my darkest days, and if I can be that source of motivation, inspiration, happiness and hope for other people, then that's what I'm going to strive for. I've literally poured my heart and soul into this album. I'm working so hard, and I know I've had this setback, but from this setback I've learnt so much. I'm even more inspired and motivated to continue this journey. I've learnt that sometimes we have to endure bad things in order to get to the good things. I know this is what I'm meant to do, and now I'm ready to do whatever it takes to succeed."

I sit up in my chair and look at my mum, who's now crying.

"I'm so proud of you, Delilah. You've come so far, especially in the last few days. I know this has been so hard for you and you've been through a lot, but you've come out stronger than ever. I knew from the moment you started singing that you were destined to help people with your music and you know we're going to support you through every single step of this journey."

"Thank you, mum. I promise this is the start of a new life for me, a much happier life. As much as it hurts, there is going to be no more talk of dad. I know where he stands now, and it's time for me to accept that and move on."

After dinner I retreat to my room. I sit by my bay window and look out at the dark blue sky covered in tiny, glowing stars. I take my guitar out of its case and sit it on my lap. *Feel the fear and do it anyway*, I say to myself as I begin to work on a new song. A few hours later I have nearly completed a song. I check the time on my phone; it's just after 10:00 p.m. I've had such a long and exhausting day, so I decide to go to bed. I get into my pyjamas and hop into my bed. I open my phone and look at the quote *"Know the darkness has to fade and the sun has to rise"* in the middle of the screen. I smile at the quote, taking in the meaning of each word. It is the perfect reminder that things will work out, and I start to feel like the person I was before my relationship ended.

I fall into a comforting sleep, something I have missed over the last few weeks. Little did I know that it wouldn't last. It is the middle of the night, and my phone won't stop ringing, I try to ignore it, but it's no use. I try to turn it off but it starts to ring again. I don't recognise the number, but something inside of me is telling me to answer it. Something doesn't feel right, and I'm about to understand why.

CHAPTER THREE
HI DELILAH, IT'S HEATHER

I'm barely awake when I answer my phone. I don't know what to expect, but I immediately know something isn't right. I never thought I'd hear from Heather, and I certainly didn't think she'd ever call me with this news. But that's exactly what happens, and suddenly my world is turned upside down.

"Hello?" I say, trying to wake myself up. I can hear someone crying and then I hear a familiar voice on the other end of the phone.

"Delilah, it's Heather."

Heather? Why the hell is she calling me at this time?

"Heather, what do you want? It's 1:30 in the morning!" Suddenly I'm feeling agitated.

"I know, and I know I'm the last person you want to hear from, but it's an emergency. Cam and I were in an accident. He got drunk out of his mind, and I tried to stop him from driving, but he wouldn't listen to me. I didn't want him to drive by himself, so I got into the car with him. He was going on about how he wanted to see you and he started speeding. He said if he drove fast, he'd get to you quicker. But then he lost control of the car and we hit a pole. I honestly don't know how we survived. I've got a few cuts and bruises, but I'm fine. Cam's in a coma though. He's at the hospital now. I'm on my way there. I know he misses you. He doesn't want to admit it, but he does. I know we're not friends, but I thought you deserve to know. If you want to see…"

Before Heather can finish her sentence, I cut her off. "I'll be there soon."

I hang up and jump out of bed, throwing on the first pair of jeans I find, a jumper and my Ugg boots. I grab my phone and my keys, and shove them into my pocket. I run into my mum's room and switch the light on, knowing I'll wake up Evan too. My adrenaline kicks in, so I don't care. I run over to mum's bed.

"Mum, wake up," I gently nudge her. Her eyes spring open and she leaps out of bed.

"What? What is it? Are you okay?" She grabs my shoulders.

"I'm fine. Sorry, I didn't mean to worry you. Cam has been in an accident. I need to go to the hospital. I just wanted to tell you so you didn't panic when you woke up to find me gone."

I try to leave, but she won't let me.

"Oh no you don't, missy."

I turn back to her, ready to protest.

"I'll drive you." She goes over to her closet, and throws on a pair of leggings, a jumper and a pair of sneakers. When she is ready, she kisses Evan, turns the light off, and closes the door. We run down the stairs.

On the way to the hospital, I tell my mum everything I know. She calls Anna and asks where they are. Anna says she was about to call. She didn't want to worry us, but she wanted to make sure my mum knew what was happening, in case we heard it from someone else.

When we get to the hospital, mum parks the car and I'm rushing to get out.

"Delilah, stop for a second, please."

I sit back in the seat and look at her. The lights from the hospital reflect off her face, and I know she can see the fear that is plastered over my face. She takes a deep breath before she asks me a question.

"Honey, I know you still love Cam, but after the breakup don't you think it's going to be hard to see him? Especially if he's not in the best shape?"

"I'll always love him, mum, and I know it's going to be hard to see him, especially in the condition he's in. He might not have been there for me when I was at my lowest, but my heart still belongs to him. I have to be here for him, and you need to be here for Anna. She's one of your best friends, and her son is in a coma. We have to put our personal feelings aside and be there for them in their time of need."

My mum's eyes shine in the light. "You're a good kid. How did I get so lucky?"

"I had the best teacher. You taught me to be a good kid. Come on, let's go and find Anna."

We go into the hospital and find Anna, William, Lucas, Gavin and Nia sitting in the waiting room. Anna spots us, runs over to my mum and embraces her, letting the tears flow from her eyes. My mum takes her over to a few empty chairs away from her family, where she tries to comfort her. I go up to the boys and Nia and hug them. When I get to Nia, she goes from looking sad to looking furious. She gets up from her spot on the floor and stands a few feet from me. I notice her eyes are red. She looks exhausted and scared.

"This is all your fault. You ruined his life, and now he's going to die. I hate you, Delilah. I'll never forgive you." She storms off without saying another word.

Lucas and Gavin get up and apologise to me before chasing after their sister. Nia blames me for what has happened to Cam, and the feeling of guilt I have been trying to fight off suddenly comes back, stronger than ever. I sink into the chair next to William and he pats my back.

"I'm sorry for that, Delilah. She didn't mean it. We don't blame you in the slightest. We appreciate you coming here to be with us. I know this is hard for you, too."

Nia is angry and scared; we are all feeling like that, and I try not to take what she said to me personally. But, no matter how much I try to shake it off, I still feel responsible and guilty. I mean, if I hadn't acted the way I did, Cam wouldn't have broken up with me, and he wouldn't be in a coma. It looks like I'm going to lose him, and there is nothing I can do to save him. That destroys me, and it takes all my strength to stop myself from crying, I know it's more important to be here for Cam's family. I have to put their feelings and their emotional state before my own.

After waiting for about twenty minutes, I spot Doctor Reynolds approaching me. I lift my head off Williams' shoulder and get up.

"Delilah, what are you doing here?"

"Hi, Doctor Reynolds. One of my family friends is here. My mum and I came down here to be with his family." I'm trying to hide the fear in my voice.

"I'm sorry to hear that. Is there anything I can do to help?"

"I don't think so. I know he's in the best care, so we just have to wait, unfortunately."

"You're not wrong about that. We have some of the best doctors in the world here, so he's in very good hands. How's the support group going, if you don't mind me asking?"

I sit down next to him and tell him about the support group; how it has been helping me cope and how I am going back to speak to Angie. I know it is important to work through my issues and let go of everything that is haunting and hurting me.

"That's great. I'm really happy to hear that." His pager suddenly beeps.

"Sorry, I've got to attend to this. It was nice to see you, Delilah. Don't be a stranger."

I thank him then go back over to William, who has been joined by Anna and my mum. A few minutes later another doctor comes out and stands in front of us.

"He's not awake, but he can hear you. Mrs Collins, if you're ready, you can go up to see him. Please try not to overwhelm him. We recommend just two people seeing him tonight. In a few days we can start sending more people in, but for now we have to keep it to a minimum."

Anna looks at William, who nods at her. She suddenly focuses her attention on me. "We want you to talk to him. We can wait. I think hearing your voice will help him. Please, Delilah, this is all I can think of doing."

I look at her, my mum and William, who all look so desperate and lost.

"Okay, I'll do it."

Anna hugs me and tells me where to go. I go up in one of the lifts to the second floor, follow the corridor, and search for his number on the doors. I open the door and walk into the room. Closing the door behind me, I stand with my back against it and observe the room. It is bland – similar to the one I was in when I was here – and the only sound I can hear is the beeping of the machines next to Cam. The repetitive sound starts to become overpowering. I shake my head, walk over and sit down next to the bed. Cam has cuts and bruises all over his face and arms. There are tubes in his nose and mouth, and he looks pale. I grab his left hand; it feels cold, but it is still soft. I miss that. I miss holding his hand.

"Hi." I don't know what to say, so I just take it one word at a time. "It's me, Delilah. I'm here. I don't know where to start, or what to say, but I can't imagine life without you. Even if we're just friends, I can't lose you. Please wake up. I won't leave your side until you do. I promise."

I lean over and kiss his forehead, then make myself comfortable in the chair. For the next thirty minutes I talk to Cam about all the fun times we shared together. I figure that hearing these memories will help him. I'm also so scared of losing him that I'm trying to distract myself. As time passes, I start to feel exhaustion taking over my body. I try to keep my eyes open, but they are starting to close, so I put my head on the bed next to Cam's left arm. I hold his hand and imagine we're back on the boat, sitting in the warm sunshine. Within minutes I'm fast asleep. Before I'm ready Anna comes into the room and whispers my name to wake me up.

"Delilah, honey, it's 3:00 a.m. Your mum has gone home. I told her you can stay with us tonight. I hope you don't mind."

I lift my head. She looks even more exhausted than she did before.

"That's fine, thank you. Why don't I give you some time with Cam? I'm sure William could use some coffee."

Anna hugs me tightly, and I feel the longingness passing through her body. She's desperate for her son to wake up.

"It's going to be okay, Anna. I promise I won't leave his side. I'm here for you all." The tears I've been holding back finally drop to my cheeks. Anna wipes them away and hugs me again.

"Thank you. We'd be lost without you."

I leave her alone with Cam, go down to the hospital café and order coffees for everyone. While I'm waiting, I notice Heather sitting at one of the tables sipping her coffee. She smiles at me sadly. As much as I don't want to talk to her, I want to thank her for calling me. That wouldn't have been easy for her to do, and I know she is worried about Cam too. When I get to her table, I sit down across from her.

"Thank you for calling me. I know that must have been hard for you."

She quickly wipes a few tears from her face, like she's embarrassed to be sad.

"You're welcome, Delilah. Umm ... I just ... can we talk? I won't take too much of your time. I just have a few things I want to say to you if that's alright."

The last thing I want to do is sit here and talk to Cam's new girlfriend, but we need to face each other at some point. I don't want to fight with her, so I know it is best to clear the air now.

"I'm happy to talk."

She takes another sip of her coffee and clears her throat.

"Technically speaking, I am Cam's girlfriend. But he doesn't treat me how he treated you, he doesn't look at me the way he looked at you, and he certainly won't ever love me the way he loved ... the way he *still* loves you. You know I've always been jealous of you. You're so stunning, Delilah. You have a beautiful personality and a heart of gold. I wish we could have been friends, and I'm sorry if I've done anything to hurt you. You're so talented. You can write songs so beautifully, and everyone loves you. Especially Cam. He wouldn't ever touch me. He didn't ever do anything, other than kiss me. Even then, I could feel it didn't mean anything. I guess he used me to numb the pain he was in."

I'm trying to process everything Heather is saying. It explains so much. She didn't act that way because she hated me. She disliked me because she was threatened by me, she was jealous of me. I've never met anyone who is actually jealous of me. I guess I've never seen myself as someone to be jealous of.

"The one thing I've taken away from my recovery is that I need to forgive people who hurt me in the past. So, I forgive you, Heather. Maybe if you focus on being a nicer person and don't put all your attention on your looks, you'll be able to open yourself up to more experiences."

"I know. I guess I've always just focused on my looks because that's what I thought mattered, but I know that's not true. Being with Cam over these last few weeks has taught me a lot, and I'm ready to change myself so I can be a better person."

I smile at her. "That's a good plan, and sometimes that's all you need."

Heather looks like a weight has been lifted off her shoulders, so I get up to leave.

"Delilah, before you go I want to tell you one more thing. I know it's confronting to talk about, but that accident was the worst experience of my life. Cam called me over to this party he was at. My mum dropped me off, and when I got there, Cam was drunk out of his mind. It's absurd to think about how drunk he was. Anyway, I sat with him, and he spent most of the time talking about you. His desire to be with you is quite strong. He was desperate to see you, so he convinced himself to drive to your house. He wanted to fix things and get back together with you. He broke up with me, and pushed me away when I tried to stop him from driving. I guess the alcohol made him feel confident enough to be honest. I told him I didn't care if we broke up, but he wasn't driving. I offered to drive him, but he refused to let me drive his car. I didn't know what to do, so I got in the car with him. He just kept putting his foot down on the accelerator. He told me his vision was getting blurry, and I begged him to slow down. He finally listened to me, but, as he was trying to slow down, he lost control and we hit a pole. I know how lucky we are to be alive. I know he's worse off than I am, but he's still alive and that in itself is a miracle. I just wanted you to know that he was willing to die to get to you. Whatever happened between you two happened, but you've both been given a second chance. No matter what he says, don't push him away. He loves you and nothing will ever change that."

I feel the tears rush to my eyes again; I can't believe what Heather is telling me. Part of me feels all the love I have for Cam shoot straight to my heart, but part of me wants to slap him for being so stupid. He knows better than that, he knows not to get into a car and drive when he's drunk, but he did it anyway.

"I know that wasn't easy for you to tell me. Thank you. I'm always going to love him, but right now we have to focus on him waking up and recovering. Everything else will work itself out."

The barista calls my name.

"I'd better get these back up to his family. If you want, you can join us."

"Thank you, but my mum's on her way to pick me up. I think it's better if you're here with his family. His family doesn't like me, you know. I went over a few times and they practically glared at me the whole time, especially Nia. She really hated me. She always talked about you. Her and Cam would always get into arguments about it."

I snicker. "Nia's like that. She's smart, and she knows what she's doing. I'd better go. But, if you want to talk, you have my number. Thank you for everything, I really appreciate it."

I hug her, knowing it is the right thing to do and that she needs it.

"Thank you, Delilah. That means a lot."

I collect the coffees and head back to Cam's family. Nia, Gavin and Lucas are sitting with William when I reach them. I hand the boys the lattes and hand a hot chocolate to Nia before sitting next to her.

"Heather told me she doesn't think you like her. Apparently you would talk about me when she was around?"

"I don't know what you're talking about." She says with a smirk.

"Well, if she was telling the truth, I should thank you. Although you know you shouldn't stir Cam up. He's a bit of a hot-head sometimes."

"Well, it's safe to say I like you better than I'd ever like her."

I put my arm around her shoulder and pull her closer to me. I can still see the fear on her face and I know she is hurting, so I try my best to comfort her.

"It's going to be okay. He's tough, and he's going to pull through."

She starts to cry. "I know. It's just the thought of losing him is so daunting. I can't imagine a life without him. I'm so sorry for what I said to you before. I didn't mean it. We're so lucky you're here for us, and I hope you guys get back together. You look as miserable as he's looked since the two of you broke up."

"I know. Right now we just need to focus on getting Cam better. The rest can be sorted out later."

A few minutes later Anna comes back down and joins us.

"He's still asleep, and we all need to get some sleep. Let's go home, and we can come back in the afternoon."

We get up and head to the car. At Anna's request, we are all heading back to her house. She tells me I can stay in the guest room, but that room holds too much pain; it is a reminder of the night Cam broke up with me. I ask Anna if I can stay in Cam's room, and she agrees. I go into his room, grab one of his shirts and put it on. I step out of my jeans and put my Ugg boots next to them on the floor. I snuggle into his bed, put my head on his pillows and cry myself to sleep, praying with every inch of my body that he wakes up.

At 1:30 p.m. my body finally wakes up. My phone is beeping, I open my eyes and remind myself where I am. I sit up in Cam's bed, hugging one of his pillows to my chest, and check the messages on my phone. The first one is from my mum, telling me she'll pick me up from Cam's at 2:00 p.m. She has to take me to a doctor's appointment, but she promises to take me to see Cam when we are done. I reply to her, letting her know I am awake, before I read a message from Ryan.

Hey, we were meant to meet today, but you didn't show up. What's going on?

Shit! With everything that's happened, I totally forgot about meeting Ryan for breakfast. I feel a wave of guilt hit me as I quickly reply to him.

I'm so sorry. I got a call from Cam's girlfriend. He was involved in an accident and he was admitted to hospital, I was with his family all night. Didn't get back to his place until 4 this morning, so I've been asleep since then.

I hit send, and Ryan replies almost immediately.

Sorry to hear that, is he alright? Why did you stay at his? I thought you guys broke up?

I read the reply, feeling protective over Cam and his family. I sense Ryan is mad at me, but, under the circumstances, I thought he would understand that I need to be with Cam's family right now.

He's in a coma. The doctors are monitoring him, I don't know how he's doing, he's not waking up, so that's concerning. I'm close to his family, they need me right now, and I have to be here for them, and for Cam. We did break up.

I hit send, and again, Ryan replies almost immediately.

Are you getting back together?

I look at his reply, questioning why he's getting defensive.

No.

I'm not sure if I actually mean it, but I don't feel comfortable telling Ryan that.

Sorry. I shouldn't ask so many questions. That's really nice of you to be there for them, it's important that they have a strong support system around them right now. Let me know if you need anything, when you're free we can meet up.

I feel slightly better after reading his reply, but I still guilty for not being there for Ryan. I know he is going through a lot and I have a feeling he will think I don't care, so I try to reassure him.

I'm sorry. I'm here for you if you need me, I just have to be here too.

I wait for his reply. It takes longer than the last few did.

Thank you. I know, I respect that. I'll speak to you soon.

There's a knock at the door.

"Delilah?" It's Anna. I get up and open the door.

"Morning ... or afternoon, I should say."

She hands me a cup of tea and sits down on Cam's bed. She looks around his room sadly. Despite both of us sleeping for most of the day, we still look exhausted, and we both have the same worried look on our faces.

"I hope he comes home so he can sleep in his own bed. I don't think I could live in this house without him. If I knew he wouldn't be here, I just couldn't come back. It would be a constant reminder. I don't know how parents do this. You never think anything like this can happen to your child. I thought I did a good job raising him. Where did I go wrong?"

She puts her head in her hands. I put the cup of tea down and move closer to Anna.

"Anna, you're an amazing mum. This isn't your fault. You raised Cam to be respectful, loving and passionate, and he is all of those things. He's an amazing person, all your children are. You should be proud, not ashamed. He made a mistake, that's all. I know it's a life-changing mistake, but it's happened now, and all we can do is pull through this together. I'm sorry for my part in all of this. I knew Cam was hurting, but I didn't know the extent of it. He pushed me away, and no matter how hard I tried to talk to him, he wouldn't let me back in."

"I don't blame you in the slightest Delilah. You haven't left us since you got the call. I know he's hurting, and I know you are too. You two are meant to be, and if Cam wakes up, you'll fix things, I just know you will."

I correct her. "I think you mean *when* he wakes up, Anna, not *if.*"

She attempts a smile.

"Your mum will be here soon. I'll leave you to get dressed. That top suits you. You should keep it on."

She leaves the room and I look down at Cam's shirt. I feel the tips of my lips curve upwards, remembering it is one of his favourites; it makes me feel close to him, and right now that's all I want. I pull my jeans back on before slipping my feet into my Ugg boots. I tie my jumper around my waist, go out into the kitchen to say my goodbyes, then head outside and wait for my mum.

~

Before I know it, I am at the doctor's waiting for a check-up. I sit next to my mum, who tries her best to stay positive. While waiting for the doctor, the sounds of phones going off, the receptionists talking to patients, and parents talking to their children echo through my ears. The sounds get louder, and I find myself getting agitated. My legs start shaking, and I'm trying to focus on my breathing, but it isn't working. I can hear all the sounds around me, and they keep intensifying. I close my eyes and think about Cam, wishing that I could be with him, away from all this chaos. I open my eyes, and my mum is watching me closely.

"What?" I say to her, trying my best not to sound rude.

"Nothing. Just want to make sure you are alright."

The doctor comes out of his office, and calls my name. I turn to my mum.

"I'm fine. Be back soon."

I follow the doctor into his office. He asks me some questions about my health and he checks my response times through a series of tests. He jots a few things down before looking back at me.

"You're all clear, Delilah. Focus on your recovery and you'll be back to normal soon."

I smile back at him and thank him while wondering what normal is. I don't even know what it feels like anymore. When I walk out of the doctor's office, my mum is outside on the phone. She's pacing back and forth, and I begin to worry.

"Delilah Walker?" The lady behind the counter is calling me.

"Yes, sorry, that's me."

I walk over to the counter.

"Sign here, Miss Walker."

I quickly sign the piece of paper. She prints a copy for me.

"You're good to go. Have a good afternoon."

"Thank you. You too."

I go outside and walk over to my mum. She looks concerned. I know the minute I see her that something is wrong. I don't think I am ready to know what it is, especially if it is about Cam.

"Mum, what is it? What's wrong? Please tell me Cam's okay?"

I look at my mum, searching for answers to my questions.

"Mum, talk to me!" I scream at her.

"Sorry. Cam's not responding anymore. Anna's concerned, and she's asked for you. Come on, we need to go to the hospital right now."

I try to walk, but my legs have turned to jelly. I practically drag myself to the car. I am even more worried now than I was when Heather called me. I am scared out of my mind. As much as I hate the thought of it, I prepare myself to say goodbye. I beg my mum to rush to the hospital and, when we arrive, I jump out of the car and practically sprint to Cam's room. Anna is standing next to his bed.

"He squeezed my hand. He woke up, but then he went back to sleep, and now he won't wake up. I don't know why but I think it's you that he needs to hear. I think knowing you're here is pulling him through. Please Delilah, talk to him."

Looking at the desperation on Anna's face, I know she thinks this is the last hope. If it brings Cam back to us, then I will do it, without hesitation. I stand at the side of the bed, across from Anna. I pick up his right hand and try to think of something to say. I can't find the right words, so I do the only thing I can think of doing, the only thing that makes any sense, the only thing I think will bring him back. I start singing the song I wrote for him. He squeezes my hand; I look at Anna, and she's seen it too.

"Keep singing."

She's practically begging me to push on, despite the tears that are streaming down my face. The tears are making it difficult to breathe, let alone sing, but I know I must push through them, singing the song with as much passion and love as I can. Cam keeps squeezing my hand, and when I reach the final verse, his eyes slowly start to open. At that moment, I know he is back. Anna looks at me and lets out a sigh of relief for the first time since being here.

"Thank you. This truly is a miracle."

I focus my attention back on Cam. I can't believe it. He is alive. He has come back to us.

Chapter Four
The Recovery

Cam's eyes open as I sing the final part of the song, and he chokes on the tube in his mouth. The nurse quickly removes it and slowly helps Cam sit up. When he feels strong enough, he lets go of the nurse and tries to breathe on his own. Anna and I keep exchanging looks. Both of us have tears streaming down our faces. We can't believe it: he is awake, and this time we know it is for good.

Anna smiles as she walks over to me and hands me a tissue.

"Thank you, for everything. I'll never forget what you've done for us, Delilah."

I wipe my eyes.

"You don't have to thank me."

We focus our attention back on Cam. He's trying to talk to the nurse, but he's struggling. The nurse calls the doctor in, who asks us to leave while he checks Cam over. He says he doesn't want Cam to focus on us, but on him, and that will only happen if he can't see us. Anna and I nod our heads and leave the room. We stand by the door and wait for twenty minutes before the doctor finally comes out of the room, closing the door behind him.

"Mrs Collins, Delilah, obviously you're aware that Cam's awake. We don't believe he will fall back into a coma. He's slowly starting to talk, but it's unlikely he will remember what happened. I briefly explained part of it to him, but he's asking for you, Mrs Collins. If you're comfortable with it, I think it would be best for you to tell him the whole story. He's very fragile at the moment, so we need to keep him as calm as possible. I'll keep monitoring him throughout the day and he will stay in the hospital until Monday, so he's here for another week. We expect he will make a full recovery, but it's best for him to stay here so we can monitor all the changes he makes. When you're ready you can go and see him."

Anna thanks the doctor and he leaves. I look at Anna and see that happiness has replaced the fear she's been feeling since Cam first arrived at the hospital. She heads towards the door, I watch her as she gets closer, and when she notices I'm not following her, she turns around.

"Delilah? What are you doing?"

I look at the floor, trying to avoid all eye contact with her. She steps back towards me and lifts my head up.

"What's wrong sweetie?"

I try to look back down at the floor, but she won't let me.

"Talk to me, please."

I try my best to hide the disappointment on my face, but I know Anna will see right through it.

"I'm scared. I don't think he wants to see me, and I doubt he will want to talk to me. I just think it's better if I go home. He needs you and the rest of his family. I don't fit into that picture anymore."

51

Anna brushes my arms and looks into my eyes.

"I don't care if he feels like that. You have been here, for not only him, but for us, and he needs to know how much you've given up for him over the past few days."

Before I have a chance to protest, she opens the door and gently pulls me in Cam's direction. She lets go of my hand, but I stand back wishing I could be invisible.

Anna approaches Cam and carefully hugs him and kisses his cheek. They start talking, then Cam looks directly at me. In a soft, yet aggressive, voice, he asks, "What is she doing here?"

I look out of the window, desperate to run away, but I know Anna isn't going to let that happen.

"Her name is Delilah, thank you very much, mister. She hasn't left your side since you were admitted. I know you've just woken up, but you're going to talk to her and sort this out once and for all."

"Where's Heather? I want to see Heather."

I instantly feel a pain charge through my body when he mentions her name. He is asking for *her*, not me. I don't want to upset him or fight with him while he is recovering, but Heather told me he wanted to see me, that he wanted to fix things with me. So, why is he trying to push me away?

"She's not here. If you really want to see her, I will call her. Until then, you and Delilah need to talk. She's been a magnificent friend to all of us."

Cam looks at me before looking back at his mum.

"Go and call Heather, please."

He reads her number out to his mum, Anna writes it down, and leaves the room to make the call. I

52

look down at my boots, suddenly remembering I have Cam's shirt on. I wrap my arms around my chest and look out of the window. The silence is deafening; you can hear a pin drop. I've never felt so uncomfortable in all of my 21 years. I finally pull my eyes away from the window, and look at Cam, who is watching me closely. I slowly approach him, pull the chair closer and sit.

"How are you feeling?" I ask, worried he will just push me away again.

"I've been better. Why do you have my shirt on?"

"I ... ummm ... I stayed at your place last night, well technically it was this morning. Your mum wanted me to, and I couldn't really say no. I don't know why I've got it on, I just ... I just wanted a shirt to wear. Sorry."

Cam rolls his eyes.

"Is it true that you've been here the whole time?"

"Yeah. Heather called me on Sunday. It was 1:30 a.m. and she said the two of you had been in an accident, so I rushed here. I ... I'm glad you're awake. The doctor said you'll make a full recovery, so that's good."

I stop talking, feeling a lump in my throat.

"Thanks for that. I'll call you when I get out."

I notice the blunt tone of his voice, and I suddenly feel angry.

"Oh, I can't take this. Stop letting your pride get in the way. I'm your ex, Cam. We dated for nearly five years! You could at least pretend to be able to stand being around me. Why are you acting like this towards me? I don't get it. Heather told me you were adamant about coming over to see me. By the way, why did you want to see me?"

53

Now it is Cam's turn to avoid looking at me. "I don't know. I was drunk, and I thought I wanted to see you. I made a mistake. Look, I'm sorry ... for everything, but nothing's changed, I don't want to be with you, Delilah. I've moved on, and I'm with Heather now."

His words cut straight through me. I remember everything Heather told me: about him not looking at her the way he looked at me or loving her the way he loved me. It doesn't make sense, but I can't fight it anymore. It is exhausting, and it feels pointless. I stand up and walk towards the door, turning to face him one final time.

"I really am glad you're alright. I thought we were going to lose you. You were at the edge of death's door."

I shake my head, feeling the tears approaching. As much as I want to cry, I know I can't in front of Cam, not anymore.

"Good luck with your recovery. Let me know if there's anything I can do for you."

I walk through the door knowing I probably won't see him anytime soon. I take a deep breath in, and then let it out as I close the door behind me.

Anna's texting on her phone when she sees me.

"How'd you go?"

I know Cam needs to focus on his recovery. If I tell his mum the truth, she will force us to talk again. I know neither of us are ready for that, so I do what I am used to doing: I lie.

"Good. We talked. Everything's fine. I'm exhausted, so I'm going to head home. If you need anything, just call me. I'm going back into the studio in a few days, but I'll have my phone on me."

"We're never going to be able to thank you for everything you've done for us over the past few days. I hope you know how much we appreciate you. I know it's not my place, but the two of you are meant to be. You might be thinking it's over for good, but believe me when I say this: you will find a way back to each other. Your mum and I both agree that we haven't seen love between two people the way we've seen it between the two of you. Time apart will fix things, I promise."

I take her words in and try my best not to show Anna how much they've hit me. I find myself wanting to tell her the truth. I want to tell her how I know it is over for good and I must find a way to move on, but she is Cam's mum. I know she has a soft spot for me. Despite not liking it, if I tell her the truth, she will distance herself from the possibility of Heather being in his life. I know he would forever blame me for that, so I thank her, hug her again and head towards the entrance of the hospital.

I pass Heather on my way out. "Delilah, hey."

"Hello, Heather."

She moves to hug me but stops, questioning if that is suitable. For me, it definitely isn't.

"Cam's been asking for you. He doesn't want me anymore. All the things you said about him not loving you? They're not true. He wants to be with you, not me. Please look after him, stay with him during this, he needs you."

Heather stares at me, and I notice the surprised look on her face. Saying those words suddenly makes all of this real, and the truth hurts. I now know Cam doesn't love me anymore; it has hit me like a tidal wave, and it is destroying me, but I don't want to talk to Heather about it. I look past her, avoiding her at all costs.

"Delilah, you know that's not true. He might act like he doesn't love you or he doesn't want to be with you, but please, believe me, he doesn't mean it. As much as it sucks for me, you two are soulmates. I'll help him through this, but I'll help him as a friend. Plus, even if something serious did happen, it wouldn't work out. His family won't ever like me."

I look at Heather and see that she believes in the words she has just said. I don't want to keep going over all of this. It is too much, too soon.

"His family will come around, just give them time. This is an adjustment for them too."

"I really appreciate that. I know this is hard for you. You've been an incredible support for him, and his family. I'll make sure he knows that. I'd better get up there. I'll see you around."

She walks away, heading towards the man I thought I'd be with forever. I stand by the entrance of the hospital, waiting for my mum to pick me up, and decide to text Ryan. I haven't been there for him, and I know he needs me. To be honest, I need him, too. I also want to call my best friends; they've been messaging me and I've seen them quite a few times since I've left the hospital. But I am still in the phase of avoiding people, which I know is a bad habit that I have to break immediately. I pull my phone out and find Ryan's name, I quickly type out a message and hit send.

Hey. Sorry I've been so distant, everything's been unusually hectic. How are you? Do you want to meet up for coffee or something?

I put my phone back in my pocket and stare at the blue sky, focusing on the clouds floating through the air, as I wait for my mum. A few minutes later my phone beeps, I pull it out of my pocket and read Ryan's reply.

I'm good, how are you? I think coffee is a good idea; maybe we could meet on Friday at 2:00 p.m.? At that café by the beach?

I'm good. Perfect, I'll see you then.

I hit send just as my mum pulls up. I get in the car and look at her.

"How's Cam doing?"

"He's awake, so that's good."

"Anna told me he woke up when you sung the song you wrote about him."

I try to focus on the clouds again. I know my mum will want to talk about everything. She is like Anna and Dakota, and everyone who wants Cam and me to end up together. I'm pretty sure Heather thinks it's inevitable that we will end up together eventually, but I know it isn't going to happen. I don't want the constant reminder, so I am blunt with my response, hoping it will stop any more questions.

"Yeah, I didn't know what to say, so that's really all I could do."

"What is it, Delilah?"

"It's nothing. I'm just exhausted."

"I'm not surprised. You've had an eventful few weeks. Let's get you home so you can sleep."

I nod my head and rest it against the window as we drive through the streets in silence. When we get home, I go upstairs to have a nap. I put my head on my pillows and my mind races through the events of the last two weeks. What were the chances that both Cam and I ended up in hospital only a few weeks apart? I never thought this would happen. I never thought I'd lose my best friend, but he is letting go, and there is nothing I can do about it. I just need to learn to do the same. I feel my eyes becoming heavy and within a few minutes, I am fast asleep.

~

The next few days come and go, and I manage to write another song. It is the only way I know to deal with things, and it helps me stay focused on getting my life back on track. On Friday I put the final touches on the song and at 1:45 p.m., I get into my car and drive down to The Coffee Café. I spot Ryan sitting at a table by the window, and when he notices me, he waves. I make my way over to him, he gets up and squeezes me.

"I ordered you a coffee already, I hope that's alright."

I thank him as I begin to fill him in on Cam's accident, and I even tell him about how he pushed me away. I see Ryan shifting in his seat on many occasions; at first I think it's because he's not comfortable, but after the fourth time, I realise it is something he is doing to avoid looking at me.

"What's wrong?"

My curiosity is getting the better of me. Ryan looks at me, then looks back at the table as he answers.

"Um, it's nothing. I just ... I've been seeing Angie quite a bit recently, and I told her about my parents. I've never told anyone about them, other than you of course."

"That's great, Ryan. How do you feel now?"

I know this isn't what he is nervous about, but it seems to distract him, so I try to get him to open up more. Since that has helped me, I figure it might help him too.

"Well, I feel better, but she wants me to get in touch with my family. She said maybe it's time I face the driver too, and I don't know if I'm ready to do that."

Ryan looks at me and I haven't ever seen this much pain in his face, not even when he told me at the support centre. I know he is trying to hide it from me – from   the world – but I can see it in his eyes, nothing is going to take away from that. I reach out and grab his hands.

"I know you're trying to hide the pain from everyone, but the eyes don't lie, you can't mask the pain from your eyes. It's scary, and this is a huge step, but maybe you need to confront the driver and your family so you can heal. It's the only way you're going to be able to get past all of this. You deserve to have your family in your life, and I'm sure your parents are desperate to have you back in their lives too. I know this might be beyond the boundaries of our friendship, but Ryan, your parents have already lost a child. I'm sure they don't want to lose you too. You can still come back from this."

Ryan pulls his hands away and looks out of one of the windows. I sit at the table, sipping on my latte, waiting until he is ready. I know not to push him before he's ready to talk, and I know the best thing I can do is sit and be here for him while he tries to process everything. When he is ready, he looks back at me and takes a deep breath, before slowly letting everything out.

"I know you're right. I hate hearing it, but it's the truth. My mum has never stopped trying to contact me, but I've never felt capable of facing her, of facing the past, so I just ignore her. I just don't know if I can do this, at least not by myself. I know it's a long stretch, but is there any chance you can come with me? I don't want to do this alone."

As much as I don't think this is something I should be involved in, I know what it is like to need someone by your side when you feel you can't face something, so I know I have to be there for him.

"Of course I'll go with you. I know facing something like this is hard, so if me being there will help, then I'll do it."

I see a sense of relief wash over Ryan's face, but he starts to shift in his seat again. I go to question the movements when he begins to explain why he's been acting weird.

"You've been such an amazing friend to me, and I need to be honest about something. After I met Cam, we started texting, then we progressed to hanging out. I told him how much you had helped me, and I helped him understand things about your dad from your point of view. I ended up telling him about my depression and, well, he was always there for me. The thing is ... he told me he was going to break up with you. He said he was doing it for you. He knew you needed to focus on yourself for a while, so he thought the only option was to end things. I tried to talk him out of it, but his mind was made up. He can tell you whatever he wants, but he's never going to stop loving you."

I sit in my seat, thinking about everything Ryan is telling me. I feel angry, sad, and slightly happy, by what he has just said.

"I don't get it. Why would he do that? This seriously doesn't make any sense. Why couldn't he stay with me? Why did he have to let me go? This is so messed up. Why did he get drunk and try to see me when he's with Heather? He's made a big deal about them being together, yet she's telling me he doesn't want to be with her. I want someone to explain to me why he threw almost five years of a relationship away! This is messing with my head."

Ryan desperately tries to calm me down, "Delilah, listen to me. He doesn't love Heather. Why do you think she called you when he had that accident? It's not because she knew about your past. It's because she knew you were the one who needed to be by his side when he woke up. She knows he doesn't love her, everyone knows it, but he won't admit it. For whatever reason, he just wants you to be free. I know you don't want that, but for now you two just can't be together."

I can't take any more of this. I know there are two sides to every story – and then there's the truth – and I know it is time to face Cam one final time. I need to hear all of this from him; I need to listen to the truth from him. I need answers to all of these stupid questions.

"Delilah? Are you okay?"

I feel my eyes widen as I pull my hands away from my coffee.

"Yeah, I'm fine. Sorry, it's been a long day. I'm going to see Cam. I've got to hear all of this from him. Thank you for being honest with me. Call your mum, set up a time to meet your parents and let me know how you go. I'll be there for you, I promise. I just need to get this sorted."

I get up to leave and Ryan tries to stop me, but I keep walking.

"I'm sorry. I have to sort this out," I say over my shoulder as I run to my car.

I head to the hospital and, when I get there, I head straight up to Cam's room. I slowly open the door, worried about seeing his reaction. I haven't seen him since Monday, and things didn't go so well then, so I have my guard up. As I open the door, I see Cam talking to Heather, who is crying. I try to get away without being spotted, but it is too late. Cam has already seen me.

"Delilah?"

I turn to face them and suddenly feel very uncomfortable. Heather is wiping tears from her eyes, and she refuses to acknowledge me.

"Hey. I just came to see how you are doing. I actually shouldn't even be here, sorry."

I try to leave, but Heather stops me.

"Don't go, please. I'm just about to leave."

She grabs her bag and walks towards me. When she reaches me, she looks straight at me.

"Thank you for being so nice to me. I didn't deserve it. I told you he loves you."

She walks through the door, closing it behind her. I look over at Cam who's sitting up against some pillows. Neither of us says anything at first, but after a few minutes Cam prepares to speak up. I brace myself for his rejection, but he gets up from the bed and walks over to me.

"I would love a coffee. Want to come down to the café with me?"

I instantly feel relieved to see him up and moving, so I happily say yes to his offer. He holds his arm out for me, so I wrap my arm around his and help him to the lift. We go down to the café arm in arm, and order two hazelnut lattes and a double chocolate cupcake which we share. At first, things feel incredibly awkward. The last time I saw him, we didn't leave things on the best terms, and we haven't spoken since then. Suddenly Cam grabs my hand, the mood changes, and it doesn't feel like we are enemies anymore; it doesn't feel tense. It feels just like how it used to be, except we aren't together as a couple. We are just friends, and that sucks. Cam picks up his coffee with his free hand and raises it into the air.

"To being best friends again."

I'm trying to hide the misery I feel when he says the word *friends*. It feels like my heart is breaking all over again.

"To being friends," I say back to him.

I know this is a step in the right direction, but I still want more. I know at that moment I have to move on from the relationship and mourn the loss, or at least try to. Maybe we were only meant to be soulmates for four and a half years. Cam suddenly interrupts my thoughts.

"I broke up with Heather. Turns out I don't love her."

I pull my hand away from his. *I could have told you that.*

"Why?"

"I think it's pretty obvious that I was just trying to fill the void I've created. I'm an ass, and I used her. No matter how hard I tried, I couldn't fall in love with her. I couldn't ever go any further than kissing her because it just felt wrong. I was mad that everyone kept telling me we were meant to be together: you and me, I mean. I just don't know how to explain all of this to you, let alone other people."

I know I have to speak to Cam about what Ryan told me, and it's now or never.

"Ryan told me everything, Cam. He told me you broke up with me because you believe I need time to find myself. He made it seem like you wanted the relationship to end purely so I could figure my life out. I'm sorry, but that's bullshit. How can you determine that? Did you not think this would hurt me?

That's not even a valid reason to break up. I know you still love me, and I don't know how many times I have to say it, but I still love you! I need you to explain why you ended it. Don't beat around the bush anymore, just tell me the truth. I deserve that."

I am practically begging him to tell me face to face. Waiting for his response is testing me in ways I don't want to be tested.

Cam shakes his head. "Delilah, Ryan needs you. He needs your help, your friendship. I need to be by myself to figure out where I'm going in life, and you need to focus on your music. I promise you that's why, and it's just how things have happened. The time isn't right, and I can't go on like this."

I don't believe him; I don't believe a single word he is saying, but I don't know what else to say or do.

"What does Ryan have to do with us breaking up?"

"I don't know. I just know he needs you."

"But *I* need *you*, Cam. Why can't you see that?"

I feel my heart sinking as I look at the love of my life.

"I'm sorry, I just don't know how to explain things anymore. We just need time for ourselves right now."

I'm not satisfied with his response, but I'm lost for words.

"Fine. Seeing as we're talking, why didn't you come and see me after my ... ummm ... my accident?" I ask, suddenly feeling embarrassed.

"Every time I saw you, I saw the pain I had caused. I know you thought you'd hidden it, but I saw right through it and it damn-near killed me to know I'd done that to you. I still see it on your face now. It's the realisation that it's really over that scares us. I know it

64

sucks, but we will get to a place where we can be best friends. It's just going to take time."

"What happened to us? We were going to spend our lives together. We broke up, and you tried to replace me. Heather took my spot, and she was the one who got to see the best things about you. She was the one who got to call you and hear your voice. It just doesn't make sense to me."

I hope he is listening to everything I am saying. I know that I am going over the same things, but I want to get this sorted once and for all.

"You've got Ryan."

That's it? That is his response? I suddenly feel angry, and I can't hold back anymore.

"It's not like that! I don't love him; I love you."

I feel like a broken record, but I can't help it.

"I'm sorry, I just can't do this anymore."

"You keep saying it's the timing of things, and that one day we will end up together. But, if we're meant to be, then we should make this work now, not later. One minute you say we're going to be friends, then you say we will get back together when the time's right. Jesus, Cam! You and I both know that when I leave today, it'll truly be the end. We won't ever get back to that place."

Tears fall from his eyes.

"I know. And I'm so sorry I've done this to you."

Finally, he's admitting we won't ever get back together. I am torn: part of me wants to stay with him for as long as possible, but part of me just wants to leave. Seeing him is too much, and it just makes leaving that much harder.

"Thank you for being honest with me. I'm going to go. You know if you need anything, you can just call or text me. You'll be out of hospital in a few days, so you've got that to look forward to."

Cam wipes the tears from his face. "Actually, I got cleared today. I'm going home tomorrow."

I force a smile. "That's great. I'm going to go now. Good luck with everything."

I get up from the table, help him back to his room, and turn to leave. He stops me and extends his hand.

"Friends?"

I look at his hand. I don't want to shake it, but I do. A shock goes through my whole body. It isn't a bad shock; it is the same shock I felt when Cam and I first started talking; it is the shock we'd often talked about. It is almost impossible to describe, but we both know it is incredible, and something we'll never feel with anyone else. I see the look on Cam's face, and I know he feels it too.

"Friends."

I pull my hand away, open the door and go through it, closing it behind me. I lean against it and try to slow my racing heart down. When I get home, I shower and call my friends. We decide to go out for dinner, and I'm hoping they'll keep my mind off everything.

~

On Saturday, I find myself thinking about Cam more. I know he will be going home that day, and I can't stop the part of me that desperately wants to be there to welcome him home. I try my hardest to stop thinking about it, so I put my headphones in and play my favourite songs. I begin to write ideas down for a new song. I have my eyes focused on the words when I feel someone looking at me. I look up and Cam is standing at my bedroom door.

He walks into my room and starts talking, but I can't hear a word he's saying. He sits on my bed and gestures to my headphones; I assume he wants me to take them out.

"Why are you here?"

"I want you back. For good this time, I think."

"You think? My God, what is wrong with you? What is wrong with us? I can't keep doing this. One minute you want to be with me, then you don't, then you do again. I can't keep up. We're bringing out the worst in each other. We're becoming shitty people. How the hell did we get like this? We were so in love. I thought you were the one. This is exhausting. You need to decide: we're either together or we're not. But, if you decide it's over, then it's over for good. I can't do this anymore. I'm broken, and going back and forth is destroying me. We had this conversation yesterday. Jesus, Cam, I can't go through this again."

Cam moves closer to me and grabs the side of my face with his hands. When he moves closer I can smell peppermint toothpaste on his breath.

"I will never stop loving you," he says as he kisses me. I think at that moment that everything is going to go back to normal, but it isn't.

"I don't know why I did that. I think I just needed to kiss you once more. Shit, I'm sorry."

I can't take this anymore; as much as I love him, I can't let him do this to me. So, now it is my turn to end it.

"It's done, Cam. For good. You should go."

"You're right. I'm sorry."

After he leaves, I look down at my bedspread and watch the tears hit the material as all of the pain I have felt over the past few days flows through my whole body and turns into tears. I know in this moment that I no longer have any other choice but to move on, no matter how much it will hurt.

CHAPTER FIVE
MOVING FORWARD

Since the Saturday when things between Cam and I ended for good, I've been on an emotional rollercoaster. I have laughed, I have cried, I am happy, and I am miserable. I have been all over the place, but I begin to throw myself into my recovery and my music. I know that, with time, I will be able to move forward, once and for all.

Before I know it, we are in the winter months. It is now July, and the past six weeks have been and gone in the blink of an eye. Learning to live without Cam has been a challenge. We often see each other out, but for the first month we acted like we didn't know each other. It was easier that way. It is an adjustment for both of us, and we both know that. In all honesty if we were given the chance, we'd fall right back into how we used to be. My heart is slowly healing, and I am focusing on my life and myself. That's how things need to be. I find therapy to be exactly what I need. I instantly connected with Angie, and knew from the beginning that I could trust her with everything. As time goes on, I find it easier to open up and be honest. I can clear my mind, and she helps me find ways to get through moments when I don't think I'll be strong enough to keep going.

I start dealing with everything I've been avoiding. It is the best thing I can do for myself, and it sets me free. I can learn to forgive my father, and I begin to go easy on myself for thinking I am never enough. I learn to love myself, to embrace every element of who I am, and I am able to work towards being a person I can be proud to be. Going to therapy and being honest means I have to face everything. I can't run anymore, and I can see how much damage I've done to myself. Angie helps me deal with life without Cam too. Whenever I want to call him or whenever I want to talk to him, I write. I write everything I'd say to him. I write down everything I am feeling and I write down everything I wish I could change about our breakup. It isn't ideal, but it gives me the chance to get it off my chest. I can still be honest and say what I want to say, but I don't actually say it to him, which means I learn to live without him, even if it is difficult. There isn't a day that goes by when I don't think about Cam, but I know nothing is going to change, no matter how much I still want to be with him. I know distancing ourselves is for the best.

I rely on my family and friends to get me through the tough days, and they are happy to help me when I need them. Whenever I am feeling down, all I have to do is text or call my best friends and we plan to do something. They always know what to say and do to distract me. I didn't think we could become any closer, or that our friendship could get any stronger, but that's happened. I realise in these days, weeks and months that, while I don't have Cam, I have an amazing support system in my friends and family. I see first-hand who is there for me when I'm at my lowest, and that's something I'll never forget. I'll never be able to repay my friends and family for what they have done for me.

At the same time as all of this, my relationship with Evan continues to get stronger. Evan and I start spending quality time together so we can get to know each other. We go out for coffee, we take Jessie for walks, and we have movie nights with Darci, my mum and my brothers. We also spend time with Evan's family so we can get to know them, and they get the chance to get to know us. Evan has moved into our house full-time now too. As a family, we became stronger. After I accepted Evan, everything felt much better: not just for me, but for everyone around us. My mum is a million times happier, and they are both able to show their love for each other without having to worry about upsetting my siblings and me ... well, mainly just me. No one has to worry about walking on eggshells anymore. We have the chance to be a family with a proper father figure, someone who isn't going to leave us, and as much as I wish it was my real father here with us, I know Evan is the best person to be in our lives. He never tries to take the place of my father; he just tries his best to help give us that fatherly support that we have desperately been searching for. Letting Evan into our lives is one of the best decisions we have made, and I know our family will continue to grow in strength and love.

When I feel like there is no other choice but to call Cam, and writing everything down doesn't work, I go straight into the studio and sit with my uncle. He has helped me to get through every bad day I have encountered since being released from hospital. He often comes with me to my therapy sessions, and he takes me out of the house when I refuse to leave my room. He picks me up when I am down, and it makes me appreciate him a million times more. He never leaves my side. I can call him at any time of the day or night, and he is there for me. I am incredibly lucky to have such a strong bond with him, and I do my best to thank him whenever I get the chance. Without him, I really wouldn't be able to find the strength I need to continue when things get tough.

With my uncle's advice and Angie's help, I can readjust my way of thinking, and focus on the path I am heading down. I decide that I want to commit to my album; I want to commit to making a career from this. I was on the right path before Cam and I broke up, but when our relationship ended I spiralled out of control, and my career was in serious jeopardy. Melody and my uncle worked tirelessly to help me get back on my feet, and they continually told me there was no rush to get the album done, even though we had agreed to stick with the original release date. I felt immense pressure from myself to get the final songs written and recorded, but I lacked motivation and inspiration. I almost wanted to quit, but I was still gaining a lot of positive attention. People were interested in my music, and the hype surrounding my debut album was astounding. I never expected this to happen to me, but it was, and after breaking down in front of my uncle I chose to embrace it, not run from it. I was suddenly motivated, and my creativity peaked. I was inspired by what I'd been through and by the end of June I had written fourteen songs.

We are now down to the final stages, and I only have a few more songs to record before the album is done. My uncle and I have worked 24/7 to get it done so quickly, and I work on posting more covers because people have been asking for more. It gives me something to do, and it reignites everything I thought I had lost.

In the second week of July, my uncle and I spend almost every hour of every day in the studio. Everything has come together and on Friday the 12th I am recording the final song. I sing the final note, and when I'm done, I stop, take a few deep breaths and take the headphones off. I go back into the office part of the studio where my uncle is waiting with his arms open.

"You did it. Oh, I'm so proud of you, my superstar! I knew you could do it."

I walk straight into his embrace, feeling my emotions creeping up on me.

"None of this would have happened without you. I'll never be able to thank you for everything you've done for me. It wasn't just me. *We* did this. There wouldn't be me if it weren't for you."

I hug him tighter.

"Darlin', it's all you. You're the one with the voice. I'm just doing what any uncle would do for his niece."

As he lets me go, he sees my tears.

"Delilah, please don't cry."

"I promise they're happy tears."

I laugh and wipe them away.

"Good. I don't want to see you cry from pain anymore. You're stronger than all of this."

He claps his hands together and winks at me.

"Alright, kiddo. I'll get these final two songs edited and send them through to Melody in the morning. If she gives them the all clear, your album will officially be done. Melody will probably contact you, but I'll keep you up to date as well."

I sit with him for another fifteen minutes, talking about everything before checking the time.

"I've got to go. I've got to meet a friend."

After I finish in the studio, I thank my uncle, again and head to my car. I turn the engine and headlights on. It is just after 6:00 p.m. but, with the change in weather, the sun has been setting earlier. I had planned to meet Ryan, so I begin to head towards the beach, except we aren't meeting at our usual spot at Cottesloe. For some reason, Ryan asked me to meet him at a beach twenty minutes away. I have been spending more time with Ryan recently too. He has been going through a lot as well, so we've been helping each other out. We've both taken comfort in being at the beach. For some reason, it calms both of us down. So, whenever we have something important to tell each other, we meet at our usual spot. I don't know if it is the comfort of being in an open space or just the calmness we get from the sound of the waves as they crash into the shoreline; either way, it helps.

As I drive to the beach, my mind is racing. I can't focus on anything other than my album, which makes a nice change because recently I have struggled to think about anything other than Cam. I go over every song I've written, reflect on every word I've sung, and think of every single event that has happened to inspire the songs I've written. I feel a sense of pride; I know it has taken a lot for me to write fourteen songs. For the first time in a long time, I feel incredibly proud of myself. I feel confident, and I feel that through my songs I can make a difference. Music has always been the one thing that never lets me down in life. It has literally changed my life, and knowing that I have the chance to do that for someone – even if it is just one person – well, that makes every single thing I've been through worth it. I always remember my uncle telling me that you're good at your job if you can make people *feel* something. I hope that my music will do that; I hope it inspires people, and can help people get through their dark days.

My mind continues to wander as I drive to the beach. When I arrive, I pull into a free parking spot and call Ryan. I've tried to spot him, but I can't see him.

"Where are you?"

He laughs before answering my question.

"Hang on. I'll come up to the car park and get you."

I put my phone into my jumper pocket, get out and stand by my car. I spot Ryan running towards me, smiling.

"Hi."

He embraces me, and I'm taken aback by his sudden affection.

"Hi."

I follow him along the walkway, and up a small hill before we make our way down to the sand.

"Why didn't we go to Cottesloe?"

I take Ryan's hand and step down from the rock I am standing on.

"Because we couldn't do this at Cottesloe."

He leads me towards a light and, as we get closer, I realise it's a flame coming from a barrel. I also notice the thick tree trunks around the bonfire. I sit down and watch Ryan grab a blanket.

"I didn't know how cold it would be, so I have a few blankets."

He hands me a thick red blanket. I wrap it around my body and sit back down, I look up and watch the stars twinkle in the clear, dark sky. Ryan sits down next to me and follows my gaze into the sky.

75

"It's beautiful here. I often come here at night-time. It's pretty popular, and it's one of the only beaches where you can have a bonfire, but I especially love the serenity it offers. It brings people together. I don't think I've ever seen an unhappy person here. Everyone's friendly, and everyone's usually smiling or laughing. I come here and sit down by the rocks over there. It's usually quiet in that spot. I look out at the water and listen as the waves hit the sand. I watch the skyline split into two as the sun disappears and the darkness takes its place, and I watch the people around me. Ever since my depression peaked, it's been something that has helped me."

I look over at Ryan, who's now looking out to the ocean. I look at his chest: it begins to slow down with each breath, I know he is thinking about something that scares him, but I don't know if I should ask about it. Ryan and I have become pretty close, especially over the last few weeks, but I know him well enough to know not to push him into telling me something before he is ready.

"I spoke to my mum today. I'm going to see her on Tuesday."

"That's amazing, Ry."

"Thanks. Will you still come with me? I don't know if I can do this by myself, at least not yet anyway."

"Of course, I'd be happy to go with you."

I smile, and pull the blanket tighter around my body as Ryan moves closer to me.

"I feel like I'm always saying this, but I need to be honest with you. There's something I've wanted to say to you for a while now, but I've always been too scared, and you've always been with Cam. But, now that you're single, I feel it's the right time to tell you. I

76

have to tell you this now otherwise I never will. I know it might push you away, and I accept that, but I can't fight this anymore."

I know exactly what he is going to say, but I don't want to hear it. I can't hear it. I am still in love with Cam. I'm not ready to deal with all of this. I look down at my shoes as Ryan gently lifts my head up so our eyes meet.

"Please, look at me."

I slowly look up and meet his eyes. The least I can do is listen to what he has to say.

"From the moment I met you, I felt something towards you. At first I didn't know what it was, but as we spent more time together the feelings intensified. I never told Cam, but I think he suspected it. I didn't ever want to be responsible for breaking a couple up, but when he ended things, I just wanted to hold you until the pain left your body. I know the timing sucks, but Delilah, I'm drawn to you. I know you've just come out of a relationship, but I want to see where this goes. I want to see if we can be more than friends."

I bite my lip as I try to listen to what Ryan is telling me. I am fresh out of a long-term relationship; I'm not even remotely close to being ready to start something new with someone else. However, something in me tells me to give Ryan a chance. I know I'm not ready, but maybe if we take things slowly, we can make it work. Maybe this is what I need to get over Cam, to prove to myself that there is still love out there, even if it's not with the person I thought I was meant to be with.

Ryan hasn't taken his eyes off me.

"Do you really want to go into…this, whatever it is, knowing I still love Cam? I mean, I know it's over between us, but that doesn't change the fact that I still love him."

"I know you do, but you've said it yourself: the two of you aren't meant to be. I don't know if you truly believe that, but maybe we are meant to be. How will we know if we don't try?"

He has just said everything I have been thinking to myself, but I am still scared. In fact, I am terrified. Loving someone after loving Cam feels incredibly uncomfortable, and unnatural, but maybe that's why I need to see where this goes.

"This is something that's going to take time, lots of time. I don't want to label this, I don't want to label us. I just want to take it slowly. We're not together, as a couple, but if you're happy to do things this way, then we can see where it goes."

Ryan leans over and, before I have time to react, he kisses me. It is a kiss unlike any other kiss I've had before. It is passionate, but it feels like it is something he needs. I kiss him back, trying to tell him it is okay. When he lets me go, he looks happier, like a weight has been lifted off his shoulders. All I feel is guilt, I feel nothing.

We spend the rest of the night talking about everything: from him going home to face his parents to my album being done. As we start talking more, the unsettling feelings slowly fade away, and I find myself getting more comfortable with Ryan. I snuggle up next to him and we sit on the beach, looking to the sky, together, as more than friends. As we look up at the stars, my phone goes off, interrupting our peace. I pull it out of my pocket and open the message I've received from my uncle.

Hi, love. Sorry for the late message. Melody wants us in the studio tomorrow. Your first song will be going out onto the radio here and around

Australia on Monday, so we need to have a business meeting. We need to figure out what song we're going to release first and we will need to come up with an album name. Be at the studio by 10:00 a.m., Melody will Skype us at 10:30 a.m., which is 12:30 p.m. for her. We can spend half an hour listening to the final two songs. I want you to hear the final product.

Oh crap! I haven't even thought about an album name. It has completely slipped my mind. Part of me wants to stay with Ryan, but I know I won't be able to concentrate on anything other than the album name.

"Sorry, I've got to go. Hey, don't be sad. I want to stay, I really do, it's just business stuff. My first song is being released on Monday, and I still need to pick an album name."

"As much as I want to stay here with you, I understand why you need to go, and I respect that. I know how hard you've worked on your album, so you need some time to yourself to think about the name. I'll walk you up to your car."

After helping him get his blankets, we walk back towards our cars holding hands. When I get to my car I unlock it, and thank Ryan for the night.

"I'll see you on Tuesday?"

"Yeah, I'm going to see my mum at 11:00 a.m., so I'll pick you up on the way through?"

I nod and hug him again before getting into my car. I wave as he heads to his car, then quickly reply to my uncle.

I totally forgot about an album name. I'll try to think of one now. I'll see you at the studio in the morning.

I hit send and start my car; my uncle replies immediately.

Don't stress too much about the album name. The right one will come to you. Get good night's sleep. I'll see you in the morning.

I know my uncle is right. I can't overthink it; the right name will come to me when the time is right. I start my car and head home. When I get home, I shower and hop into bed. As I drift off, I keep trying to think of an album name, but nothing is jumping out at me. I continue to throw words out into the world, hoping I'll stumble upon the perfect one. But, the more I think about it, the more I become frustrated with the whole thing.

~

As I drive to the studio on Saturday morning, I try to distract myself from thinking about the name, *again*. I turn the radio on and turn the volume up, singing along to all the songs I know. When I get to the studio, I go inside and find my uncle. He is waiting with a coffee and some breakfast for me. As I sit down to eat the pancakes he has made me, he begins to explain what we will be doing.

"Melody basically wants to discuss the album name, the announcement of the album and what song we're going to drop first. When we've got all of that sorted, a day and a time will be picked. Your song will get replayed throughout that day and over the week, before an official lyric video will go up online next Friday morning. At some point, we will shoot a music video, but that's still a way off."

He continues to explain the gist of things, then plays the songs we have recorded over the last few weeks. It is surreal to hear them, but I am happy to see the album finished. I feel proud of what I've accomplished. I just hope that other people like my music too.

At exactly 10:30 a.m. my uncle's computer alerts us to Melody's Skype call. We wait for her to appear on the screen, greet each other, then she starts filling me in on the plans too.

"Delilah, your album is amazing. You should be really proud of what you've produced. We need you to pick the first song to release. We want to get it out onto radio stations on Monday, and we want to release the album name at the same time. You're about to get a schedule for Monday too. It's going to give us a chance to generate more hype for the album. You've got quite a following as it is, but we want to push your album more. You've been through so much, and you've worked so hard. You deserve every ounce of success. You've done all the hard work, now it's our turn to get this album out there for the world to hear."

We then begin to try to pick an album title. I know it must be the right word or words. We go through what seems like a million different words. Word after word keep popping up as we brainstorm, but nothing sounds right, nothing feels right. I am ready to give up when I look between my uncle and Melody.

"I've got it! *Rise*."

As soon as I say it aloud, I know it is the right word. Everything I've been through has led me to this moment; I have risen from everything that has nearly destroyed me, and now, I stand tall and proud of everything I have overcome.

"It's perfect," my uncle says, beaming at me.

"I agree, it's perfect," Melody says on the computer. "It's settled. *Rise* is the official title of your debut album. Now we just need the right song to release."

I don't even need time to think about that one; I already know what song I want to debut first.

"Let's go with *Wildfire*,"

My uncle looks at me, surprised.

"Are you sure?"

I know he is hesitant. That song was the first song I ever wrote, and Cam and my dad inspired part of it. I wrote it after Cam and I started dating, and I used my dad leaving as motivation. The words in the song are powerful, and it shows what I have to offer: not just through my vocals, but through my lyrics too. I know without a doubt it is the right song to go with, even if it is difficult to hear.

"Yes, I'm sure."

"Okay, let's go with *Wildfire*."

Melody claps her hands together. The sound makes my uncle and I jump, we look at each other and laugh.

"Perfect. It's settled. *Rise* will be your debut album and *Wildfire* will be your debut single. Congratulations, Delilah."

I thank her before asking her the question I'd almost forgotten to ask.

"Hey Melody, what do I do about my job at Boom Clap? I spoke to Hayley - my boss - this morning. I haven't worked a shift for a few weeks now, and she asked if I want more hours. Do I take them or do you think it's time to move on?"

"Well, Delilah, that's entirely up to you. If you need the money to support yourself, then I'd stay there. But, when your album drops, I think you'll find it'll be time to quit. Now, while I remember, I need to tell you about Monday. As far as the day goes, you'll need to be in the studio with your uncle from 8:30 a.m. to 3:30 p.m. Over the morning, you'll do live announcements, for each state separately. Then you've got interviews with the biggest stations in Perth, Sydney and Melbourne. These will all be live, so make sure you're prepared. They will ask you questions about the album and what inspired the songs you've written. Your personal life is off limits, so don't worry about that. You'll get a break from 1:00 p.m., but you'll need to be ready to go at 1:30 p.m. From 1:30 p.m. until 3:30 p.m. you'll be doing newspaper interviews in Perth. You'll be talking to five different journalists. They have questions ready to go, but the same deal applies as before: your personal life is off limits. Your song and interviews will continue to play throughout the day too, so, by 4:00 p.m. when it's peak time, all of Australia will be aware of who you are and what you are offering. I know this is a lot to take in, but we've got to get moving so we can meet the deadline for your album to be released. The more press we generate now, the better your sales will be when the album drops."

I try to take in everything Melody's saying, I didn't expect all of this to happen so suddenly, and while I'm nervous, I'm also beyond excited for these opportunities. I shake my head as my uncle hands me the schedule. I start reading the printed copy and see something scheduled for Tuesday, which is when I'm meant to go with Ryan to see his mum. He'll be devastated if I can't go.

"Um, Melody, what is this thing scheduled for Tuesday?"

"Oh, how could I forget? You're scheduled to film a segment for MTV Australia. They want to document your journey before the album drops. They'll do an interview with you and then film some things, like you at home and you walking at the beach. It's a great opportunity for you."

I look back at the schedule.

"You're probably going to hate me, Melody, but can we do it another day? I've got something really important that I need to attend to on Tuesday."

I feel my whole body tense up as my uncle looks at me, I know by the look on his face that he wants to know what I am talking about. Just as he is about to ask me about it, Melody interrupts him.

"Delilah, this is your career here. This is important. Anything else comes second. I know that might suck, but we need to do this on Tuesday. Everything's already organised. The camera crew and the reporter are ready to go. It's too late to reschedule now."

I feel guilty, and sad too.

"I understand, and I agree. I'll, ummm, I'll reschedule."

I know that Ryan's going to be hurt, and I am torn. I want to be there for him, but Melody is right: this is my career, and that has to be my number one priority right now. Everything else has to take a back seat. Despite knowing that being there for Ryan should be a priority too, I decide not to go against Melody's schedule. I know she's worked hard to get all of this organised, and an MTV interview is incredible, so the least I can do is follow the schedule.

"I know this is happening quickly and I know it means sacrificing other things, but you only get one chance at this, Delilah. You have to put the hard work in to reap the rewards. You've already worked so hard. This is the final step before the album is released."

"I know. It's just hard for me to cancel on people. I always feel bad."

"I know, but it's only one day. Also, please keep Wednesday free. I've organised the photo shoot we need to get your album cover done too. I'll fly to Perth for the day, so I will be there with you. It will be a half day shoot, but by the end of it, we will have the album cover done. I'll spend a few hours after the shoot with Chris, who's the photographer. He's going to be flying to Perth with me. I use him for all my client shoots. He's one of the best photographers in Australia, so you're in good hands. We will get the final design down and get your opinion from a range of options. When you've picked one, I'll take it back to Sydney and then we will begin to produce copies of your album. That may take a while, but we will be ready to go for the release date in a month's time. I think that's everything I need to cover. I'll let you have some time to process all of that. I know you're probably overwhelmed. I'll talk to you again on Monday, but feel free to call me before that if you need anything."

I thank Melody again before she disconnects from our conversation. After my uncle turns the computer off, he faces me.

"Go home and try not to think about everything too much. Just do your best to relax. I'll see you tomorrow night for dinner."

I get up from my chair and head to my car. I immediately get my phone out and call Ryan. I know it is best to tell him the truth now and get it out of the way. The phone line rings three times before he answers.

"Hey, you. How'd everything go?"

I take a deep breath before trying to gently explain the situation.

"It was good. Intense, but good. I've got a pretty hectic schedule. I've got radio interviews and newspaper interviews, and we picked the album name, so that's exciting."

I squeeze my eyes closed, feeling frustrated that I haven't told him straightaway.

"That's awesome. What name did you settle on? When are these interviews?"

He sounds excited, and my guilt begins to build again.

"I thought *Rise* would be a good name. It sounds right, and it fits the songs I wrote. The interviews are scheduled for Monday, but I, ummm, I have another interview with MTV. That's on Tuesday."

I feel incredibly anxious as I wait for Ryan to reply.

"Tuesday? As in, this Tuesday? The Tuesday when we're meant to go and see my mum?"

I hold my phone with my right hand and lift my left hand to my head, slowly rubbing the middle of my forehead.

"Correct. This Tuesday. I'm so sorry. I want to be there for you, but Melody wouldn't budge on the schedule and I can't exactly bail on everything." I bite my lip, hoping Ryan will understand, but I prepare myself for him to react badly.

"Oh, okay. What about Wednesday? I can call my mum and change the day if that works?"

I feel even worse; now I have to say no to that too.

"I'm so sorry. Wednesday isn't any good either. I have to shoot my album cover."

Ryan goes quiet again.

"I didn't want to face this without you by my side, but your career is important. I'll go by myself and I'll keep you updated."

"Ryan I'm really sorry. I can call you before you go and I'll call you after. I'll be there with you in spirit. Please, don't be mad at me."

"I'm not mad at you. Honestly, it's fine. I know how important this is to you."

I let out a sigh of relief, but I still feel bad.

"Thank you for understanding. You're amazing."

"You're amazing too. I love you. Shit, sorry, I didn't mean to say that. I've got to go. I'll call you tomorrow."

Before I even get a chance to reply, he hangs up. Did he really just say what I think he said? Surely I heard that wrong. He doesn't love me. He can't love me this quickly, can he? My mind races and I feel weird; I didn't ever think I'd hear those words from anyone other than Cam. I shake my head before heading home, trying my best to ignore what has just happened.

When I get home, I go into my room and find Dakota sitting on my bed waiting for me.

"Dakota! What are you doing here?"

I run towards her.

"Surprise! I'm here for a few weeks before I fly to New York. I made mum keep it a secret. I'm staying here in my old room until I fly out."

I hug her tightly.

"I'm so glad you're here. I've missed you."

"I've missed you too. Sit. Let's talk and catch up."

She sits on my bed, patting a spot next to her. We lie down on the bed, looking up at the roof which becomes darker as the grey clouds cover the sun outside my window. The faint sound of rain falling starts growing louder as my sister and I have one of our famous D&M's. She tells me about New York and what she'll be doing, while I tell her about my album and, of course, Ryan.

"Confession time. What was he like as a kisser?"

That's my sister: never one to beat around the bush; she's just straight to the point.

"He was a good kisser, not the best, but I imagine that's what happens when you don't kiss a lot of people."

"How do you feel about it? Do you like him?"

I look over at my sister, who's still looking at the roof.

"Honestly, I do like him, and I guess I see the potential for a relationship. It just scares me, when I look into his eyes I see someone who's falling in love and I just ... I don't even know how to finish that sentence."

My sister tries to give me a reassuring look.

"What do you mean? It sounds like you're trying to convince yourself that there is potential for something more. Do you not feel the same?"

I throw my hands in the air before being completely honest.

"No, I don't feel the same. I guess I've been trying to force myself into trying to like him romantically, and I've been focusing on the idea of trying to love him in general, but I can't. Every time I try to, I'm reminded of the reason why I can't. He's not Cam. Dakota, I don't know what to do. I like Ryan, but I love Cam. Ryan wants to be with me, and Cam doesn't. How am I supposed to move on or figure out what to do if the person I love doesn't want to be with me? I feel stuck. Physically, mentally and emotionally I can't get over Cam. I thought I was making progress, but I don't think I am."

"Delilah, you can't force yourself into loving someone. But, at the same time, you're not going to know if there's potential if you don't allow yourself the chance to explore this option. Your heart is still healing, and I know it sucks, but you're just confused. Give things with Ryan a chance. Stop looking for Cam when you're around Ryan. He's not Cam, he's Ryan. It will take time, but Ryan deserves a chance, and you deserve a chance at happiness again. After a few months, if you still feel the same, then you'll know it's not meant to be. You're not going to know if you don't try."

I know she is right. I guess I just don't want to admit everything she's just said. I giggle.

"He told me he loves me."

"He what? Already? Geez, he's not wasting any time, is he?"

I giggle again.

"He didn't mean to say it ... at least, I don't think he did. He hung up on me once he said it. I think he felt embarrassed. I think he's going to avoid me now."

Dakota lifts her hand into the air and flips it back and forth.

"Boys! So keen to jump into things heart first, aren't they?"

We burst into a fit of laughter, then spend the rest of the day planning things to do while she's here. Having my sister home makes me feel so much happier, and spending time with her is exactly what I need.

~

As we sit down for our usual Sunday night family dinner, my uncle hovers over me.

"So, Evan's one of us now. Think he will last?"

He's trying to sound serious, and I try to hide my smirk.

"If he does, he must really love mum. I wonder how he will deal with all of our pranks. I don't think he knows we're a bunch of pranksters."

My mum looks at us.

"What are you two laughing about?" she asks as she hands a bowl of bread rolls around.

"Nothing, sis. Just special uncle/niece business."

I watch everyone pass food around the table. Everyone at the table is happy, and there is so much love in the room. Evan looks at my mum with love. When he sees me looking at him, he smiles at me and raises his glass.

"To Delilah! Congratulations on your album. We're proud of you."

Everyone cheers as our glasses hit.

"Thank you," I say, getting up and hugging him. "Welcome to the family, Evan. We're lucky to have you."

We all sit at the table and talk, laughing and enjoying each other's company. I am proud of not only how far I've come, but how far my family has come too. We have become a strong unit, and nothing can break that.

After many conversations with Dakota over the weekend, I am still confused about what to do. Monday is quickly approaching, and I know it will be the start of a new chapter in my journey. I promise myself it will be a fresh start for me and my mind. As I snuggle into bed with my sister by my side, I think about what the week will hold. Little do I know that while Ryan faces his past, I'll unexpectedly have to face mine too.

Chapter Six
Closure

I know the next month of my life is going to hectic, and I know I'll be taking more proactive steps towards my dream. I have so many things to look forward to, and I am excited to see where the next month of my life will take me.

On Monday morning, my alarm sounds at exactly 6:30 a.m. As much as my body longs to stay in bed all day, I know I have to get up. I have a long day ahead of me. I am due to be in the studio at 8:30 a.m., so I have an hour and a half to get ready and have breakfast. I head downstairs and decide to make myself a smoothie; it feels like the only thing I can stomach. My nerves are running rampant, and the last thing I feel like doing is eating, but I know my body needs fuel, so a berry smoothie will be enough to keep me going until lunch. I am sitting at the table and slowly sipping my smoothie when Dakota walks into the kitchen.

"Morning," she says as she yawns. "Can I have the rest of this?"

She points at the extra smoothie liquid that sits in the blender. I nod my head as I finish off the last of my breakfast.

"What are you doing up so early? I didn't wake you up, did I?"

"No, you didn't. My body still thinks I'm in Sydney, so I wake up thinking I'm still two hours ahead."

She yawns again and sits down. I giggle but stop when Dakota looks at me with an aggravated look. I clear my throat as she lets out a deep sigh.

"Sorry. I'm just tired. What are you doing up so early?"

"I've got to go into the studio. I'm announcing my album name and releasing my first single on the radio, then I've got some interviews. Do you want to come? I'm so nervous, so having you there will help."

"Of course, I'd love to be there with you. What are you going to wear?"

"Um, I don't know, gym clothes maybe?"

Dakota laughs, "Delilah, you can't wear gym clothes. If you're doing interviews, you should look professional. Otherwise, people might think you don't care."

"Shit. I didn't even think about that. I certainly don't want to give off the wrong impression. I don't know what to wear though. I don't ever overthink my outfits, and I don't even know if I have anything professional."

"Don't stress. You can make most clothes look professional. You just need to find the right pieces. Let's go and look at what you've got."

I follow my sister back to my room and sit on my bed as she begins to go through my clothes.

"The key is not to wear something that's not you. You should look professional, but if you don't feel comfortable or you feel it's not right, then it's pointless."

I nod my head, trying to help my sister pick pieces I think will work. Dakota keeps putting clothes on my bed and when it is all but covered, she asks me to get up.

"Decision time. These are the kinds of looks you want to go for, but remember it has to represent you, and you have to feel comfortable. Is there anything you're drawn to?"

I focus on the pile of clothes. "Dakota, I obviously like all of these items, since I own them, but I didn't ever see them as *professional* clothes."

"You're overthinking this. Just pick whatever you want to wear."

I finally settle on an outfit.

"Let's go with the faux leather leggings. They're my favourite. I like the light grey peplum top and, um, I don't know what shoes or jacket to go with."

Dakota looks at the clothes and picks out a faux leather jacket.

"Here, this hooded motorcycle jacket will be perfect."

I try to hide my laughter, "Huh? Motorcycle jacket? Isn't this just a jacket?"

"Yes, but technically speaking it's a motorcycle jacket. It basically has a distressed finish and a removable hood, plus it's got extra lining on the inside, so it's warmer."

I hold the jacket up. "Well, that explains it then. I guess I should read the tags when I buy clothes."

"Now you just need shoes."

I look at the options my sister has put out, and settle on a pair of black ankle boots. I hold them up and show Dakota.

"What about these?"

"Um, I guess. You've gone with blacks and greys though. Don't you want any colour?"

94

I look at the shoes then back at my sister. "I like blacks and greys. They suit me better than colour anyway."

"As long as you're comfortable."

"Thank you for helping me, and for being here for me. You're my best friend, and I'm so proud of you."

"Ditto. We're in this together, for life. I've always got your back."

I release my sister and check the time on my phone. It is 7:20 a.m.

"I'm going to shower then do my hair and makeup. If it gets closer to 8:00 a.m., come and get me. I can't be late today."

"No problem. I'm going to find something to wear too. I'll keep an eye on the time."

I thank her again before going into the bathroom. At 8:03 a.m. Dakota comes down the stairs.

"Ready?" she asks as she gets to the bottom of the stairs.

"Yep. Let's do this." I unlock the front door and head towards the car.

"Let me drive," Dakota says. I don't hesitate; I throw her my keys and get into the passenger side of the car.

When we reach the studio, we head inside and find our uncle busily getting everything set up.

"Morning, ladies," he says before kissing our cheeks.

It is just after 8:20 a.m., so my uncle tells me to sit down by the phone that is set up in the studio.

"You're going to talk to Stacey O'Donald and Louis Parker. They run the morning show on one of the biggest stations in Sydney. They usually finish at 9:00 a.m., but they're staying on for longer. Melody had to pull some strings to make it happen, but she's expecting it'll help with promoting everything. Also, pre-orders for the album will open tonight. Seeing as the official date has already been announced, Melody wants to get sales going. Melody will call you in about five minutes, and she will connect you to the station."

I take a few deep breaths, suddenly feeling nervous. A few minutes later, the phone rings. I answer it and talk to Melody.

"If you're ready, I'll put you through now."

I give her the all clear, and she puts me through to the radio station.

"Welcome back. I'm Stacey, and I'm joined by my co-host Louis. We have a special treat for our Sydney listeners now. If you haven't already heard Delilah Walker's amazing voice, you've been missing out. The talented 21-year-old from Perth started posting covers online, became an internet sensation, and was soon signed to BrookeHouse Entertainment where she's been busily working on her debut album. We're going to talk to Delilah, but first have a quick listen to some of her covers."

Parts of my cover songs begin to play and after thirty seconds, I hear Louis.

"What a beautiful voice! We've got Delilah on the line now. Good morning Delilah, how are you?"

"Good morning. I'm good, thank you. How are you guys?"

"We're great, thank you. Your voice is incredible. How has posting these covers changed your life?" Stacey asks.

"Thank you. Well, they got me a contract, so they've definitely been life-changing. I've been able to take my passion for music and write songs for my debut album, which has been such an indescribable experience."

"Now, we understand you're joining us to announce your album name and then you're going to release your first single. So, we will hand it over to you."

"That's correct. I'm proud to announce my debut album is titled *Rise*, and this is my debut single, *Wildfire*."

I smile at my uncle and sister as I make the announcement, and the butterflies I've been feeling suddenly disappear.

"You heard it here, folks. Congratulations, Delilah, and thank you for joining us. Ladies and gentleman, here it is: the debut single from Delilah Walker."

I thank the hosts and, when the song begins to play, I hang up. I sit with my uncle and sister and talk to them about the interview. We couldn't listen to the broadcast since it would interfere with the line, and now we can't get the station loaded in time to hear the song, so we have to wait until I speak to the Perth station to hear it.

After the Sydney announcement, I do the same for the Melbourne station, and then the Perth station. After the announcement for Perth is done, I sit back with my uncle and sister, and we listen to *Wildfire* play through the radio. I feel tears of happiness escape my eyes as Dakota embraces me.

"So proud of you, sis. You did it!"

She holds me while I cry. It feels nice to cry from happiness and not sadness, for a change, and I feel proud. I've accomplished something I didn't think I'd ever be able to accomplish and I really am on the path to a better life. I am constantly improving on the person I am and I am heading to a much happier place. Everything is falling into place, just as it should be, and I know that as long as I continue to believe in myself and focus on getting myself closer to my dreams, I'll succeed. In the end, that's all that matters.

Throughout the rest of the day, I promote my album and do a number of interviews. The more I talk about my album, my journey and my songs, the more confident I become. After the final interview is over, my uncle and I speak to Melody. She tells me how proud of me she is, and she tells me that so far the song has been a huge hit. She has been inundated with comments and feedback from the radio stations and from listeners. My song is making an impact, and that is the most amazing part of this whole thing. I am finally doing what I've always wanted to do: I am singing songs that make people feel something, and I am suddenly more determined than ever before.

After agreeing on the photo shoot time for Wednesday, I am done for the day. Melody tells me that the pre-order option will open at 5:30 p.m. Perth time. She says that from what she's heard, we should get quite a few pre-order sales. I smile at the thought of people buying my album before it's even been released. I honestly don't care about the money side of things. I just care about people enjoying my music and, from the sounds of things, they are.

~

On Wednesday, Dakota, my uncle and I meet at Cottesloe beach, where we'd agreed to meet Melody for the photo shoot. Dakota and I spent all of Tuesday with MTV, filming a mini-documentary about my journey. The producer told me it would air in a few weeks, but I will get to see the final cut as soon as it's edited, which I'm excited about. After the interview, Dakota and I went home. I tried to contact Ryan, but he didn't respond, so we ended up trying to think of the perfect album cover. We brainstormed a ton of ideas, and we were trying to think of the perfect location.

"What about the beach? You love it there. I mean, you're always there. You could get a photo of you looking out to the ocean. Everything could be grey except the water? That would look awesome!"

I looked at Dakota, who looked proud of her idea. I thought about her idea and tried to envision it.

"I like it, but what does it have to do with rising? I mean that's the focus point. It has to be powerful. If I were on top of a cliff with my guitar by my side looking out into the ocean, then I'd go for it."

Dakota looked at me, "I love that idea! Why don't you do that? There's that area at Cottesloe, you know where the rocks are? You could stand on that and look out to the water!"

I try to visualise the area my sister was referring to. She's right: it would be perfect, and it would embrace every element of me. I'd written multiple songs at that beach, and being up on a ledge looking out to the water would embrace the rising aspect.

"Let's do it," I said as I grinned at my sister.

We called Melody and told her the idea. After we explained our concept, she agreed to it.

"Your album cover has to show you and give a glimpse of what the listener can look forward to, so you need to go with something that sums everything up. If you feel that's what's going to fit the album, then that's what we will go with. Make sure you've got clothes that represent you too. Don't go overboard with your outfit, it will take away from everything else."

After I finished my conversation with Melody, I got up and went to my closet, where Dakota was trying to sort through my clothes, again.

"This dress would be perfect! You could wear your black heels, and you could curl your hair. That would look stunning!"

"Dakota, stop. I already know what I'm going to wear. I'm often in jeans, a plain top and my Converse, so that's what I'm going with."

I pulled a pair of light blue skinny leg jeans and a plain white oversized top from one of my clothing racks, and picked up my white pair of Converse. I placed them by my door and sat back on my bed. Dakota leant against my closet door and smiled at me.

"You've developed quite a backbone. Usually you don't like fighting."

I laughed, "Dakota we're not fighting. If you want to say I stand up for myself more, then I'd agree with you."

My thoughts about yesterday are interrupted.

"Delilah, Melody's here."

When she reaches us, she hugs my sister and me before shaking my uncle's hand. She introduces us to Chris – the photographer – who recognises Dakota; he's worked with her before. After he's finished catching up with my sister, he sets up while I get my guitar out. When I'm ready, I head over to the spot by the rocks and Chris starts clicking away.

An hour later we have settled on some photos. Chris edits them so that only the ocean is in colour, adds my name and the title of the album, then makes them bigger so I can see a rough edit of the final product. We have images of me sitting cross-legged facing the camera and turning my back to the camera; we have images of me standing towards the camera and with my back to the camera; we have images of me standing without my guitar. Chris and Melody go through all of the images, and it is now up to me to pick. I stand there, looking at two covers for close to twenty minutes. I am torn, trying to pick just one image isn't easy. In the end, I ask Dakota and my uncle to help me decide. We continue to debate which one to go with before we finally settle on the one where I'm standing up, facing the water, with my back turned to the camera. My guitar is in my left hand, and it sits gently on the floor, next to my left leg. My long hair is straight, and it sits in the middle of my back.

I'm proud of the final design, although it's not exactly how it'll look when it goes on the album. Melody and Chris inform us that they're going to lunch, where they will add the final touches. When it's done, I'll get the final copy to approve, and then my album will have a title and a cover. My excitement for everything that's happened over the last few weeks continues to build, and I know things can only get better from here on out.

After the photo shoot, Dakota and I go to lunch with my uncle, then spend most of the afternoon with him. At 2:30 p.m. Dakota and I head home; when we pull into the driveway, I notice Ryan's car in the street. I haven't seen or spoken to Ryan since Saturday, even though I've tried to contact him. I tell Dakota to go inside, and I slowly approach Ryan's car. When I get to the passenger side, I slowly open the door and get in. Ryan looks over at me and tries to smile, but I instantly notice the redness around his eyes. He looks happy and calm, but he looks like he's been to hell and back. I know he's been to see his mum, but I don't know if it went well. I slowly tuck my hand into his left hand and look at him.

"How'd it go?"

"It was good. My dad was there, and we went to lunch before we met the driver that killed my brother. He's obviously in jail, so we had to go to him. He kept apologising for what he'd done. He said that since being in jail he's been able to see how much damage and pain he's caused. He said he's working on fixing himself and his life, but he couldn't do any of that until he'd personally apologised to us. I sat there at first, not saying a word, I really didn't know what to say. I felt so much anger when I went into the visiting room. Delilah, part of me wanted to kill him. He didn't just take my brother's life; he took my family's lives too."

I see Ryan getting tense, so I try my best to comfort him.

"There's nothing wrong with feeling angry. He made a mistake, a fatal mistake…"

Before I can finish my sentence, Ryan interrupts me.

"I know all of that, but I've never felt rage like that. He sensed it, so he asked me to be honest with him. I was. I told him I hated him and I wanted to kill him, and he said he didn't blame me. But he also said that he can't take any of it back, as much as we wish he could. What's done is done. He could see that I've been suffering, and he told me that I should live my life as best as I can. My brother doesn't get that chance anymore, but I do. I sat there and spoke to him for as long as I could. When it was time to go, I found the strength I needed to forgive him. When we left, I talked to my parents, and we agreed to work on our relationship. We're going to take it day by day, but it's a step in the right direction."

"That's amazing, I knew you could do it. How do you feel now?"

"I feel like a weight has been lifted off my shoulders. I feel like a new person. I feel like I have a second chance and now I can change my life, for the better. Before today I presented myself as one person, which is the person I wanted people to think that I am, but I was hiding who I really am. I was fixated on this idea that I couldn't let the world see how damaged I am. If you can trick your family into believing you're okay, you can do the same thing to the rest of the world. I didn't like myself. In fact, I hated myself. But, seeing my parents today, well, it helped. It changed the way I view myself, and the world. I feel like I can go back to the person I was before. The Ryan I was proud to be, the Ryan who was happy and loved life."

I feel tears form in my eyes, and when Ryan sees me getting emotional, he leans over to hug me.

"Why are you crying?"

"I'm just happy for you. I know how much your depression has dictated your life, and over the last few weeks, I've seen the real you: the one you've been too scared to show. You're an amazing person, and I'm lucky to have you in my life."

Ryan wipes the tears away from my face.

"You showed me how to be this person again. If it wasn't for you, and Angie, I never would have faced the past. I would have just kept running."

We sit talking in his car for another twenty minutes, before I decide to do something I haven't done before.

"You know, in all the time I've known you, you've only ever met one of my family members. Why don't you come inside? You can get to know Dakota more until the rest of my family gets home, then maybe you could stay for dinner?"

"I'd love that, thank you."

We spend the rest of the day at my house. Ryan and Dakota get to know each other, then when Darci, my mum and Evan get home, I introduce them to Ryan too. My mum invites him to stay for dinner, which he accepts. As we sit down for dinner, my family chat to Ryan; I know they are doing their best to make him feel welcome and comfortable, and I know we both appreciate that. After dinner, I help my mum clean up and she turns to me.

"I have to tell you something. Please don't be mad, but Evan and I have set a date for the wedding."

Mum looks nervous. I know she still has hesitations talking to me about her life with Evan. Despite our relationship growing stronger, she knows I am still adjusting to having a male – a father figure – around 24/7.

"That's great, mum. I'm really happy for you. When is it?"

"It'll be a Saturday, at 2:00 p.m. The date is the 3rd of August."

Now I understand why she looks so nervous! The wedding is happening within the next three weeks.

"Mum, why didn't you tell me sooner? I would have helped you plan it. Is everything planned? Do you need to find a dress? Have you even invited people? You didn't have an engagement party. Isn't that something you're supposed to do?"

Shit, slow down, Delilah. One question at a time! I say to myself.

"I didn't tell you sooner because Evan and I wanted to do the planning ourselves. We didn't want anyone to worry about it. We've planned everything, so there's nothing else to do. We've already sent out invitations and no, Delilah, you don't have to have an engagement party. Evan and I just want to get married. As far as the dress is concerned, I've already got one. Well, I'm waiting for it to come back. It's having a few alterations. I'm going to try it on next week, and I'd really love it if you and your sisters come with me. Your brothers are going with Evan to get suits. They've agreed to be his best men. I'd love it if you and your sisters would be bridesmaids."

I want to be happy for her, I *am* happy for her, but part of me feels hurt that she's planned all of this and invited people before telling me. I question if my siblings knew about it. She said my brothers had agreed to be Evan's best men, so surely that means they knew. I must look sad; my mum lifts my head up and looks right at me.

"What is it?"

"I am happy for you mum, but why am I the last to know? I'm your child. I should have been one of the first to know."

"Honey, it's not that I didn't want you to know. I was just worried you'd think this was happening too fast. I mean, in a way, it is, but we don't want to waste any time. Everything just started working out for us, and before we knew it, everything was planned. I was going to tell you earlier, but then everything happened with your father, and you were in the studio so much that we didn't want to distract you. We wanted to wait until we felt you were ready."

I haven't thought about things that way, and I guess she is right. I would have been distracted by everything going on and that would have taken away from what I was trying to accomplish. To be honest, I really didn't need any distractions, especially when I had to focus on myself and my album.

"I understand. I'd love to be a bridesmaid. Thanks, mum. Wait, who's your maid of honour?"

I'm suddenly interested to know who she picked out of Dakota and Darci.

"Anna," my mum blurts out.

I look at her and feel my stomach drop. I obviously know her and Anna are best friends, so I understand why she had asked her. But, does that mean Cam will be there too? My mind starts racing, and I feel the heat rise to my cheeks. My mum grabs my hands.

"I don't even need to ask what you're thinking about. Cam is going to be there. I'm sorry honey, but I invited the whole family. I couldn't leave him out. He's going by himself, and he will be sitting with his family, so he won't be close to you. Why don't you bring Ryan?"

"Mum, are you crazy? My ex-boyfriend and my current, um, friend, in the same room? Sounds like a recipe for disaster!"

I know I am worrying about nothing as Cam already knows Ryan, but the thought of being with him in front of Cam makes me feel uncomfortable. I know I'd try to avoid both of them on the day.

"It will be fine."

She heads towards Ryan in the next room.

"Ryan, love, Evan and I are getting married at the start of next month. Would you like to come? We could put you on the table with Delilah's uncle Derek. He's my brother, and he'd be happy to take you under his wing for the day."

I look between my mum and Ryan, who are now both looking at me.

"Don't feel pressured, but if you want to come, you're more than welcome."

Ryan hugs my mum and accepts the invite.

"Thanks, Ms Walker."

"Call me Deidra, please."

"I'd better get home, but thank you for having me. I'm sure I'll see all of you soon."

I follow him towards the front door.

"Thank you for asking me to meet your family. It's been fun. I'll see you soon. Goodnight."

~

It is now two weeks out from the end of June, and my mum has her final wedding dress fitting. Dakota, Darci, my Aunt Debra, and Anna join me and my mum at a bridal shop in Perth, where we try on bridesmaids' dresses. After my mum has decided on our soft pink, long gowns we sit down and wait while she tries on her dress one final time. While we are waiting, my phone starts to vibrate. I take it out of my bag and see an unknown number flash across the screen.

When my first single dropped I received calls from magazine companies, radio companies, TV companies and everything in between. It seemed everyone wanted to contact me to organise a time to talk about my album, but Melody has put a block on my number. Businesses have to call her, so I don't know who is on the other end. My gut is telling me to answer it, so I do.

"Hello?"

"Delilah? Is that you?"

I recognise the voice straightaway. It's my dad. I look over at my sisters who are watching me.

"Sorry, I've got to step outside and take this."

I head outside, and put my phone back up to my ear.

"Delilah? Are you there?"

I try to answer, but my there's a lump in my throat.

"Ye-yes, I'm here. Why are you calling me?"

I try not to sound rude, but the last time I saw him, he did kick me out. He pushed me away and made it clear he didn't want to talk to me.

"I know it's out of the blue, but I was wondering if we could meet? I know after the last time you're probably hesitant, but I'd really like to see you once more."

Once more? What does that mean? I don't know if I can face him, not after everything that has happened, but nothing can change the fact that he is my father. Despite the part of me that wants to yell at him and hang up, I know I'll regret it if I don't see him. Anna comes to the door and opens it, signalling that my mum is ready to show us the dress. I nod and she goes back inside.

"I have to go. I'll meet you. When? And where?" I ask.

"Tomorrow, 12:30 p.m., the park by our old house."

I'm flooded with memories. We spent so much time at that park; he used to take me there every day. When he left us I started to hate that park. I couldn't even go there when my siblings went. I haven't been back there since then, but maybe facing it now after all this time will help.

"Okay, I'll see you then."

I hang up and go back inside. When I re-join everyone, Dakota looks at me.

"Who was that?"

"It was Melody's assistant, just business stuff. Is mum ready?"

Just as I ask, my mum walks through the curtain. She's wearing a full-length dress with stunning lace detailing; it suits my mum's body type flawlessly. She looks so radiant and, as she stands there, everyone is silent.

"Well, how do I look?"

My mum looks between the five of us. When I notice everyone's crying, I get up and approach her.

"You look stunning. It's perfect."

"Thank you, my love. I'm so glad you're here for this. I couldn't imagine my life without you. The best thing out of my marriage to your father was my children. I'm so blessed we get to spend such an amazing day together as we welcome Evan into the family."

I know today is all about my mum, but it's incredibly awkward that she mentions my dad right after I've spoken to him. I quickly turn around and sit down as everyone gets up to take a closer look at my mum's dress.

After the day of bridal shopping, we go home. I know that when the sun rises in the morning, I'll see my father again. I just don't know if I am ready to face him, especially if he has decided he wants one more chance.

Chapter Seven
The Face-Off

At 12.20 p.m. I sit on a bench seat in the park, waiting for my dad to arrive. I didn't tell my mum where I was going, and I begin to question myself. I don't know if I should be here; it feels wrong. It feels like I am back to sneaking around, and I guess I am.

I distract myself by thinking about my music. My song, *Wildfire*, has continued to rise in the Australian charts; it has even started playing internationally, which is insane! The pre-order sales for the album are climbing, and the hype surrounding my album is continuing to build. I have started doing more interviews and Melody has been flooded with offers. We are struggling to fit everything in. I've been ridiculously busy, and I've been given some amazing opportunities. Dakota and I have even shot a cover for a magazine, where they focused on the two of us being 'successful sisters'.

I am generating a lot of interest, and I begin to wonder if my father suddenly wants to see me now that I am succeeding. I suddenly spot him and watch him slowly approaching me. When he sees me watching him, he grins and waves. I wave back at him and look back down at the grass.

When he reaches me, I don't know what to do. I stand up and he tries to hug me, but I step back. I feel my legs hitting the chair, but I force myself to stand back up.

"Sorry. We're not at that stage yet," he says.

I take note of that fact that he said 'yet'. What does that even mean? I sit back down on the bench, and my father sits next to me, although he keeps his distance. We sit there for a while before, finally, he speaks up.

"I've listened to your songs. Your covers and your single, I mean. They're beautiful. I won't lie: at first, I tried to ignore it, and I tried to ignore you. But, every time I got in the car or turned the radio on, your song was playing. I couldn't escape you, and I saw it as a sign to see you again, to try to fix things, to find a way in which we can both forgive ourselves and move on."

He looks genuine, and the anger I felt is slowly fading away. I know I owe it to him to hear what he has to say.

"I want to apologise to you for what I said when you came to see me. The truth is, I haven't been in a place where I was ready to face my past, to face you, or anyone for that matter. I've been preparing for this day since I left. I knew one day you'd find me, but I didn't think it would be so soon. Since seeing you, I've had time to think. There's a lot I wish I had said to you, but I panicked."

I try to speak, but he doesn't let me.

"Please, let me talk. I need to say all of this. I need to get it off my chest. I regret leaving, Delilah. Believe me, I have beaten myself up every day for walking out on you all, but I had to. At least, at the time I did. I never thought I'd stay away for good, but time just went by so quickly. Things got so bad that I didn't think coming back would be a possibility, so I didn't. I've regretted it ever since. I don't want to hurt you any more than I already have, that's why I'm here. I want to sit here and talk to you about everything. You can ask me whatever you want and I will answer it honestly. There must be a lot of things you want to ask me."

I look at him as question after question pops into my head. He is right: there are a lot of things I want to ask him. I want honest answers, and I want to know exactly what was going through his head when everything happened. But, I am scared to hear what he will say. I have to stop and think; I can't let my fear of his answers stop me from asking the questions that have haunted me for so many years.

"I have a lot of questions." I take a deep breath. "Why didn't you come back? Why did you leave me?"

He moves closer, but I still need distance so I stand up. He shakes his head before answering.

"I couldn't, Delilah. I wasn't capable of being a good father to you, to any of you. Your mum was the only one who could raise you. Don't ever think I didn't, or don't, love you. Out of all the bad things I've done in my life, I wonder how I ever got so lucky to have five beautiful children. No matter what happens from here on out, I won't leave. Unless that's what you want. I know I can't make up for lost time, but I'd like to try. I'll never, ever stop loving you, Delilah. Nothing in this world could ever make me not love you."

"So, what happened to make you leave?"

"My mum, your grandmother, died. She didn't understand why your mother and I had so many children when we weren't financially capable of looking after you all. Your mum and I had so much love to give, at least at that time anyway, and we always wanted a big family. When my mum didn't agree with it, I pushed her away. Eventually, we were financially stable and your mum tried to fix things between my mum and me, but I couldn't let her back in. I don't know why, but I couldn't. Then she died, and I felt so guilty. I started spiralling out of control, and your mum knew I was in a bad place. She asked me to leave, and I did. I thought that's what was best for you."

"Okay … why did you get a house on our old street?"

He shifts on the seat.

"I felt close to everyone there. I've always had this vision that one day you'd all turn up at my door, asking to come inside. I guess that's why I never came to you, until now. I wanted that vision to come true, so I waited. Of course, when I realised you weren't going to turn up, I figured it was too late to do anything about it. So, I stayed there, hoping one day I'd find the courage to do this. I'm just sorry it took this long."

I don't allow myself time to overanalyse anything before I move onto the next question.

"Were you mad at Adrian and Helen for allowing me over? They were pretty honest with me. I asked them all these questions I'm asking you, but they didn't know how to answer. They told me I should ask you."

"At first, I was mad. It wasn't their decision to make, but I know they were only trying to do what was best. They knew it was time for me to face all of this. I was just too stubborn to do what they knew I needed to do. I've since spoken to them about things, and I don't blame them for any of it. I actually appreciate what they did. It made me realise what I was missing out on. I know this is overwhelming. Do you want to continue? Or have you had enough?"

I decide to sit back down next to him.

"No, I want to continue. Why did you feel you had only Helen and Adrian?"

"Delilah, something I have learnt from all of this is that family is all that we have. Your mother raised you to believe that too, and she was right in doing so. When I was at my lowest, they were there for me. They picked me up, and they saved my life. They never gave up on me, even when I had given up on myself. They loved me through all my bad days. They never let me go a day without telling me I was worthy, even after everything I had done. That's something you get from people who really love and care for you. Sometimes in life you're only lucky to have one person to care for you, so I know how lucky I am to have two. I know I had the chance to have more, but I screwed that up."

"You know Helen used to come into my work? I recognised her when I saw her."

"I know. She told me about it every time she saw you. She always talked about how we looked alike, and she always tried to convince me to go there with her."

My father isn't holding back. I know he is being truthful, and I know it is hurting him. The more we talk, the more I feel his energy change. It's like he is finally admitting to his wrongs and he is finally forgiving himself for all of the damage and hurt he has caused. I know we are getting to a point where I need to tell him I forgive him, but I still have a few more questions I need answers to.

"Why didn't you?" I'm curious to know why he hadn't ever come to see me at work. "I don't think I would have recognised you, if that's what you were worried about."

"I almost went with Helen one day. She convinced me that you wouldn't recognise me, but I knew you would. You say you wouldn't, but you would know your own father. I was always too scared to face you. I knew that when I did, I'd have to face my past and I was running from it. I didn't want to face it, so I made up any excuse that I could to avoid going there."

I nod, understanding why he stayed away. I have one more question, and I need him to be really honest with this answer, I hope with everything in me that he does just that.

"Are you happy?"

I know it is a question he wasn't expecting. It has thrown him off, and he suddenly gets nervous. He shifts in his seat and takes a number of deep breaths before finally looking up at me.

"No, I'm not. I haven't been happy for a long time. Delilah, when I held you in my arms for the first time, I felt the most unbelievable sense of happiness, pride and love. I wanted to protect you from every bad thing and person in this world. I promised myself, and you, that I would do just that, that I would be a strong dad for you. We were inseparable. We were best friends, and you never left my side, no matter what I was doing. I was determined to keep you safe from all the scary things life throws at us, and I'm so sorry I couldn't do that for you. I'm sorry I couldn't be the father you needed and deserved. I'm sorry I abandoned you and I'm sorry I never came home to explain why. No matter what happens from here on out, I just want you to be happy. I want you to live the best life possible. I know you're going to succeed. You've always had the potential to do anything you want. I wish I could have been a part of your journey through life. I just hope one day you can forgive me."

The tears are welling up in his eyes as he talks and gets to the root of everything. I slowly move closer to him.

"I wish you could have been there for me, but I understand why you weren't. I don't hate you. In fact, I love you very much. I'll forgive you, but only if you can forgive yourself."

I feel the tears fall from my eyes too and, at that moment, everything feels like it did when I was little. My dad leans over and hugs me tightly, and I stay in his arms for five minutes while we let years of pain out. Finally, everything that has happened starts to fade away.

"Thank you, for hearing me out. I hope we can start over. I would love a second chance. I know it will take time, and I'm willing to work at it."

I move back into the spot where I was sitting before. My father looks happier and I know he has finally forgiven himself. I want to give him a second chance, but I am scared. I don't want him to hurt me again, and I don't know if I can trust him.

"You're my father. I want to give you a second chance, but I don't know if I can. You have to know I'm scared to do this. I'm scared you'll hurt me again, and I'm scared you'll leave again. If you're going to do that, I don't want to give you a second chance. But, if you can commit to making this better, then I think it's time we move forward."

"Honey, I won't ever make that mistake again."

I know I have to ask him if he has any questions for me.

"Is there anything you want to ask me?"

"I only have one question. It's, um, it's a sensitive one. Please don't feel like you have to answer it. When you ended up in hospital, your mum told Helen. She asked her to tell me. When she did, I felt my heart break. I dropped to the floor and I couldn't bring myself to get up. I wanted to be there, but I knew you were better off without me, at least at that point in time. What happened?"

I knew this question would be asked at some point, but I still don't know how to talk about the whole situation without feeling incredibly uncomfortable.

"Well, I saw you and you pushed me away. You made me think you didn't want me, and my ex-boyfriend didn't want me either. I was madly in love with him. I thought I was going to marry him, and then he just dumped me out of the blue. It crushed me and suddenly everything was turning to shit and I didn't see how I could get through it all. I honestly wasn't trying to kill myself. I've explained this a million times. I just wanted to numb the pain. I drank alcohol, which I don't ever do, and I made the stupid decision to mix it with sleeping pills. I made a mistake, and I know how lucky I am to be alive. I wish I could take it back, but I can't. All I can do is try to move on from it, from everything."

"I'm sorry I made you feel that way. I wish I could take that day back. I wish I had told you all of this."

"It's okay, it's done now. We just need to move on. Um, I have to be honest about something else though: I always remember you smelling of cigarettes and whiskey. I hope you don't rely on those things anymore."

"No honey, trust me. I don't drink or smoke at all. I was in therapy for a long time and that was one of the things I focused on. I was dependant on drinking and smoking, but now I'm not. It's healthier for me and I'm able to think clearly, so it's been beneficial for me."

My father and I sit in the park for another half an hour, talking about where to go from here. He asks me to wait until the time is right to tell my family, although I admit I will be telling Dakota that night. We agree to meet up again, in a month. I also tell him he needs to see Dakota, which he agrees to. He tells me he wants to see all his children, and he is determined to make things right, one by one.

When our conversation ends, I get up and hug him, reminding him that I forgive him and that he needs to forgive himself too. I tell him I'll call him in a month and we can arrange another time to meet. I watch him walk to his car and drive away; as he leaves, I feel like a weight has been lifted off my shoulders. I feel happier, and I know things with my dad can only get better from here on out. I just hope he sticks to the words he has said.

When I get home, I find Dakota and we sit outside, under the patio. I fill her in and tell her everything my dad and I talked about. We both agree not to tell our mum just yet. Her wedding day is coming up, and we don't think the time is right. I give Dakota our dad's number, and I tell her to contact him as per his request. We sit outside and talk about giving him a second chance. We both agree that it is time our family moves on, once and for all.

After seeing my father, I feel a wave of relief. We were brutally honest with each other. After all these years, we can finally move on. I know it will take time, but eventually we will get to a place where we can work on our relationship again. I know we won't ever be as close as we once were, but I also know he deserves a second chance. I am willing to give him that. I smile, knowing that good things will continue to come my way, until my family finds out about my dad.

Chapter Eight
The Wedding

Before we know it, the big day has arrived. Months of preparation has paid off, and my mum and Evan are finally going to unite as one.

On the Friday night before the wedding, my mum, Anna, my aunt Debra, and my sisters head to a hotel in the city. I have my final shift at Boom Clap; I have reluctantly quit after many conversations with my mum, uncle and Melody. We know it is in my best interest to focus solely on my career. With my album due to debut in a matter of weeks, I know it is time to move on, even if it is bittersweet. I have loved working at Boom Clap, and it has become a sanctuary for me. I've made amazing friends, and I've brought my love for music into the store. I've been so passionate about my job, so it never felt like work to me. I've met so many people, and I've served more customers than I can count. I've worked long hours – including in the middle of summer when I always longed to be at the beach – but I wouldn't have it any other way.

Boom Clap offered me the best job I could have asked for as a 16-year-old aspiring musician. It gave me a platform to be around the one thing I loved more than anything. I learnt about different instruments, and I listened to every genre of music. I am so grateful for everything that I've gained from working here and I am leaving on good terms. When my final shift comes to an end, I say goodbye to everyone, including Hayley who I've grown attached to over the years.

"You know, I knew the minute I hired you that I'd lose you to your dream of being a singer. I knew one day you'd become the singer-songwriter you've always been destined to be. You're going to go so far in life, Delilah. Please don't ever doubt the amazing gift you have, and don't forget me when you're living like a rock star!"

"Thank you, for everything. I couldn't imagine this job without you. You're the best manager ever, and I promise I'll visit you when I'm a rock star."

I take one final look around the store and say one last goodbye before I head to my car.

When I get home, I text my uncle and tell him I'm ready when he is. He has agreed to drive me into the city so I don't have to worry about driving home before the wedding. An hour later we pull into the car park at the back of the hotel. I text Dakota and ask her to come down and meet me. I haven't been to this hotel before, and I am staying in a room with her and Darci. Plus, I'm terrible with directions, so I assume it will be easiest if Dakota comes down to get me. I thank my uncle for driving me, hop out of the car, grab my bag and wait for Dakota. When my sister reaches me, I notice she looks incredibly relaxed.

"Finally! You've been missing out on all the fun."

"Fun? What fun? I thought we were just relaxing and getting an early night before the big day tomorrow?"

"Well, that's what we were supposed to be doing, but Anna brought some fancy champagne with her and mum ordered way too much food, so now we're having an epic girls' night! Anna even organised massages, manicures and pedicures for us. A lady she knows owns a beauty bar, and she's going to bring some of her staff here so we can get pampered before tomorrow."

Dakota looks beyond excited; she loves this kind of thing. I do too, but I'm ridiculously tired. The last thing I feel like doing is drinking and getting pampered late into the night.

"Firstly, don't ever say 'epic girls' night', it sounds weird. Secondly, it's nearly 7:00 p.m. Isn't it a bit late for all of this? I mean we have to be up early …"

"Firstly, it's not even that late, and secondly, stop being such a bore and have some fun! You're allowed to relax and enjoy yourself, Delilah. This isn't meant to be a boring night! Come on, let's go up to the room."

She drags me inside and I can't help but laugh. My sister is certainly persistent, and maybe she is right: I should relax and have fun. This night is all about celebrating a new chapter in my mum's life.

When we get to the room, Dakota unlocks the door and I follow her inside. There are two queen-sized beds in the middle of the room, two couches, a TV on the wall, and a big window. We have a clear view of the city, which is lit up like a Christmas tree. We have a fairly big bathroom too. Darci is sitting on the couch watching TV as Dakota shows me around. When I've seen everything, I ask Dakota who's sleeping in which bed.

"Well, since we're only here for one night, Darci and I agreed to share one bed, which means you've got the other one all to yourself."

"I like that plan. So, where's mum's room? I suppose I should go and see her."

121

Dakota jumps off the bed and walks towards a door that's in the middle of the room; she unlocks it and knocks on another door that's a few feet behind the first. My mum opens the door and walks through, holding a glass of champagne in one hand and a potato chip in the other.

"Delilah! You're here! Oh, I'm so happy to see you. Did your sister tell you about the pre-wedding present Anna got me? Well, she got it for all of us. How nice is that?"

I raise my eyebrows and look at Dakota before looking back at my mum.

"Are you … drunk?"

She leans against the door, popping the chip into her mouth and trying to hide her laughter.

"I certainly am not! I've only had a glass or two … or was it three?"

I giggle and approach her.

"Mum, as much as I want you to let loose and have fun tonight, I don't think you should drink anymore. You don't want to have a hangover tomorrow. Save it for then. You can drink as much as you want after the wedding."

I take the glass from her, expecting her to protest, but she doesn't.

"That is true. Anna's friends will be here soon. While we wait, I want to talk to you about something. Come and sit down with me."

I quickly hug Anna before she goes downstairs to wait for her friends.

"Evan mentioned something about the wedding the other night, and then we were talking about the DJ we've booked. We got onto talking about your music, and well, that brings me to ask you a question. I know it's late notice, and don't feel pressured to say yes, but we were wondering if you'd sing our favourite songs tomorrow. We both picked a song, and it would be extra special if you sang them."

I look at the glass of half-drunk champagne I still have in my hand and, without thinking, I lift the glass to my lips and drink the rest of it.

"Well, that's a good sign," my mum says as she takes the now empty glass out of my hand. I look at her face, and I know it will mean a lot: not just to her, but to Evan too. After all they've done for me, this is the least I can do for them.

"I'll do it," I say aloud, without giving myself any more time to hesitate. My mum's face lights up.

"You will? Oh, thank you, honey! This means so much to me, and it will mean a lot to Evan, too."

"What songs do you want me to sing? I'll have to go home in the morning to get my guitar, and I'd like to run through the songs before the reception, although I doubt I'll have time. Shit, I don't want to just roll with it. I need to practise."

I feel uneasy, and regret agreeing to sing, but it's too late to back out now.

"Calm down, Delilah. I'll ask Uncle Derek to get your guitar in the morning, and you don't need to practise. You're already perfect, honey. As far as the songs go, Evan wants you to sing *A Sky Full of Stars* by Coldplay and I'd love you to sing *Can't Help Falling in Love with You.*"

As soon as my mum tells me the songs, I instantly relax. They are two songs I'm very familiar with, and I've played them plenty of times before. So, going over them before the reception, while ideal, isn't necessary. I am confident enough that I can do them without rehearsing, and for once in my life, I decide to suck it up, relax and just enjoy the moment instead of fearing it.

"So, are you still okay to do it? If you really don't want to then ..."

"Mum, it's fine. I'll do it."

Anna walks into the room.

"Sorry, I hope I'm not interrupting. My friends are here. This is Lindsay, she owns the beauty bar. These are a few of her top staff members: Fiona, Louise, Julie and Kelly. Lindsay, Fiona and Julie will be doing nails, while Louise and Kelly will be setting up in the corner to do the massages. Feel free to do whatever. It's on me, ladies. Enjoy!"

We spend the next few hours gossiping, drinking champagne – although we now monitor our intake – and eating food. When our pampering session is over, we thank Lindsay and her team again before they head off. At 10:30 p.m. we call it a night. We have an early start in the morning, and we all need a good night's rest. Just before Dakota, Darci and I go into our room, our mum stops us.

"Girls, come and sit with me for a second. I want to talk to you."

We do as she says and, before we know it, we are snuggled up in her bed just like we used to do when we were younger. I'm lying on the end, with Darci snuggled up against my chest. When our mum starts talking, Darci squeezes my hand, almost as if she feels nervous about what our mum is about to say.

"I know this has been a transition for all of us, and I know at times it has been difficult, but I hope you know how much I appreciate the three of you welcoming Evan into our family. I know it hasn't been easy, especially for you Delilah, but I'm so proud of my girls. I hope you know that neither of us ever wanted, or want, to replace your father. We know that no one can do that. But I look to Evan as someone who can, and has tried to be, a father figure to *all* my children. I know that, over time, in your own way, you've dealt with this and it's been so lovely to see you all bond with him. It's not just the two of us that are about to start this new chapter in our lives. It's all of us, as a family, and that includes your brothers too. No matter what happens in the future, the five of you are my priority. That's the way it's always been, and that will never change. Watching you all grow into strong, independent, loving, compassionate and caring people has been the most amazing thing for me, and I am so proud to be your mother. I love you all so much, and I hope tomorrow is just as special for you girls as it will be for me."

I slowly lift my head off the pillow and look at Dakota, who is wiping tears away from her eyes. Dakota rarely cries, but these days her and my mum set each other off. I roll my eyes before I respond to my mum's beautiful words.

"Mum, we're honestly so happy for you. I know for me this has been something that required a lot of time to adjust to, but Evan is a great guy. We're all lucky to have him in our lives. We know you've always done what is best for us, and we appreciate that, and you. You've never put yourself first, but tomorrow, it's all about you. We're blessed to be standing by your side as we start this new chapter."

After a few minutes, my mum lets go of us.

"Okay girls, we need to get some sleep. Don't forget to set the alarm. I'll see you in the morning. I love you all, so much."

She kisses each of our cheeks as we get up, we say goodnight to her, and head back to our room.

That night, I sleep peacefully for what feels like the first time in forever. I dream about Cam, and I don't know if that's why I am sleeping so well. In my dream, I am with him, and that feels like the most amazing thing in the whole world. I see Cam in a crowded room – when I first walk into the room I immediately spot him – and then I'm instantly drawn to him, unable to take my eyes off him. He spots me, and he smiles as he slowly approaches me. I feel nervous. As he gets closer I notice a seductive smile on his face. When he reaches me, he wraps his arms around my waist as he pulls me into his chest. "I've missed this, I've missed you," he says as he moves his lips closer to mine. I can feel his breath on my face, and I notice how ridiculously happy I feel. In fact, it's the happiest I have felt in months. I'm desperate to be with him, I want to be close to him again. I slowly move my head forward, edging in on his lips. We're now only inches away from each other's lips when ...

"Hey sleepy head, wake up." I hear Dakota say.

"No, go away. I'm having the best dream," I murmur, desperate to get back to my dream.

"Well, I'm sorry about that, but you've already slept through the alarm. We've let you sleep in as much as we can. Breakfast is here and the makeup and hair people are on their way, so get up, shower and come into mum's room."

I slowly open my eyes and roll from my side onto my back. As my eyes open, I see Dakota standing over me.

"Dakota, seriously. If you get any closer to my face I'll be able to perfectly describe the nice pimple you've got on your chin."

I know pointing out her pimple will annoy her, so I do it on purpose. She woke me up from the best dream, and now it is her who is inches from my face.

"Ha ha, very funny. I'm already self-conscious about this stupid pimple, which just so happened to make an appearance today!"

"It's not that bad. The makeup will cover it, and it's only small."

"Seriously though, go and shower, then go into mum's room. She'll start freaking out soon."

I slowly get out of bed, grab my bathrobe and head into the bathroom. After closing the door, I turn the taps on and wait until the water is warm. Once it's at the perfect temperature, I step into the cubicle and stand under the middle of the shower as the water falls over my body. The water feels incredible, and I instantly feel relaxed, although I can't shake the memory of the dream, which keeps replaying in my head.

After my shower, I hop out and secure the bathrobe. I go back into the room and look at Darci, who looks different, although I can't figure out why.

"What?" she snaps when she notices me looking at her.

"Nothing. You, uh, you look different."

"I know. Mum made me get a stupid spray tan. Apparently having our nails, hair and makeup done isn't enough. Now I have to look orange too!"

I try to hide my laughter. I can tell how upset she is about being forced into doing things she clearly doesn't want to do.

"You don't look orange. You look beautiful."

I head into my mum's room. After saying good morning to my aunt, Anna and my mum, I join Dakota at the table. We share a vegetable omelette and some orange juice. When we've finished eating, we quickly brush our teeth before getting our spray tans done. As we are drying off, the hairdressers and makeup artists arrive. We each have our own makeup artist, while the hairdressers rotate between us.

After almost three hours of tanning, getting makeup done, and having our hair styled, we are finally done. The bridal party has their hair styled into loose waves, and our makeup is full coverage, complete with a smoky eye and false eyelashes. We then get changed into our dresses, which are stunning. My mum settled on full length, baby pink dresses. They sit under our armpits, with a piece of material sitting over our left shoulders.

When we're ready, we wait patiently for my mum to come out of the bathroom. This is the first time we'll see her with her completed look, so we are all excited. A few minutes later, she appears. As soon as she walks out, we are all blown away by how beautiful she looks. I mean, my mum always looks beautiful, but she has this glow surrounding her today. I've never seen her this happy and I know this is everything she has ever hoped for. Her makeup matches ours, and her hair is curled and half of it is up in a loose ponytail. She stands in the middle of the room and looks between the five of us.

"Well, what do you think?" She sounds desperate.

"Mum, you look stunning," I say to her as I get up to hug her.

"Thank you, honey. You all look beautiful. Oh, I'm so excited! We'd best be going, otherwise we're going to be late."

When we reach the church, we are taken into a room at the back of the building, where we sit and wait until we're told we can go. We're given the go ahead, then we hug my mum and head out towards the closed doors that lead into the church. As the music hits, the doors open and one at a time, we walk through them and head down the aisle. As I'm the eldest daughter I'm the last to go before Anna. When it's my turn, I take a deep breath, slowly walk into the church and head down the aisle. I feel the guests' eyes on me and I pray I make it to the altar without falling over. As I reach the front of the church, I spot Ryan, who's sitting with Cam. I get chills up my spine, but I can't figure out who is causing this reaction. I focus my eyes back on the altar, where I see Evan, who is smiling at me. When I reach the altar, he helps me up four steps and then he kisses my cheek.

"You look beautiful, Delilah."

"Thank you. You look very handsome."

I stand next to Dakota and look up the aisle as Anna makes her way towards us. When she reaches us, everyone stands. We turn to the back of the church, where my mum is slowly walking down the aisle. She decided to walk down by herself since her father – my grandfather – passed away almost ten years ago. She knew if he couldn't be here to walk with her then she didn't want anyone else to do it. When she reaches Evan, he takes her hand and helps her up the stairs too. They stand side by side, and the ceremony starts.

The ceremony is beautiful, and before we know it, it is time for the vows. Evan goes first.

"Ever since you came into my life, you have showed me how to love another person. You've taught me to be a better person, and you've taught me how to live a life where happiness and family are top priorities. You don't ever push me away, and you love me unconditionally. I truly am a better man because of you, and my promise to you is never to let a day pass without telling you how much I love you. I promise to always be there for you, and I promise to always support you. I also promise to be there for you children too. I'm incredibly blessed to say they're now my step-children and I promise I will love them unconditionally and protect them as if they were my own."

Most of the people in the church are now crying, myself included. When my mum starts saying her vows, I feel a sense of pride. She speaks so beautifully.

"I often wonder how I got so lucky. I've been given a second chance at love, and I'm so very blessed to have you in my life. You've not only embraced me, but you've embraced my children too. You've been there for them, and you've worked tirelessly at being a positive influence in their lives, even if it was tough at first. I cannot wait to spend the rest of my life with you, I cannot wait to come home to you after work, I cannot wait to travel the world with you, and I cannot wait to grow old with you."

As Evan and my mum tell each other all these beautiful things, I feel emotions running through my body. I look out at the sea of people sitting down; they're smiling as they watch my mum and Evan proclaim their love for each other. My eyes are drawn to Cam again. He looks so handsome in his suit. He is sitting a few rows back from the altar, and he has a beautiful smile on his face. His eyes slowly meet mine and, for a minute, we don't take our eyes off each other. All the feelings I thought I'd managed to fight off over the last few months come rushing back, stronger than ever. I remember my dream from this morning and I long to be in his arms. I wish more than anything that I could go to the reception with him, dance with him, and enjoy the rest of this day with him by my side. I wish he would embrace me, kiss me, and tell me he wanted to start over and give our relationship another go, but I doubt that will ever happen.

I don't want to take my eyes off him, and I think he feels the same. The more we look at each other, the harder it becomes to fight these feelings. As much as I want to stare into his eyes for the rest of the wedding, I know I should focus my attention back on the words that are being spoken. I pull my eyes away from him, try to listen to the rest of the words throughout the ceremony, but I can't concentrate on anything other than Cam.

Thankfully, the wedding is coming to a close. When Evan and my mum are officially married, the bridal party and the groomsmen head to the back room we started in. When the guests are outside, we head outside and join them. We take photos and mingle with the guests. Ryan approaches me and kisses me.

"You look stunning," he says.

I thank him and we talk about the wedding. My mum approaches us and, as she starts to talk to Ryan, I find myself looking around, desperately trying to find Cam. I finally spot him, and I begin to walk towards him. My mum stops me.

"Honey, we've got to go to the reception. Say goodbye to Ryan and then head to the car. I'll meet you there."

I sigh and do as she says, heading to the limousine. Everyone is in the various cars singing and drinking as we head to the reception.

The reception seems to go quicker than the wedding, and soon it's time for the speeches. Anna gets up to deliver her speech, but nothing can prepare me for what she is about to say.

"I know it's tradition for the maid of honour to make a speech, but I'd like to invite Deidra's eldest daughter, Delilah, to come up here."

I look at Anna and my mum as everyone in the room turns to face me. I hate public speaking, and I haven't prepared anything, so I feel completely thrown off. Everyone in the room begins to clap as I slowly stand up. I walk over to Anna, who pulls me into her.

"Speak from the heart, beautiful girl."

She sits back down next to my mum, grabs my mum's hand, and they look at me, smiling, as I try to think of something to say. I am clearing my throat when Cam approaches me, and hands me a glass of water before heading back to his seat. I look up and find him in the crowd; I smile at him, take a sip of water and put it down before I start to speak.

"We're gathered here tonight to celebrate the marriage of my mum and Evan."

I instantly regret starting like that; I sound just like the priest when he began the ceremony earlier. I know I'm overthinking things, so I take a deep breath and decide to let my words come to me, just like Anna said.

"My mum has always put her kids first. She's always done what's best for us, and she's built a life for us. She never forced us into liking her past boyfriends, and believe me, we tried to sabotage most of her relationships!"

Everyone in the room laughs, including my mum and Evan. Knowing I am being truthful makes me feel confident, and I feel a natural instinct to keep going.

"Evan came into our lives a short time ago, and in that time he's shown us just how loyal he is. At first, we didn't get along. In fact, I don't think it's a secret that I hated Evan. I believed he was trying to replace my father, and I resented him for that. But, as time went on, he got to know me, and I opened myself up to get to know him too. Believe me when I say I'm so glad I did. I've personally been through quite a lot over the last few months, and during that time I've found comfort in Evan. He has become a father figure to me, and over the last few weeks, our bond has grown incredibly strong. I now look to Evan as my father, and the only thing I wish is that my mum had found him earlier."

I turn to my mum and Evan as I wrap up my speech. "I know the two of you are going to spend the rest of your lives together. You've shown me what true love is, you've taught me how to be a better person, and you've reminded me that no matter what we go through, good or bad, family will always be there to celebrate with you, or pick you up. I love you both. Congratulations. To mum and dad!"

I raise my glass, and everyone stands up, cheers and hollers.

"To Evan and Deidra!"

After my speech, I look around the room and I spot my dad. At first, I think I'm seeing things. When I close my eyes, squeeze them, and reopen them, he's still standing there. *Oh shit, this can't be good.* I head towards him, but he turns around and walks through a door. One of my mum's friends tries to talk to me, but I quickly apologise and continue towards the spot where my father had stood. I turn into the corridor and find him. I get to him just as he makes it outside.

"Dad, stop!"

He stops dead in his tracks and turns to face me; I expect to see a look of anger, but when he looks at me, he looks sad.

"What are you doing here?" I ask him.

"Dakota told me where you were going to be, so I thought I'd come by and see everyone. I wanted to congratulate your mother and fix things with her too. I didn't expect to hear of all of that though. Did you mean it?"

I bite my lip and turn my head to the side before looking back at him.

"I don't think now is the right time for that ... for you to confront mum, I mean. I'm sorry you heard that, but yes, what I said is true. You left me, dad. I tried to fight for you, and I tried to welcome you back into my life, but you pushed me away. Everything was spiralling out of control and Evan, he just ... he was there for me, for all of us. He has never tried to take your place – no one could ever do that – but what was I supposed to do? I needed a father, or at least a father figure, and you weren't there. I know we're starting to repair things now, but..."

"But it's too little, too late, isn't it?"

"No, it's not too late, but I I need more time to think."

"I had a feeling we wouldn't make it work. I understand if you don't want me in your life anymore, and I respect your decision. I hope you stick to your word of forgiving me."

I step towards my father and grab his hands.

"Of course I do. I do forgive you. I want you in my life, I really do, but I need to focus on myself and my career right now. That has to be my priority. I'll always love you, you'll always be my father, and nothing will ever change that."

He squeezes my hands.

"Thank you for being honest with me. I know how hard all of this has been for you. You were willing to give me a second chance, and I blew it. I know you need time, and I will step back and give you all the time you need. Your mum did a damn good job raising you, and I know you'll succeed with your music. I love you, Delilah. Call me when you're ready."

"Thank you, daddy. I love you."

We slowly let go of each other, and I watch as he turns around and walks back to his car. I wave at him before he drives off and, after a few minutes, I muster up the strength to turn around and go back inside.

I almost jump out of my skin when I turn around. Cam is standing right behind me, waiting for me.

"Jesus Christ, Cam, you scared the shit out of me!"

I place my hand on my chest.

"Sorry, I thought you heard me coming. Who was that?"

I look at the spot where my dad's car was.

"It was my dad."

"Your dad? As in your real dad?"

"Yes, Cam, as in my real dad. I don't really want to talk about it. Is there something I can help you with?"

"You know at the wedding I couldn't take my eyes off you. You looked right at me and I felt it. I know you felt it too. It was the same feeling we used to get when we were together. Even in a crowd of people in the church, and in that room tonight, you are always the first person my eyes are drawn to. The whole time I've been thinking about you, about us. I thought this should be us, but it's not, and it kills me to see you with someone else. Does Ryan make you happy?"

I feel startled by Cam's confession and his sudden question about my relationship with Ryan.

"Firstly, I don't know what you're talking about, and secondly, yes, I am happy with Ryan."

I don't believe a word of it, but I'm too scared to face the truth, to admit to Cam that everything he said is exactly how I feel.

"You know I can't keep up. One minute you want to be with me, then you don't, and now you do? I just…"

Cam interrupts me, "I know. I'm sorry. Just being here, at a wedding, well it reminds me of when we used to talk about us getting married. I know you've moved on but …"

I desperately want to tell Cam the truth: that I don't see a future with Ryan, that I don't love him, that I love Cam and I want to be with him forever. I almost do, but I notice Ryan is watching us. When he sees me looking at him, he walks over to us. I see a look I've never seen on Ryan's face before; he looks angry. I feel like the boys are about to get into an argument, but when Ryan stands next to me, Cam extends his hand and addresses him.

"Take care of her. She deserves the best, and only you can give that to her now. I pushed her away, and I know I made a mistake, so please just love her like I did – like I should have – and tell her how you feel every day. She's an amazing person, and she deserves the best."

I'm blown away. It isn't like Cam to give up, and I almost feel hurt that he doesn't want to fight for me, especially if he means what he has just said. I look at Ryan, who looks at me before going towards Cam. They shake hands, and at that moment, I truly believe all hope of Cam and I ever getting back together has just been blown away.

After the boys wrap up their conversation, Cam stands in front of me. A few tears slip from my eyes as we hug. This feels like home, this feels like my safe place. I don't want to lose this feeling, but I don't know what to do. We're about to walk away from each other, and I feel like there is nothing I can do to stop it from happening. I want to hug him forever; I never want to let him go; I want to yell my love for him into the dark sky. But, I can't find the strength to be truthful, so I just stand there, hugging Cam, wishing he wouldn't ever let me go.

After a full minute passes, Cam releases me and smiles as he wipes my tears away.

"Don't cry because it's over. Smile because it happened."

Without saying another word, Cam turns around and walks away, leaving me with Ryan. I know I am only hurting him. He is falling deeper in love with me, but nothing I can do will ever change how I feel. I don't care about anyone the way I care about Cam, and that makes me feel horrible. I don't want to hurt Ryan, but I know that by carrying on like this, I will continue to hurt him even more.

"Did he actually quote Dr Seuss? Isn't that a kid thing?"

Ryan interrupts my thoughts and grabs my hand.

"I loved Dr Seuss when I was a kid, he knew what he was saying."

"We'd better get back inside. You're due to sing soon."

He's trying to ignore what just happened, and maybe I should too. I fake a smile and nod as I follow Ryan back inside.

Thankfully, I don't have to focus on anything other than my nerves as it's time to sing the songs my mum has asked me to sing. I position myself on a stool and my uncle hands me my guitar. He lowers the microphone for me and taps a knife against a glass to get everyone's attention.

"Hey guys. If you don't mind, I'd like everyone to take a seat. We have a special surprise for you all. Delilah, over to you."

I thank him and look up at all the guests, who are watching me eagerly.

"As the night draws to a close, I want to take the time to end things with a few songs. Evan and my mum have requested a song each, and it's my pleasure to sing not only for them but for all of you too. Thank you so much for being a part of this day. This song is called *A Sky Full of Stars*."

I start playing the song on my guitar as Evan and my mum get up to dance. After the first song, my mum invites the guests to get up and dance with them as I play her song choice, which everyone happily does. As I finish the second song, everyone stands around me and starts to clap. When I play the final chord, the applause gets louder. I hug my mum and Evan and put my guitar back on the stand as the DJ plays the final few songs. Everyone in the room dances and everywhere I look I see happy faces. I feel a sense of incredible happiness, despite my feelings about my relationships with Cam and Ryan. I feel happy to have been a part of such a special day.

As the wedding ends, I sit down and yawn. It's been incredible; the room has been filled with so much love, and I know this new chapter is going to be the fresh start we all need and deserve. We are going to move on, as a family, with someone who my siblings and I look up to as our second dad.

CHAPTER NINE
TWENTY-TWO

After the wedding, things finally settle down, but before I know it it's nearly the end of August and my 22nd birthday is fast approaching. I want to have a quiet day and night with my family and friends, but I soon realise that the start of my birthday means the start of a new Delilah.

I'm sitting with Ryan in his lounge room and looking through photos from the wedding. My mum and Evan are still on their honeymoon. They've been gone for almost a month now, but they're not due back for another three weeks. They've been enjoying some much-deserved quality time together in Europe, where they've been travelling around, sightseeing and enjoying their new life as newlyweds.

"It was a beautiful wedding. Everyone looked so happy, especially your mum,"

"Yeah, she does, doesn't she? She deserves it though."

Ryan continues to look through the photos as I look out of one of the windows. I get up and head into his kitchen, put water into the kettle to make some tea.

"Hey babe, I was wondering if you want to come to dinner with my parents on the weekend.

They're going to come here. They've never seen my place before, and my mum really wants to meet you."

"Ummm, my birthday is on Saturday."

"Oh shit, I totally forgot about that! I'll ask if they can make it on Sunday night instead. What are we doing for your birthday? I feel like we haven't even talked about it."

I look down at the kettle as it finishes boiling.

"We did talk about it, the, uh, the other night. I'm having my family and friends over, remember?"

Ryan gets up and walks over to the kitchen as I pour the hot water into two mugs. I place two tea bags into them and swirl them around with a teaspoon.

"Oh yeah, I remember now. Sorry."

He watches me put milk in the mugs before I hand him one.

"You don't have to apologise. It's fine, I know you've had a lot on your mind."

I walk back over to the couch and sit down, sipping my tea, Ryan joins me and places his cup onto the coffee table.

"Can I invite my parents to your party? They'd love to meet your family."

I feel my eyes widen, and try my best to avoid looking at him.

"It's, um, it's not really a party. It's more of a casual get-together, and I'm, um, I'm not sure that I'm ready for that yet ... to meet your parents, I mean. Sorry."

I want to explain my reasons, but Ryan cuts me off.

"I know this is new to you, but I also know that you had a close relationship with Cam's family. You still have that with them, but I want you to have that same bond with my family. Why do I get the feeling that you don't want that at all? Do you even want to be with me?"

His question hits me out of nowhere. I almost don't know how to respond to it, but I've been expecting this conversation ever since Ryan became close to his family again. I've known that at some point I'll have to tell him the truth about why I don't want to meet his family. I just hope that he understands, and I hope I don't hurt him. I put my tea next to his on the coffee table.

"It's not that I don't want to meet them, but I just, I don't know how to explain it. Breaking up with Cam broke me, and you're right, I was so close to his family. I *still am* close to them. That's made getting over him harder than it would've been. I just don't want to be in that situation again. I know that's difficult to hear, but I just need time. We've only been together for a few months, and I don't want to rush into anything. I know it's important for me to meet them, and I will ... just not yet. I think it's more important for you to spend time with them and work on your bond again before I meet them. They deserve to spend quality time with you. It's been so long, and I know they've missed you. I don't want to take away from that. I'm sorry."

I look at him, hoping he won't be mad at me, but he isn't showing any emotional response.

"You didn't answer my question: do you want to be with me or not?"

"If I didn't want to be with you, I wouldn't be sitting here, would I?"

He finally looks at me, and although he looks hurt, he smiles. I can't help but feel terrible for what I've just told him, but I figure it's better to tell him the truth, rather than lie to him. I've now begun to question our relationship, and I no longer know if I want to be with him. I want to talk to him about it but I just don't know when the right time will be. Mind you, I doubt there ever will be a right time.

"I understand. Maybe you're right. Maybe I need to spend more quality time with them first. But, about your birthday get-together: who's going?"

I notice his tone of voice has changed, and I'm suddenly scared to tell him. I fear his reaction, especially when he finds out that I've invited Cam.

"Well, my mum and Evan obviously won't be there, but my uncles and aunts will be there with my cousins. Dakota and James, my brothers and their girlfriends and Darci will be there too. I've also invited Cam's family. Hadley and Rosie are coming, and I think Owen and Jacob are coming with them. It'll be the first time you meet the boys, and I'm sure you'll get along with them."

I grab my mug and finish my tea as I wait for Ryan to reply. I noticed his body tensed up the minute I mentioned Cam's name. I figure he needs more time to process everything. I finish the rest of my now-cold tea, get up, take the mug back to the kitchen, wash it and place it on the bench to dry. I lean my palms against the bench and watch Ryan. He has his back turned to me as he faces the television, which isn't even turned on. Finally – after what seems like forever – he gets up, picks up his mug and comes into the kitchen. I turn around to face him, this time leaning my back against the bench as I watch him empty his half-drunk tea into the sink. When he's finished washing his cup, he slowly turns to me. I notice my heart rate has picked up.

"Why did you invite Cam's family? Is *he* going?"

I've never heard Ryan speak like this before; his whole demeanour has changed again.

"Yes, *he* is going…"

"Why do you want him there?"

I look at my chipped nail polish before looking back at Ryan. He's watching my every movement.

"Because I've known him for almost 22 years. I've always celebrated my birthdays with him. It just doesn't feel right for him not to be there, and I can't exactly invite his whole family and exclude him. My mum isn't going to be here, and Anna's like a second mum to me. So, it means a lot to me that they're here to help me celebrate my birthday. It's the next best thing to having my mum here. Why are you so mad about it? I thought the two of you got along?"

I try to speak in the nicest way possible, but the more I try to explain things to Ryan, the more I feel his whole body shift. I don't want to keep aggravating him, which is what I'm clearly doing.

"We do get along, but not when he's around you. It's like a competition, and I'm not stupid, Delilah. I know if it came down to it, you'd pick him over me. Anyone can see that."

I bite my lip as I look at Ryan. He still looks annoyed, but I notice he now looks sad too. The last thing I want to do is hurt him, but his words have hit me. I start to question why he would say that, but then I realise that maybe he's right. Maybe I need to come clean about the truth, right now. My feelings have changed. Deep down I know he is right: If it came down to it, I'd choose to be with Cam without hesitation.

I feel like the worst person. I don't want to string him along, but the more we progress in our relationship, the more I feel our connection dying. I don't think that we're meant to be boyfriend and girlfriend; we're meant to be friends. I know that deep down Ryan feels the same too. We got along better when we were friends, and we were certainly more honest with each other too. All we do is fight now, and I know that's not healthy, but for some reason neither one of us can find the strength to just end the relationship once and for all. Ryan stands in front of me, startling me.

"The fact that you're not even responding to that just proves that I'm right. I think you should go home. I think we need time apart right now. I'll see you on Saturday. I think three days apart will be best. It'll give you time to think about our future, and it'll give me the chance to do the same too."

Without saying another word, Ryan walks to his room and slams the door, leaving me alone in his kitchen. I look at the door he has just slammed, and I find myself wanting to go and open it, to try to comfort him, to just get everything out in the open. But, he needs time alone. I grab my bag and my jacket from the couch and as I head home, I begin to cry out of confusion and frustration.

~

On Saturday morning my sisters and brothers wake me up.

"Happy birthday to you, happy birthday to you, happy birthday dear Delilah, happy birthday to you!"

I open my eyes as they finish singing. My four siblings are smiling from ear-to-ear, and I notice they're holding balloons and gift bags. I spy a cup of coffee in Dakota's hand.

"Your favourite: one mocha with soy milk, no sugar."

"Thank you."

They all sit on the bed and give me my presents. Darci throws her gift bag at me as quickly as she can.

"Open mine first!"

She sits on her knees, looking at me with an excited expression. I laugh and open the pink gift bag. I pull out some pink tissue paper before pulling out a photo frame. I look at the photo that sits perfectly in the beautiful rose gold coloured frame. It's a photo from Darci's 16th birthday party, when I sang *Beauty and a Beat* for her. I look incredibly happy, and all the memories from Darci's party flood back.

"It's a photo from the very first time you performed a song live. I thought it would be nice for you to have a photo of that moment, and I didn't have a lot of money, so I couldn't afford anything else. I'm sorry."

Darci looks embarrassed.

"Hey, don't apologise. I love it! You're right, it is nice to have a photo of that moment. Do you want to put it on my desk for me? That way when I sit down to write a song, I can look at it for motivation."

Darci hops up off the bed and walks over to the desk.

"To remind you of how far you've come in the last few months."

She places the photo in the left-hand corner of my desk.

"Exactly! Now come here and give me a hug."

She jumps back onto the bed and hugs me as tightly as she can. I kiss her forehead as my brothers smile at me. Declan hands me a card, and Dylan hands me another gift bag.

"We didn't know what to get you, but we wanted to get you something special. We hope you like it."

I smile at them as they watch me open the card. I read the message first.

"To our beautiful sister, Delilah,

We hope you have a great birthday. We're so proud of you, and we know you'll be a great success in the future. We're proud to be standing by your side, and we can't wait to see how far you go. Make sure you always follow your heart and don't ever settle for less than you deserve. We're blessed to have you as our sister, and we love you.

Dylan and Declan xx."

I look up at my brothers, who are still smiling at me. Their words have hit me harder than I expected: *make sure you always follow your heart and don't ever settle for less than you deserve.* I think of the problem I'm currently facing with Ryan, but I don't want to think about that right now, so I quickly shake my head.

"Thank you," I say as I place the card next to me.

I open the gift bag and pull out a blue jewellery box; I pull the lid off and, sitting inside the box, is a solid gold music note on a gold necklace.

"Thank you, it's beautiful."

Declan tells me to turn it over, and I notice there's a 'Dx5' engraved on the back.

"The D represents the first letter of our names, and the 5 represents the five of us, so no matter where you go in life, or where you perform, we will always be with you."

"Thank you, to both of you. This means so much to me. I'll keep this with me every single day."

I put it around my neck before sitting back down next to Dakota, who hands me another gift bag. I start to pull things out as she explains what she got.

"I didn't really know what to get you, but I remember you mentioning you needed some new writing supplies, so that's what I got for you. I got you music sheets, lined pages, pens, pencils and highlighters, and I got you a new pair of headphones. I know your pair hasn't been working very well. Now you won't have to keep borrowing mine!"

"Thank you, Dakota. I appreciate it."

As I thank my siblings again, there's a gentle knock on my bedroom door. I look past my brothers, and I'm blown away when I see my mum and Evan standing in the doorway.

"Oh my God!" I say as I jump up from my bed and run over to my mum and stepdad. "What are you guys doing here? You still have three weeks of your honeymoon left!"

My mum laughs.

"We were always going to come back for your birthday. We just didn't want to tell you. Otherwise, it wouldn't be a surprise, would it?"

I laugh and beam at her. Evan hands me my guitar case; I take it from him, wondering why he's giving it to me.

"Open it," he says with a warm smile.

I take it over to my desk and pull out my chair. I sit down and open the case. When I open it, I notice my guitar isn't in it; instead, it's been replaced by a new acoustic guitar. It's a glossy black colour, and it has my name engraved in gold. I notice there's also a gold star next to my name. It's stunning, and it's just like the one I've been looking at buying myself for a while now, minus the engravings.

"Mum, how did you know?"

"Evan and your uncle were having lunch one day before the wedding. Evan asked Uncle Derek if he knew of something special we could get you. He mentioned that you'd been looking at buying this guitar for yourself, and after everything you've been through – and everything you've achieved – we decided you deserve to be treated. So, we got it for you. The star was Uncle Derek's idea. He said he always tells you that you're his superstar, so we thought it would be an extra special touch."

I run my fingers over my name and the star on the guitar.

"I love it. Thank you both, so much. I can't believe you're here, and that you got me this! It's too much."

Evan pulls a tissue packet out of his pocket and hands me a tissue.

"You deserve it, love. We're happy you love it."

~

At 5:00 p.m. Dakota and I are in the bathroom, getting ready for my birthday celebration. I've spent the day with my family, which has been amazing because we haven't spent time together like that since the wedding. My mum and Evan told us all about their honeymoon, and showed us photos. My siblings and I filled them in about what we'd been up to while they were gone. As we sat at the lunch table, I thought about how close we were. We felt like a family: one that has been bonded since we were kids, but it's almost like Evan has always been around. Every single person in my family was smiling and beaming with happiness, although I still couldn't distract myself long enough to stop thinking about Ryan. I still haven't spoken to him. At this point, I don't even know if he is coming tonight.

"Delilah? Did you hear anything I just said?"

Dakota stands with her hands on her hips.

"Uh…"

"What's going on? You've been out of it all day."

I sigh as I put my moisturiser down.

"It's Ryan."

"Still haven't heard from him?"

"Nope. I thought by now we would have spoken, but we haven't. I know he said we need a few days apart, but I don't even know if he's still coming tonight."

"Well, have you tried contacting him? Maybe he's been waiting to hear from you?"

"No, I haven't. I hadn't even thought of it like that. I guess I just assumed he'd want to talk to me. I never even thought about him giving me space. He's probably waiting for me to contact him. *Shit.*"

"Delilah, listen. I know we're insanely close, and I know I may hit a nerve with what I'm about to say, and I'm apologising in advance if I do. I think it's safe to say that, in a way, you're stringing Ryan along. I know you're not doing it on purpose, but you don't love him ... at least not the way that you loved Cam. Ryan's a nice guy. Don't you think he deserves to be told the truth about how you feel?"

I've been dreading this conversation too, but I'm glad I'm having it with my sister. While she has been harsh in her words, I know she is right.

"Of course he deserves to know the truth. I'm not trying to hurt him, but I know I'm not the person he's meant to be with, and I think he's starting to realise that too. I don't love him the way I used to, the way I *still do* love Cam. I know that's not fair on Ryan, and he deserves so much better."

I look down at the sink, too scared to look at my sister.

"I think you're settling because you're scared you won't ever love someone as much as you loved Cam. Correct?"

"I guess I was, or am, settling. I never thought about my fears of not loving someone as deeply as I once loved Cam, and I thought I'd moved on from those feelings. But, every time I see Cam, the love I have for him comes rushing back. I've told myself a million times to just walk away, to move on, but no matter how hard I try, *I can't*. I don't want to imagine a life without Cam. I've tried that before, and I hate it. Deep down, I know we'd make it if we gave things another shot. I can't explain how I know, but I do. I love him, Dakota, and nothing will ever change that. I just feel so horrible for putting Ryan through this. I'm such an awful person! I never meant to hurt him."

I sink to the floor before pulling my knees to my chest. Dakota sits next to me and pulls me into her arms.

"Delilah, you're not an awful person, and you didn't do this on purpose. We don't choose who we love, it just happens. You and I both know that. In the end, you have to do what's best for you. You deserve to be happy. If Cam makes you happy, then that's what you have to fight for. I know you don't want to hurt Ryan, but you need to be honest with him. Like you said, it's not fair for him to be put through this if you know it's truly over."

I wipe the tears away from my eyes. My sister offers me a comforting smile and hands me a tissue from the box.

"Here," she says. "It'll be okay, I promise. Just enjoy your night. I know it'll be difficult now, but just try to relax and have fun, okay?"

"I'll try. Thank you."

At 7:00 p.m. everyone starts to arrive. I'm standing with Hadley and Rosie when Ryan walks in. At first, I'm surprised to see him. Then I realise that I'm not as excited as I thought I'd be when I finally saw him. I thought that after three days apart, I'd be happy to see him. In a way I am, but I wish he was just my friend again. I force a smile onto my face as he approaches me.

"Hi, happy birthday," he says as he hugs me.

"Thanks, how are you?"

I try to pull away from him, but he doesn't let me go. After almost thirty seconds, he finally releases me. I notice he has bags under his eyes, and he looks ridiculously tired. I also notice he looks nervous and uncomfortable.

"I've been better. I know it's not the right time, but I think we need to talk."

"I know. We do need to talk, just not tonight. Let's just try to enjoy the night, and after the weekend we will talk, I promise."

He smiles back at me, shakes Owen and Jacob's hands, and hugs Rosie and Hadley. We stand together and talk, then I see Cam's family walk in. I already knew Cam's brothers weren't coming, but Cam said he was; I can't see him though. I excuse myself from the group and go inside, where I greet William, Anna and Nia.

"Happy birthday, beautiful girl!" Anna says as she embraces me.

I thank her before hugging William and Nia. As I'm hugging Nia, she whispers something to me.

"Don't worry, he's on his way. He's driving himself."

"How did you know?" I whisper back to her.

"I saw the disappointment on your face when we walked in here and you didn't see him."

"What are you two whispering about?"

I look up and see Cam walking over to us.

"Nothing. I'm going to find Darci," Nia says as she winks at me.

"Hi," I say as Cam reaches me.

"Hi. Happy birthday. Here's your present."

"You didn't have to get me anything."

I take the wrapped box out of his extended hands.

"Of course I did. Open it."

I sit at the kitchen table and unwrap the box. As soon I pull the wrapping paper off, I know what it is.

"Oh my God, I can't believe you still have this!"

Inside the cardboard box is a pile of things from our childhood. There's a small teddy bear Anna and my mum gave Cam and me when we were five, sea shells we collected at the beach and a bunch of photos of us: from when we were babies, to when we started school, to our time in high school, photos from our first date – and more from other dates too – and recent photos. My favourite is a photo from the night when his house lost power, which was the first time we held hands. It was the night I knew I loved him. I notice a book at the bottom of the box; I pull it out and smile as I read the cover.

"Remember when we were nine? We wrote that book the night your parents ... you know…"

I know the night he is talking about. My mum had given birth to Darci that year, so she was still a baby. My parents were in the middle of another

152

intense fight, so Anna came over to pick the five of us up. At the time, we didn't understand what was going on. All we knew was that we were going for a sleepover. I had seen my parents yelling at each other, so I was upset. I remember Cam tried to cheer me up, but nothing he did worked, so he suggested we make a book.

"The night my parents knew their marriage was over. I remember."

I stare at the book. I open it and start looking through the pages.

"Boof the dog and Toby the cat. I forgot we even made this. Where did you find it?"

I look at the pictures we had drawn. They weren't the best, but I remember how much fun we had when we were drawing them. We made a story out of them, and it was exactly what I needed to distract myself from the fight I had witnessed earlier. The dog and the cat didn't like each other at first, but by the end of it, they were the best of friends. It's almost like we knew that's how we were going to end up one day.

"My mum kept it, and she found it the other day when she was cleaning the hallway closet out. She said I should give it to you. I thought it would be nice to give you the photos too. It's crazy how much of our lives we actually lived together."

I want to tell Cam the truth about how I feel, and he looks desperate for things to go back to the way they were too. But he suddenly gets up from the table.

"I can't stay long. I promised Marc I'd hang out with him. I totally forgot about it when I told you I could make it for your birthday. I tried to reschedule, but he's going away with his family in a few days, so it's the only night he is free."

I feel so disappointed, but maybe it's for the best if he's not here now, especially considering how I was feeling towards Ryan.

"It's fine, don't stress. Do you want me to walk you out?"

"Yeah, that would be nice."

I follow Cam outside. When we reach his car, he stops and leans against the door.

"Can I ask you something?"

I nod my head.

"How are things going with you and Ryan?"

"Honestly? They're not very good. We got into a fight a few days ago. His whole mood changed within a few seconds, and it scared me. I know he's going through a lot and I know I haven't been very present in our, um, our relationship, but I just don't see a future with him. All we do is fight."

Cam grabs my hand and looks into my eyes.

"I figured. You look miserable. Delilah, listen, there's something I have to tell you. I need to tell you now. Otherwise, I never will. I'm sorry. I thought I was doing the right thing when we broke up. Ryan needed you. He was suffering, and I knew you were the only one who could help him. He needed a friend like you, and I had to let you go so you could be there for him. I didn't expect him to fall in love with you. When we spoke, he didn't mention that he was falling for you. I thought it was the right decision. I thought letting you go would help, but now I know that us breaking up, well it was a mistake. I know Ryan's made progress. You've helped him to find what he needs. He's at a point where he can finally find his happiness, and that's amazing. But, like you said, you know you two don't belong together. We do though. Taking time away from you made me realise how stupid I've been. You didn't just save his life, Delilah, you saved mine too. You were there for me when I was at my lowest, and even after I tried pushing you away, you refused to leave. I should never have let you go when you needed me the most, but I want you to know that I'll never make that mistake again. I love you. I've never loved anyone the way I love you, and I know I'll never love anyone this way again. I want every piece of you, good and bad."

Cam is still holding my hand. This is everything I've wanted. I've been waiting to hear these words ever since we broke up. I want nothing more than to snuggle into his chest, but I'm still scared. I don't want him to hurt me again.

"How do I know you won't walk away again? How do I know you won't hurt me? How do I know that you won't break my heart, again?"

Cam takes a step towards me and kisses my cheek. I feel him standing close to my face, and I feel the same inexplicable feelings that I feel every time I'm this close to him. I want to face him, but I'm too scared to move. I'm too scared to lose this moment.

The chemistry between the two of us is insane. I know how rare this is, to be *this* in love, but my doubts keep haunting me. Cam suddenly places his face closer to mine, he slowly edges towards my lips, and he tries to kiss me, but I pull away from him.

"No, not like this. I can't do this to Ryan. I want to be with you, Cam. I want this more than anything in the world, but I'm not hurting him like this."

Cam nods as he takes a step back. Before I can even think about what's going on, Ryan is by my side.

"What the hell are you doing? Are you trying to take *my girlfriend* away from me?"

Ryan gets up in Cam's face and, before I know it, they're arguing.

"Ryan, back off. I'm doing what I should have done a long time ago. I love her, and I want her back, and that's what I'm going to fight for."

Anger takes over Ryan's body and Cam notices it too. I know I have to step in and pull Ryan away. I know I'm hurting him, and Cam's words are just making it worse. He doesn't deserve to be hurt like this, so I have to get him inside as quickly as I can.

"Cam, just go, please. Ryan, come on, let's go inside."

I grab Ryan's arm and try to pull him away. He moves a few feet away from Cam, and I think he's going to follow me inside. But he suddenly walks back towards Cam and punches him in the face.

"Ryan! Stop!" I yell as he tries to hit Cam again. Cam goes to hit Ryan, but I step between them again.

"Cam, leave it. Please, just go."

Cam looks at me and backs away from Ryan before getting in his car and driving off. I try to walk back inside with Ryan, but he tells me he's leaving.

"I'm going home. I'll call you in a few days. I'm sorry I ruined your birthday."

"Please, don't apologise. Do you promise we will speak in a few days?"

"I promise. Please enjoy the rest of your birthday."

I watch Ryan get into his car and leave as I stand at the end of the driveway, looking into the dark street. I replay everything that has just happened over and over until I hear the front door open. I look to the top of the driveway as Anna approaches me.

"They both left, didn't they?" she asks me as she puts her arm around my shoulder.

"Yeah, they got into a fight. Oh God, this isn't how I wanted this night to go. What have I done?"

"Honey, it doesn't take a genius to see that you and Cam still love each other. I know you think you're hiding it, but it's written all over your face. Your body language completely changes when Cam is around. When it's just you and Ryan, you look miserable. If you don't want to be with Ryan then, out of fairness to him, you should end it. Cam feels the same way about you, and as everyone has said all along, you two are meant to be. Now you must decide if you want to be with him for good, or if you want to move on for good."

It feels like everyone, myself included, is saying the same thing, and that scares me more than anything.

"You're right. I agree with everything you've said. I just don't want to hurt anyone."

"Love, you're torturing yourself. Either way, someone is going to get hurt. In the end, you need to do what makes you happy. Leave it for tonight. Let's go inside and enjoy the rest of the night. You can deal with everything else tomorrow."

I follow Anna back inside, where I spend the rest of the night with my family and friends, trying to forget what has happened. Although, no matter what I do, I can't stop thinking about how I can get through the next few days without hurting two people I genuinely care about.

~

Something in me changed that night. I don't know if it was seeing Cam and Ryan fighting, me realising that I can't fight my feelings for Cam, or Anna telling me that her – and everyone else – can see that we belong together, but I finally know what I have to do. I don't want to hurt Ryan, but at the same time I'm not happy, and neither is he. I know my shot at happiness lies with Cam and my music career and, if I want it all, I have to risk it all. I start to think of ways that I can minimise Ryan's pain when I end things for good. All I know is that all my life I've put other people's feelings before my own. I always hold back on what I want to say and do, out of fear of hurting those around me, especially those I care about. Ryan deserves to be with someone who truly loves him, and that person isn't me.

CHAPTER TEN
THE DAY THAT FOLLOWED

After the ordeal of my birthday, I find immediate comfort when my head hits the pillow in the early hours of Sunday morning. I keep replaying the words Cam said to me. I can't help but smile. He has finally confessed his true feelings, and that makes me so happy. However, I can't stop the feeling of guilt I've had since I made the decision to sit down with Ryan and end things for good.

The rest of my birthday went better than I expected. After calming myself down, I did my best to enjoy the rest of the night with my family and friends, although everyone kept asking me where Cam and Ryan had gone. At first, I didn't know how to respond, so I just changed the subject. Eventually, everyone stopped asking me about it. I spent quality time with those closest to me. We talked about my album, which is set to drop in a few days. I made plans to spend more time with my best friends, and I spent as much time with Dakota as I could as she's leaving for New York on Wednesday night. I tried my best to ignore the booming headache I had, and I tried my best to stop overthinking every single detail from Ryan and Cam's confrontation and all of the words that were exchanged between the three of us. I kept closing my eyes, trying to stop the constant replays, and after calming my breathing down, I managed to push things to the side long enough to enjoy the rest of the night.

After everyone had gone home, I went straight into the bathroom to shower. I washed the makeup off my face and let the warm water relax my body before I got changed into my pyjamas. At 2:00 a.m. I finally crawled into bed and fell asleep almost instantly.

On Sunday morning, Dakota wakes me up, much to my displeasure.

"Why? I'm tired, Dakota. I just want to sleep." I say as I open my eyes and look at my sister.

Dakota raises her eyebrows as she walks over to my desk and sits down in the chair that sits under the wooden frame.

"You've been asleep for nine hours. How are you still tired?"

"I don't know. I just am. Anyway, what do you want?"

"Well, Dylan has a soccer game today. I was going to watch the game and, because I'm leaving soon, I thought I'd see if you want to keep me company? You know I'm not into sport, so I don't understand how soccer works."

"Dakota, I don't understand soccer as much as you don't understand it, but I'll come with you. What time is the game?"

Dakota jumps up from the seat and claps her hands.

"Awesome! It starts at midday. It's not far from here, but we need to leave soon."

"Okay, let me get dressed. I'll meet you downstairs in ten minutes."

After Dakota heads back downstairs, I get changed. When I'm ready, I grab my phone and my Ray Bans and head downstairs to find Dakota.

"I'm ready, Dakota."

She's in the kitchen, flicking through a magazine.

"Sweet. I like what you're wearing. You look nice. Here are your keys. You're driving."

She throws my car keys at me. I catch them, put my phone in my pocket, and follow my sister to my car. As we drive to the ground, we talk about everything that happened last night.

"I know you might not want to tell me what happened, but I'm here if you want to talk about things."

I flick through the radio stations, before settling on one that's playing *Save the World* by Swedish House Mafia.

"It's not that I don't want to talk about it. I just don't know if I can keep going over it."

I tap my fingers on the steering wheel.

"It's about Ryan, isn't it?"

"Yes, it is. I may as well just tell you, since I've confided in you about it already. Cam confessed that he wants me back. He wants to give our relationship another go, and that makes me so happy. It's everything I want, but the thought of hurting Ryan sucks. I know the longer I leave it, the worse it'll be. I think he knows it's over anyway, but this just isn't who I am Dakota. I love so deeply, and I care about those around me so much. I really do love Ryan, but I love him as a friend. Knowing that I'm going to hurt him just feels shit. You know I wouldn't ever intentionally hurt someone, especially when they've made such a positive impact on my life, I just know what I want, and what I want lies with Cam."

161

"Delilah, everyone who knows you knows how caring, loyal and loving you are. Sometimes it's a curse to have those qualities, especially when you feel them so deeply. But, if you don't do what makes you happy, then you're not living a fair life. Will Ryan be hurt? Of course he will. You can't avoid that. No matter what you do or when you do it, he's going to be hurt. But that hurt will continue to build if you don't end it now. Ryan knows it's over, Delilah, but I think he is just as scared as you are. You're both facing the reality of losing what you had when you were friends, but you need to do what you need to do. I know how much you care for everyone but, for once, you need to put yourself first."

Everything my sister says to me hits me on such a deep level. I know everything she is telling me is true, and it's exactly how I've been feeling, especially since last night. Deep down I know that things need to change.

Dakota and I continue to talk until we reach the ground. When we arrive, we head towards the pitch. As we make our way towards the seats, I notice a very familiar person, and it's not my brother. I take my Ray Bans off and look closer. I stop walking to make sure it is who I think it is.

"Dakota, what is Cam doing here?"

I follow her over to the grandstand, and we sit three rows from the front. I stand next to my sister and put my sunglasses back on. She gently tugs on my oversized top, pulling me down into the seat next to her.

"Um, well, one of the players is sick so they needed someone to fill in for him. Dylan knew about it last night, and because he's the captain he called Cam after he left. He was going to ask him when he was there, but Dylan didn't get a chance to."

"You knew he was going to be here. Why didn't you tell me?"

"I wanted you to get out of the house, and I want to spend time with you too, especially because neither of us knows how this game works! I did also think you'd want to see Cam without everyone around. This is the only game here today, so when it's over, everyone will leave and you two can talk in private."

Cam has spotted me. He waves as the referee blows his whistle, signalling the start of the game. I wave back at him.

"Thanks, I guess."

"What? Are you mad at me?"

"No, Dakota, I'm not mad at you. I just thought I'd avoid Cam until I ended things with Ryan. It's too hard to see him right now. All I want to do is hug him and kiss him, and I refuse to even entertain that idea until things are over between Ryan and me for good. Every time I see Cam, though, I find myself wanting to throw that idea out of my mind. I know it's wrong. God, I sound so stupid!"

Dakota grabs my hand and squeezes it.

"Hey, you're not stupid. It's going to work out, Delilah. You know what you have to do. Just talk to Cam after the game, get things sorted once and for all, and then talk to Ryan. I know it's going to be difficult, but just try not to focus on any of that. Let's just try and figure out how this game works."

She winks at me.

"What am I going to do when you leave me for New York?"

"Hey, I'm only on the other side of the world for a few months. I'll be back in no time, and it's me that's going to struggle without you!"

"Please! You've got James, so you'll be fine!"

"And you've got Cam, so you'll be fine too!"

When the game finishes, Dakota gets up from her seat and stretches.

"Well, I don't know about you, but I'm glad that's over. I still don't understand how soccer works. I think I'll just stick to tennis."

"Sounds good to me."

We head down to the pitch, where Dylan and Cam are waiting for us. When the rest of the team has left, Dakota turns to me.

"I'm going to go home with Dylan. See you soon?"

"Yep, I'll see you soon."

Cam and I watch my brother and sister leave. When they're gone, I look at him and smile.

"Nice black eye."

I look at the bruise around his right eye.

"Thanks. It's my battle wound. Want to go and talk?"

I follow him back to the seats and, as soon as we sit down, the silence falls upon us. I watch a few leaves getting dragged across the floor as the wind picks up, and I listen to the sound of the breeze as it makes its way through the trees. I get lost in the sounds the wind makes, but Cam finally ends the silence.

"Do you feel it?"

"Feel what? The breeze?"

"No, not the breeze. *It:* that feeling, that energy, that charge between us."

I know what he's talking about. It's the same thing I feel every time I'm around him, and I'm never sure of how to explain it. It makes my heart sing when he explains the same feeling. It shows that he believes in us again, that he really does love me.

"I always feel it when I'm around you," I whisper.

Without even thinking, I blurt out a question that I've asked before. I've never believed Cam's response, so I'm trying again.

"Why did you do it? Why you did you break up with me? You broke my heart, Cam. I've never been the same since then. I know we're talking about getting back together, but I can't do that until I know why. I need you to explain it to me."

I look back down to the ground and wait for him to answer my questions. He puts his hands on my face, and gently lifts it up so our eyes meet.

"If you want me to tell you, you have to look at me."

He removes his hands from my face and puts them in his lap.

"I know I hurt you. I know I broke your heart. I made a mistake, and it has cost me nearly everything. I can't tell you how many nights I lie awake, crying and cursing myself for ending things. I thought we needed time apart. I thought we needed to focus on ourselves for a while. We did, and still do, but I realise we can do that together."

"You cried?"

"Of course I did! I love you, Delilah. Nothing's ever going to change that."

It makes me so happy to hear him say that; to hear him tell me he loves me. It makes every bad thing we've been through worth it. It shows me that true love does exist. When something's truly meant to be, it will always work its way out.

"How do I know you mean all of this? How do I know you're not just saying what you think I want to hear?"

I want to believe him, but I'm terrified of going through that pain and heartbreak again.

"Delilah, I know we've discussed this before, and I know we're repeating these things, but we're doing that for a reason. In the end, you have to decide what you believe. You have to do what's best for you. I've said it so many times in the last 24 hours, but I really do love you. If you feel the same, then we'd be stupid to not give our relationship another chance. I regret doing what I did to you, and I'll never be able to fix that, I know that. I'm being honest with you, because I want to be with you for the rest of my life. Nothing will ever change the way I feel about you. I know I'll never feel this way about anyone, and I know you feel the same. If we're both honest, we jumped into new relationships almost immediately because we wanted to fill the void of not being with each other. I know that's what I did, and I've regretted it ever since."

Despite going over things, Cam and I have never truly spoken about him and Heather, not in depth anyway. I know that if we're going to move forward, we need to talk about it so we can move past it once and for all.

"You're right. We did do that but, Cam, you have no idea how hurt I was when you were with Heather. It killed me. I saw how she looked at you, and when I first saw you together, I thought you'd moved on for good."

"I know, and I regret all of that. I bumped into Heather the day after me and you broke up. I was obviously a mess, and she saw that as an advantage. She started hitting on me, and I was desperate to numb the pain. I agreed to get a drink with her, and we ended up getting drunk. Before I knew it, we were together. I say together, but it was more like she had a boyfriend, and I had a friend to numb my pain."

I didn't know he felt this way about ending our relationship. It makes me feel angry that he put both of us through all of this when it could have been avoided. But, that's life, and there's nothing I can do to change the past.

"Did you, ummm, did you, you know, ummm …"

I want to know how far he went in his 'relationship' with Heather.

"Did we have sex? Yes, we did, a few times near the end of our relationship. We hadn't done it before then, to be honest I don't even know why we bothered, we both knew it meant nothing. It certainly didn't help. It just made me feel worse, so I stopped doing anything with her. I didn't even kiss her. I decided a long time ago that I wanted to end things with her. She knew just as much as I did that I wanted to be with you. I guess we just stayed together because we were both lonely. I promise it meant nothing."

I look into Cam's eyes as he answers my question, and I can tell he's being honest. His eyes don't light up when he talks about Heather or the past that they share. In fact, he looks guilty every time I ask about it. I know that going over things a million times isn't going to help, and I know he's sorry, so I choose to forgive him. I choose to move on from it all. In the end, all I want is to be with him. I know that I can't walk away from this: from loving him. Not again.

"Are you really going to break up with him, with Ryan?"

"Yes, I meant what I said. I don't love him the way I love you. It's not fair to continue in a relationship when I know it's not what I want. In saying that, did you mean what you said? I mean it when I say this Cam: regardless of what you want to do, my relationship with Ryan is over, but I don't want to get back together with you if you're just going to walk away again."

"Delilah, I meant every word that I said last night. I know I've just said the same thing, but I see the doubt in your eyes. I'll say it again. I mean it when I say the time apart confirmed that you're the love of my life and the person I want to spend the rest of my life with. I love you more than I can even begin to explain. We're meant to be, Delilah, and I've never been so certain of anything like this in my entire life."

For the first time in a long time, things feel perfect between us again. That is the best feeling in the world.

"I've got to get home. I've got an assignment due in a few days, but I'll walk you back to your car."

I follow him back to my car, and on the way he startles me.

"Delilah, stop!"

I think something is really wrong, and I look around to see why he reacted like that. I can't see anything, so I look at him.

"What is it?"

"Your shoelace is undone. I don't want you to trip on it."

I watch him as he ties my shoelace, grinning. He stands back up on his feet, and walks me back to my car. We stand there, face to face, staring into each other's eyes, not saying a word. It feels like neither of us wants this day to end, but I know deep down it's not the end. Instead, we're on the verge of rekindling our relationship. As hard as it will be, I know that ending things with Ryan is the right thing to do: not just for me, but for him too. After another minute of looking into each other's eyes, I finally build up the courage to get into my car. I wind my window down.

"I'll see you soon?" he asks as he smiles at me.

"Yep, I'll see you soon."

"Good luck with Ryan. I hope he understands."

"Me too. I just hope I don't hurt him."

"Well, that's going to happen regardless of what you say, but you're sparing his feelings in the long run. If you really don't love him and you don't want to be with him, then it's something you have to do sooner rather than later."

I look down at my hands in my lap.

"Delilah, don't worry. We're going to get back together. The time just has to be right. We will know when that time comes, okay?"

I start my car.

"Get home safely."

"You too. I'll see you soon."

I pull out into the quiet street. Despite going separate ways for now, I know that things are going to work themselves out. I know that when we're ready, we will find our way back to each other. For once, I don't fear waiting; this time round it doesn't seem scary. In fact, it feels the complete opposite. It feels like things are finally falling into place. Things are happening exactly how they're meant to happen, and I can't help but feel excited about the future, even with the conversation with Ryan looming over me.

I turn the radio on and realise that my song is playing. No matter how many times this happens, I'm always overcome with emotions. I still can't believe this has happened to me. Despite all the shit that I've had to deal with recently, I know it's all just steps towards a brighter and happier future. My debut album is about to be released, and everything I've ever wanted from my life is about to take full effect. Knowing this helps me deal with my struggles. And I'm about to face more struggles: not only is Dakota leaving for New York City, but I'm also about to end my relationship with Ryan. I'm hoping that everything doesn't go as badly as I'm expecting it will.

CHAPTER ELEVEN
THE TURNAROUND

I sit at my bay window and watch the sky as the sun rises on Monday morning. The last few days have been hectic, but every part of me is now at peace. I know that my relationship with Ryan is over for good, and as much as I feel scared of hurting him, I know that it's for the best. With my decision to end my relationship with Ryan, rekindling my love for Cam, helping my sister prepare for her trip to New York, and waiting for my album to debut, things are intense. But, I've learnt to balance things out and, with time, I don't think that my turnaround will be as bad I expected.

I'm lost in my own little world when there's a knock at my door. I look up as Dakota walks in, holding two cups of tea. She hands me one of them and sits on the opposite side of my bay window. We don't speak for a few minutes; we just look outside and watch as the sun lights up the deep blue morning sky.

"It's such a beautiful day already," Dakota says with a smile as she takes a sip of her tea.

"It is, isn't it?" I say to her as I do the same.

We continue to sit in silence as we finish our tea, then put our cups on the floor and look at each other.

"So, how are you feeling about your album being released this week?"

My album is dropping on Wednesday. Melody and I have agreed on a mid-week release. She said it would be more beneficial, although I didn't really understand the meaning behind that. At the time I just wanted a release date, so I knew it was actually happening and I wasn't dreaming, so I agreed with whatever she said. Now Wednesday is nearly here, and my nerves are skyrocketing. I don't know how the public will respond to my album. I always remind myself that my covers and *Wildfire* were hits, so I hold onto that as a level of comfort when I think about all the things that could go wrong when the album drops.

"I'm pretty excited. I can't wait to see what everyone has to say about it. I hope people like it, and connect to the words. I worked really hard. I poured my heart and soul into this album, so I hope that shows."

"I'm sure it will. I pre-ordered a copy."

"You did? Why? I could have just given you a copy."

"I know you could have given me a copy, but I wanted to buy one. I want to support you, and I know I don't have to buy your album to do that, but I know how hard you've worked on this. You've been through so much lately, and I'm just so proud of you. To see your name and your album pop up on iTunes is so surreal. I wanted to be one of the many people that buys your album."

I notice how proud Dakota looks, and it makes me feel a sense of pride too. I lean over and hug her.

"Thank you."

We then begin to talk about her big trip to New York.

"So, you're only going for a month, right? Is it a trial or does the agency think you'll be able to move there permanently?"

"It's a four-week trial to begin with. The agency wants to see how many jobs I can book. After the four weeks is up, I'll sit down with my manager and the agency and we will look at how I went. Based on that, we will make a decision about if I should move there full-time."

She sounds sad. I've never seen her respond like this; usually when we talk about her job she lights up. This time it's different.

"What's wrong?"

"Nothing's wrong. I'm just scared. I only just moved to Sydney, so I don't want to jump into anything. If I'm honest, I'm quite happy to travel between Sydney and New York. I know that's crazy – New York is so far away from Sydney – but it just makes more sense to me. There's a ton of work for me in Sydney, and I don't know if I'm ready to give that up just yet. I love working in Australia, and I love working for Australian brands. I've learnt so much. So many doors have opened for me here. I know I can find jobs in New York ... I just don't know if it feels right."

This is the first time I've seen her lose the spark in her eye. It's the first time in so long that I've seen her doubt herself or look scared. I think back to all the times that Dakota has helped me. No matter what I've been going through, whenever I needed her, she was there for me. From the process of Cam and I splitting up, to recording my album, to going through everything with Evan, and recently the issues I've been facing with Ryan, Dakota has been the one consistent person who has helped me get through it all. She never left my side. Even if she was in Sydney, she made time to call me every single day, regardless of how busy she was. We aren't just sisters; we are best friends too, and I know it's my turn to pick her up.

"Dakota, do you know what I've always envied about you? Your passion, your determination, and the way you fight for what you want. I've learnt so much from being your sister. If it weren't for you, I never would have found the strength and confidence I needed to fight for my dreams, to fight for the chance to succeed as an artist. I know that this could all fail. I know that my album could debut and everyone could hate it. I am aware that I might be a one hit wonder, or only good enough for a short period. Despite all of that, I made a choice to do it anyway. *You* taught me that we only get one shot at life, and if we don't follow our dreams – no matter how impossible they may seem – we waste our lives doing something that we're not passionate about. You may doubt yourself right now, and I know that because it's written all over your face, but believe me when I tell you that you're going to succeed, no matter where you go. I've never met someone who is so passionate about what they do. You light up whenever you talk about the jobs you've booked, and you're so dedicated to what you do. Everyone around you sees that. I know this is scary for you, but you once told me not to let fear stop me from doing something out of my comfort zone. Now I'm giving you the same advice. Go to New York and show them what you're made of. You can do this, Dakota."

My sister's trying to hide her tears from me. She hates how emotional she has become.

"You can do this. You're so strong, Dakota. Don't let the voices telling you you're not good enough win. I know you don't think it feels right, but you're never going to know if you don't try."

I wipe the tears away from her eyes. Just as Dakota starts to speak my phone rings.

"It's Melody. Sorry."

I answer the call.

"Hi, Melody."

"Good morning, Delilah. How are you today? Excited for the album release?"

"I'm good. How are you? Yes, I'm very excited, and nervous!"

"I'm good too, thank you. Oh, don't be nervous. That's why I'm calling. I wanted to tell you about the pre-sale numbers. You should be very proud. You've had a lot of interest in the album. I can't give you an exact number because it's constantly changing. Every time I get one number, it changes straight after. We can't keep up. But the last I heard there were over fifty-five thousand pre-orders already submitted on iTunes, and that's just from the online store. We've had a lot of interest in music stores too, so you'll be pushing a higher number. As far as I know, that was only for the Australian iTunes orders too. The international orders have been coming through rapidly as well, but I don't have an exact number for you. I know it's quite overwhelming, but it's an incredible start. We think this is really going to take off. We're excited to see where this goes, and you should be too."

I look at Dakota as I try to process what Melody is telling me. *Fifty-five thousand?* That doesn't even sound right! I never expected this many people to pre-order something they haven't even heard. It makes me feel so happy; this is a dream come true. Knowing that my music will be heard by the world gives me goose bumps, but in the best way! As I'm trying to calm myself down, Melody continues.

"Now, while I have you on the line I have to talk to you about the MTV documentary that you filmed last month. There was a slight delay in the airdate. I can't tell you exactly why because even I don't know. Anyway, I asked them to schedule it for tonight. With your album dropping on Wednesday, it will help generate more hype and hopefully help with the sales. I've sent a copy to your uncle. He received it this morning, so I imagine you will hear from him soon. Watch it with your family. Enjoy this moment. You deserve it. Give me a call after you've watched it. I'll speak to you then."

I thank Melody before hanging up.

"Whoa, that was intense." I say aloud

"What did she say?"

"She just told me that the pre-orders are going well. She said the orders keep coming in, and they can't keep up with the numbers anymore. Let's not talk about that. It's giving me a headache. How are *you* feeling? I know crying helps me, and you look slightly better."

Mum comes into my room, interrupting our conversation.

"Morning girls. Uncle Derek will be over soon. He has a copy of the MTV documentary. I'm going to run to the shops to get some food. I'll be back soon."

We head downstairs as our mum leaves.

"You can do this, Dakota. You just have to keep believing in yourself. You've come this far."

She looks like her normal, happy self again.

"Thank you."

"You don't have to thank me."

We go into the lounge room, where Darci is sitting with Evan, James, Dylan and Declan. We play a few rounds of Jenga, then my mum walks in and joins us, closely followed by my uncle, aunt and cousins. We sit down and my uncle puts the disc into the DVD player. I turn to my mum.

"Where's aunty Deb? I thought she was coming?"

"Oh shoot, I forgot to tell you. They're not going to make it. Aunty Deb has a virus, and the whole family has caught it. They don't want to spread their germs. She said to tell you she's very proud of you, and she will call you later."

A few seconds later, the documentary begins. When it finishes, I discuss it with my family. I'm overcome with emotions. The documentary was surreal, although I found it awkward to watch myself on television. As my family discuss the documentary and my album, I get up and head outside to call Melody.

"You're scheduled to go into the city on Wednesday afternoon for another radio interview when your album has dropped. Your uncle knows about it, and he will go with you seeing as he's your co-manager. Delilah, this is going to open so many doors for you. You're getting the chance of a lifetime, one that most aspiring singer-songwriters don't ever get. You've worked so hard, and that will all pay off. Your dreams are about to come true, so prepare yourself. Your life won't ever be the same again. I mean that in the best way possible. This is the start of your professional music career, and I'm not just saying this because I'm your co-manager. You really are the next big thing in music."

I never expected this to happen to me. I didn't ever think I would get a shot at making my dreams a reality, at least not like this. It's the scariest, yet most exciting feeling, and I know Melody is right: this is going to change my life. For once, I'm ready to embrace every single aspect of this journey, no matter how good or bad it is.

When I get off the phone with Melody, I head back inside and run through the final details about Wednesday with my uncle. He's agreed to pick me up before we head into the city for the interview.

"Thank you, for everything. None of this would be possible without you. I'm so glad you're on this journey with me."

He waves me off.

"Honey, this wouldn't be possible if it wasn't for you. You're the one with the talent, you're the one who wrote the songs, you're the one who fought for this. I should be the one thanking you for letting me come on this journey with you. I'm so damn proud of you, kiddo. I knew you could do it."

I feel tears prick the corners of my eyes.

"We make a good team."

We head into the kitchen where my mum has made lunch for us. We sit down and chat, but I'm suddenly overcome with a feeling that I can't shake. I try so hard to ignore it, but I can't. I've been avoiding Ryan since Saturday, and I feel horrible for doing that. I guess I've just been too scared to face the reality of ending things with him, but the time has come. I can't keep running. I know that if I don't end things now, I never will. I get up from my chair, hug everyone, say goodbye, and leave. I'm not surprised when my mum chases after me.

"Where are you going?"

"I'm going to see Ryan. It's time, mum."

I haven't spoken to my mum about what happened on Saturday, but I know she's spoken to Anna. She is up-to-date with the whole situation ... well, until my birthday anyway.

"Are you okay? Do you need me to come with you?"

I raise my eyebrows at her.

"Sorry. Stupid questions. We will be here for you when you get back."

"Thanks, mum. I'll be fine. I'll see you soon."

I grab my keys, get into my car, pull my phone out and dial Ryan's number. After three rings, he answers.

"Hello?"

It sounds like he's just woken up.

"Hi. Sorry, did I wake you?"

"No, but I've only been awake for twenty minutes. I was going to call you soon. You've been avoiding me."

"I'm sorry. I just needed some time. Can I come over?"

"Sure. I'll see you soon."

Without waiting for me to respond, Ryan hangs up. I put my phone down and start my car before driving over to Ryan's house for the last time.

When I arrive, I raise my hand to knock on the door, but Ryan opens it before I even get a chance.

"Hi."

I notice the stubble that has formed around his chin and mouth. He has dark circles under his eyes, and he looks miserable. *Look what I've done to him.*

"Hi."

I step inside, Ryan closes the door and embraces me like it's what he needs to survive.

"I'm sorry about how I reacted on Saturday. I sent Cam a message and apologised to him too. I know I ruined your birthday, but I'm glad you're here."

I hug him back, sensing that he needs a hug more than ever right now.

"Please don't apologise. You didn't ruin my birthday, I promise."

I know deep down that I should be the one apologising to him. After all, I'm the one who has caused all of this. I follow Ryan into the living room, where I sit down on the couch as he makes me a cup of tea. I look around the room; I notice there are new photos on his coffee table. I pick one of them up: Ryan's sitting in the middle of two other people, who I assume are his parents. They look so happy.

"My mum has come back to life," Ryan says as he hands me a steaming cup of tea. I put the photo back down on the table and smile at him.

"I bet she's happy to have you back in her life. How are things with them?"

I'm trying to avoid the reason why I'm here, although I do genuinely want to know how things have progressed since we last spoke about it.

"Good. Really good, actually. I've come a long way, and so have they. We're finally a family again. Everything's almost perfect in my life, except for us."

I take a sip of the hot tea. Despite it being boiling I find myself wanting to down it so I can leave, but I remind myself why I need to do this. I put the cup down and turn to face Ryan.

"I've cursed myself more times that I can count about doing this, so bear with me. You're amazing Ryan, you really are. You're funny, caring, loving, loyal and you're the best listener. You're everything a girl wants in a boyfriend. There's just one problem: you're not Cam. My heart has always belonged to him. We have talked about seeing where things go from here, but I don't know how that will pan out. If things don't work out this time, it may mean I'm single for the rest of my life. If that happens, then that's just how it's meant to be. I can't be with someone else when I'm always going to wish it was him. That's not fair on you."

I brace myself for him to yell at me, but he doesn't. In fact, he looks relieved.

"I've been expecting this for a while now. I've known for a long time that we weren't going to work out. I guess I just thought it would change with time, but I know we can't force things like this. In the end, we're both in an unhappy place and that's not fair on either of us. We were better off as friends, weren't we?"

"Yeah, we were. I know it will take time, but eventually, I hope we can reconnect and be friends again. No matter what I do, I hurt someone. It really does upset me that I know I can't avoid that. I'm so sorry that it's you I'm hurting. You don't deserve this."

I feel sick to my stomach.

"Delilah, you have to do what's best for you. If you're not happy, there's no point. Don't worry about me. I'll be fine, I promise. Despite everything, I really do just want you to be happy. I see the way you look at Cam, the way you light up whenever he's around you. That's who makes you happy, and that's who you need to be with. If, or when, the time is right we can be friends again. For now, we both have things we need to concentrate on. I really do want the best for you. You're an amazing person. If it wasn't for you, I would never have gone home. I would never have found my way back to my parents. I would have just kept running and making things worse for myself, and my family. Because of you, I stopped running, and I faced everything. Now I'm in a much better place. I'll be okay, Delilah. I promise. Please don't feel bad."

It makes me happy that I've helped Ryan and, despite the difficult times we've recently faced, we really were lucky to find each other, even if it was short-lived.

We spend the next two hours talking. After our conversation ends, I get up and hug Ryan one last time.

"Good luck with everything. Promise to keep in contact?"

"Of course. I hope everything continues to work out for you. You really do deserve the best. Thank you for being there for me. You helped me get through such a difficult time, and I'll never forget that."

He walks me to my car and opens the door.

"Just friends."

"Just friends," I agree.

I start my car, feeling a weight lifted off my shoulders. The conversation I just had with Ryan was a million times better than expected. I feel like I can finally move on with my life, and Ryan is free to do the same.

~

Wednesday soon arrives, and at 12:30 p.m. my uncle picks me up. We stop at Stripes on our way through to get coffee. My uncle places our order and I look around the busy seated section. As I glance over the crowd, I spot a familiar face and smile when I see Cam. My uncle spots him too and, without even thinking, he walks over to him. They start talking and Cam waves at me. I slowly walk over to join them.

"Hi," he says before gesturing me to sit down.

"Hi," I say back as I sit across from him.

"What are you doing here?"

"I've got a radio interview soon. We wanted to get a coffee on the way."

"That sounds fun."

Before I can even respond, my uncle chimes in.

"If you're not doing anything, would you like to join us? Delilah's pretty nervous, so the more, the merrier I say."

I feel the heat rise to my cheeks as I look between my uncle and Cam. Thankfully one of the waitresses brings us our coffees, so I have an excuse to look away from the two of them.

"I'd love to."

I take a sip of my coffee, and try to think of something to say. This is ridiculous. I feel the same nerves I felt when I first started getting feelings for Cam. It's like I'm falling for him for the first time. Before I can think of anything to say, my uncle stands up.

"We'd better get going. Cam, why don't you come with us? I can drop you off at your car when we're done."

Cam agrees and, when we reach the car, my uncle turns to us.

"You two sit in the back. It's safer." I look at him and raise my eyebrows. He winks at me, and Cam and I hop into the back of the car. We start the trip to the radio station with talk about my album, although it makes my nerves worse. Then my uncle and Cam talk about sport: something they bonded over a long time ago. I look out of the window as I drift in and out of the conversation. Cam grabs my hand and holds it. I look at him, and he smiles at me before continuing the conversation with my uncle. For some reason, it helps calm my nerves.

When we reach the studio, we head inside to meet the hosts, who I spoke to last month when I did my phone interview. They brief me on what we will be talking about before Renee, one of the hosts, asks about Cam.

"Is this the famous boyfriend of yours?"

"He's a friend, a very good friend."

I worry Cam might react badly to me calling him a friend, but he smiles and nods his head.

"Is your boyfriend coming in today?" Renee blurts out.

I look at her and notice she looks embarrassed by what she has just asked. I laugh before answering, hoping it will make her feel less embarrassed.

"No, I'm single now. I want to enjoy this time of my life, and when the time is right, I'll make the transition into a relationship,"

Renee smiles at me before showing me to my seat. I sit down, put on my headphones, and we start the interview.

As we wrap up the interview, Renee announces that my album is officially available.

"You heard it here first, folks. Perth's own singing superstar, Delilah Walker, has officially released her first album. *Rise* is now available, and it's going to take the world by storm!"

I smile as the interview comes to an end. When it's over, I thank the hosts, take a photo with them and head back to the car with my uncle and Cam.

After we drop Cam off, my uncle drives me home. When we reach the driveway, my uncle checks his phone.

"I just got a text from Melody. She said your album is doing incredibly well. She's getting a lot of good feedback, and the people who have purchased the album are loving it. She says everything is going better than expected. It looks like you're going to be an overnight sensation, again! Congratulations, kiddo."

This still doesn't feel real; it feels like a dream. A very unexplainable dream.

"Wow, that's incredible." I feel stupid for saying that, but it's all I can manage I'm overcome with emotions. My uncle gently taps my shoulder.

"I know this is overwhelming, but you don't have to worry now. Everyone loves your music, Delilah. Your talent has finally been exposed, and you deserve this. Enjoy this moment. It's the next step of your journey, so embrace it."

I take in every single word he is saying.

"You're right, thank you. I'd better go inside. I'll see you tomorrow. Thank you for coming with me today."

I head inside, go to my room, and grab my laptop. I go onto iTunes, type in my name, and start to read the reviews of my album.

I am on cloud nine. Everything is working out perfectly. I'm finally in a good place in my life, and I'm nothing short of happy. I know this journey is going to be incredible, and I can't wait to see where it takes me next. The positive response to my album has been astounding, and I can't wait to continue my career as a singer-songwriter. But, all of that needs to briefly be put on hold as we prepare for Dakota to head to New York.

CHAPTER TWELVE
SECOND CHANCE

On Friday morning, I'm woken up by screaming voices. At first, I think I'm hearing things but, as I sit up in my bed, I notice the voices are very real and they're getting louder. I jump out of bed and run downstairs, where I find Dakota and my mum in the kitchen having a heated argument. I try to step in to help, but it's no use. I sit down at the kitchen table and listen to what they're saying. Within seconds I realise that Dakota has mentioned the one person who can make my mum crumble: *my dad*.

As the fight becomes more intense, I find myself becoming increasingly uncomfortable. Out of nowhere, Dakota says something that stops my mum dead in her tracks.

"I want you guys to be able to get along. I want him to be able to be a part of my life, and I want him to be at any events I have in the future. He's my father, and I know you haven't been on the best of terms, but he deserves a second chance. Why won't you just see him and hear what he has to say? He has changed, mum. He's not the person you remember."

I see my mum tense up. It reminds me of when I mentioned finding my dad a few months back.

Her reaction was understandable, but I remember how much it hurt when she asked me not to see him. It's like déjà vu, except now it's Dakota who's in the firing line.

"For goodness sake, Dakota. You're just like your sister. You have to have things your way when it comes to your father. I don't want to see him or hear what he has to say. I don't care anymore. If you kids want to give him a second chance, then that's your decision, but I will not give him that chance. I gave him more chances than he deserved and I'm not going back to that place, not again. Now, we need to talk about your going-away dinner on Sunday night. I know you fly out on Wednesday night, so I want you to spend some quality time with your family before then, but on Sunday night your friends are welcome to join us, like I said last week when we discussed it. Who did you end up inviting?"

Dakota doesn't even respond. She turns on her heels and storms out of the kitchen mumbling to herself. My mum leans against the kitchen bench, puts her head in her hands and shakes it from side to side. After a few minutes, she looks up at me.

"Do you think I was too harsh on her?" she asks in a quiet voice.

"Well, I don't know the extent of what happened."

"She wants your father to come over today. She came into the kitchen this morning and asked me, like it was no big deal. I don't understand why you and Dakota have suddenly gone on this tangent to have him in your lives."

I try to approach this conversation with caution. I know my mum still struggles to understand why we're desperate to have our father in our lives, but maybe it's time we face this problem and deal with it once and for all before it destroys us. I slowly lift my head to face my mum again, and I see a look on her face that I've never seen before. I know I have to approach her with ease; she looks furious.

"Mum, I don't know if this is my place to say this, but since we've been through it before, maybe I can shed some light on this whole 'dad' thing."

She looks at me and waits for me to continue.

"Um, well, when we were, you know, going through our issues with me trying to find dad, you told me I should pursue it. I know why you told me to do that. Considering how much I was struggling with the breakup and everything else going on, it made sense for you to let me do that. I know we've been through this a million times before, but we need him, mum. And, deep down, he needs us too. I know things will never be the same. We're never going to truly be a family, and that's okay. Evan is the perfect person for you, and he fits into our lives. You know we love him but, like everyone's said before, nothing replaces your real dad. I know you think he's still the same person, but he really has changed. His old life, his old self: it's destroyed him. He's not the person you remember. I know it's asking a lot of you, but you were given a second chance when you found Evan. Don't you think dad deserves a second chance too? We're not trying to hurt you. We just want him back in our lives."

I leave my mum alone in the kitchen, and head upstairs to Dakota's room. I find her sitting on her bed, flipping through some magazines. I stand by the door and, just as I'm about to speak, my mum comes into the room.

"Dakota, I'm not doing this for him. I'm doing it for you. We will go to him. I don't want him knowing where we live. Call him and tell him we will be there in an hour. Delilah is coming with us."

Without saying another word, or waiting for Dakota to reply, my mum leaves the room, slamming the door behind her. The thud of the door makes me jump.

"She's angrier now than she was when I told her about finding him."

"I know. She was furious this morning. Right before you walked in I saw this look on her face. I was scared of how she reacted. I thought she was going to lose her shit, and she did. I really thought she would have taken it better since you spoke to him. Apparently, I was wrong."

Dakota slumps into her bed as I sigh and take a magazine from the pile.

"Dakota, you have to understand how hard this is for her. I know exactly where you're coming from, believe me I do, but this is so hard on her. We've gone behind her back to find someone she has tried so hard to protect us from. Yes, we're old enough to make our own decisions but, at the end of the day, she's our mum and she wants to protect us from everything she thinks is damaging. For her all she remembers of him is the person he used to be. Those memories are still raw for her. She doesn't know who he is now, and that's going to take time for her to adjust to. We just have to be patient. What she just said is huge. I never thought she'd be willing to face him, but she's going to. We have to play it cool if we want her to give him a second chance."

Dakota puts her magazine back on the pile.

"I know. I just thought she'd be more open to the idea of him being in our lives after you saw him. I'd better call him and see if he's home."

My sister picks up her phone and calls our dad. When he answers, she explains things to him.

He's surprised, but he agrees to us coming over. After settling on a time, Dakota ends the conversation.

"It's done."

Our parents are about to come face to face for the first time in over ten years.

~

At 1:30 p.m. we pull into the driveway of my father's house. I'm flooded with memories of the last time I was here; I shudder at how badly things went. As I step out of the car, I notice the house is still the same. It looks abandoned: the grass is brown, and the curtains are still dirty. From the outside, there is no sign of life. There is no sign that anyone would actually call this place home, and that makes me sad. I wish my father cared enough about the place he lived in to look after it. It makes me question if he's looking after himself. I shake the thoughts off as I walk towards the door with my sister. As Dakota knocks, I notice my mum isn't standing with us. I turn around and spot her standing by the car. I watch the expression on her face change as she slowly walks towards us. Just as she joins us, my father opens the door. Dakota walks in first, hugs him and waits as I do the same. When we're standing behind our dad, we look at our mum, who's still standing outside the door. She walks in and our dad tries to hug her; she abruptly stops him.

"Don't. I'm not here for you, I'm here for them," she says as she points at us. We try our best to remain calm.

"Would you like a cup of tea?"

We follow him to the dining room table, which is nice and clean, unlike the rest of the house.

"No, thank you. Let's just get this over with."

When we're all seated, the silence consumes us. The four of us don't know what to say, so we just sit there waiting until someone feels brave enough to speak. I look between my parents. My mum looks scared and uncomfortable; she doesn't look angry anymore. I think seeing the state of the house, and my father, has been enough to show her why Dakota and I have tried to give him another chance. I know my dad doesn't know what to say either, so I decide to end the silence.

"Dad, I know Dakota briefly mentioned why we're here this afternoon ... you know that the two of us are willing to let you back into our lives. We don't know about Declan, Dylan and Darci. That's something you have to work on with the three of them. But, in fairness to mum, we thought that in order to move forward, the two of you need to sit down and talk about everything. This is your chance to clear the air and put everything out on the table so we can *all* move on. We're very lucky to have Evan, and we love him dearly, but he and mum, as well as us kids, know that nothing replaces your real father. We're ready to have you in our lives. I know it's taken a lot of soul searching for you to get to a place where you want the same too, but we need you to be honest and communicate with mum. We don't want to go behind her back, so we made the decision to be honest with her about everything. We need you to do the same."

Being in this situation is overwhelming for all of us, but I know dad's ready to move on too, so encouraging him to open up is the only thing I can think of doing.

"I'm sorry. For everything. I can't ever express how apologetic I am for what I put you through,

Deidra. For what I put our children through. I never meant to hurt anyone, but I know that ultimately that's what I did. I know I caused permanent damage, and nothing I can ever say or do will change that, but I want to right my wrongs. The biggest mistake I ever made was walking away from you, from all of you. I know you've moved on with Evan, and I'm so happy for you. I'll never do anything to get in between the two of you but, at the same time, I want a relationship with my children. I've said the exact same thing to the girls, and I'll say it to you now. Out of all the bad things I've done in my life, I question how someone like me managed to end up with five amazing children. Granted, I only have a relationship with two of them, for now. I really do know how lucky I am to have that, to have a second chance. I just want you to know how truly sorry I am. I hope one day you can forgive me."

I look at my dad as the last words leave his lips, and I see tears run down his face: something I've never seen before. I know how hard that was for him, to admit that he made a mistake and he was wrong. I know that he's working on forgiving himself, something he deserves to do. It took a lot for my sister and me to forgive him for leaving us behind, but now we are old enough to understand why he did. We've made peace with the past, and now we're able to move forward. I just hope my mum can find the strength she needs within herself to do the same thing.

My mum looks at Dakota and me before she sets her sight on our father. Within seconds, she's unleashing years of pent-up anger.

"I don't know why it's taken you so long to apologise. You should have done it earlier but, for the sake of my children, I will forgive you."

My dad tries to talk, but she cuts him off.

"No. Don't say anything. Now it's my turn to tell you a few things. I hated you, Tony. You didn't just destroy my life, but you destroyed the lives of five innocent children. You have no idea how hard it was for me to raise them on my own. Thank God I had my family. Otherwise, I don't know how I would have coped. For years, I had to deal with one of my children having this unspoken hatred towards me. For years, I had to find a way to deal with Delilah hating me for you leaving. Even though I'm the one who stayed to raise them, I was the enemy. She never said this to me. She never once told me she hated me, but I could see it written all over her face. It was burned into her eyes."

I listen to my mum opening up for the first time, and I feel guilty. I know what she's talking about. I thought I had hidden it, but I hadn't. I didn't hate my mum, but I did blame her for my dad leaving. Over time, I knew it wasn't her fault, but I still resented her. Eventually, I could move on, but it took a huge toll on our relationship.

"For all of these years, all they have wanted has been one thing: *you*. I can't tell you how many nights I spent trying to comfort hysterical children who didn't want anyone but you. Every birthday and Christmas wish was the same. They all wished for the same thing every single year: *you*. That's what *you* did to them. *You* ruined their lives. It took so much strength for me, and them, to get through those dark years without you. I had to find it within myself to let you go, and I did that a long time ago. I've never been able to forgive you, and when I found out Delilah was trying to find you, I wanted to scream. I worked so hard to protect them from you, to keep them safe. I never wanted them to find you, but I saw the pain in our daughter's eyes. She was broken, and *you* were the only person in this whole world that could help her. So, I let her find you, and then you pushed her away like she didn't even matter. I wanted to kill you. I was angrier than I've ever been in my whole life. Then she was in the hospital, and not once did you try to contact us. At that point in time, I decided never to forgive you. I made the choice that, no matter how hard they tried, I would never ever let you back into our lives. Yet, here we are."

As she finishes talking, I see a few tears drop from her eyes too. She quickly wipes them away. She refuses to break eye contact with my father.

"I don't blame you for hating me, but I don't know what else to say. I can't apologise enough. I know what I did. I know I stuffed up. I know I destroyed their lives. I'm sorry you were left to pick up the pieces, but I'm not that person anymore. I'm not the Tony you remember. I'm someone new. I'm different, and I want you to forgive me, but only if you want to. Don't do it for them, Deidra. That won't bring peace to anyone. If you really don't want to forgive me, then don't. I want a relationship with my children, and I'm willing to work for it. I know it won't happen overnight, but I'm willing to try my hardest because the biggest mistake I ever made was walking out on the people who loved me the most. I know you don't believe it, but I really did ... I really *do*, love these children with every single bit of my being."

My mum still has her eyes on my father as he lets all his emotions out. She seems to relax her shoulders as she sighs.

"I loved you, and you broke my heart. You hurt me in ways I didn't think were possible, and I was scared. In fact, I was terrified. I always knew deep down that you would leave. I knew I would be left to raise five children by myself. I didn't think I could do it, but I didn't have a choice. I had to do it, because you left. You made a selfish decision, and you abandoned us – your family – when we needed you, when *I* needed you, the most. You left me to raise four children and a newborn who doesn't even remember you. Do I want to forgive you for them? Of course. I wouldn't be here if it wasn't for them. But *I* see the difference in you, so I forgive you. Not for them, but for *me* and for *you*. I forgive you, Tony. I didn't want to believe it, but *our* children are right. It's time we move on."

I can't believe what we are hearing. Is this really happening? I never thought I'd see this day. I thought my mum would just say what we wanted to hear, but for the first time in a long time, she has stopped putting us first. She has done something that we've all hoped she'd do. She has forgiven the one person who hurt us, who hurt her, the most.

My dad smiles and cries again; this time he doesn't try to hide it.

"Thank you. I really mean that. I didn't think we'd ever get to this place, but I appreciate it more than you'll ever know. I don't want to go over the past anymore. We do need to move on, but I just want to know one more thing. Why did you not let them have my last name?"

The question surprises all of us and, to be honest, it's not something I've ever really thought about. I always assumed my dad had been on board with us having our mother's last name.

"I'm not stupid. I was never going to give them the name of someone who would leave, who would just abandon them. I knew it would hurt every time one of us would have to write their last name, or say their last name. It would be a constant reminder of the man – the father – who left them. So, that's why I refused to give them your last name."

"That makes sense. I don't blame you for that."

I know that having this conversation, while difficult, has done him the world of good. Not only can my siblings move on, but now my parents can move on too. That's all I've ever wanted.

After another hour of discussion, my mum gets up from the table.

"Okay, we have to go now. I'm glad we got to have this talk. I don't know if the girls have told you, but Dakota is leaving for New York on Wednesday night. We're having a get-together on Sunday evening. I don't think that we're ready for you to be around the whole family just yet. But, on Sunday afternoon, maybe you could stop by for a coffee? You can meet Evan and spend some time with the girls and Dylan, Declan and Darci too, if they want to. If things go well, maybe you can join us at the airport on Wednesday night when we say goodbye to her. I'm warning you now though, don't force the other three children into anything they don't want. It's up to them. They decide if they want a relationship with you. They decide if this is what they want. They're not to be influenced by the four of us, especially not Darci. This is their decision, not ours."

Dakota looks as shocked as I am. The last thing I expected was for our mum to invite our dad over. She had made a big deal about him not knowing where we live, so to see her extend an invite like this shows that she really has forgiven him. She isn't just doing it for us, and I appreciate that more than I'll ever be able to explain. My father gladly accepts her offer, and promises he won't force his other three children into anything they're not ready for. They organise a time, and my mum gives him our address. Dakota and I follow our mum out to the car, and we hug our father. We get into the car, wave and head home.

We thank our mum over and over again for finally making peace with the past, and our father. She has seen the changes in him and, to our surprise, they managed to get along much better than expected. Maybe my parents are meant to be friends and not lovers, and that's okay because I've learnt that not everyone is destined to be with the person they think. Now we have the chance we've all been looking for; we're able to move on.

~

On Sunday morning, my mum and Evan sit down with the five of us Walker kids. My mum clears her throat as she starts to talk.

"On Friday afternoon, I went to visit your father ... as in, your real father. Delilah and Dakota asked me to do this for them, so I did. I didn't want to do it, but I saw him and we sat down and spoke. We put everything out on the table and cleared the air. I no longer hold any resentment towards him. In fact, I feel the complete opposite now. I've forgiven him, and we are finally able to put the past in the past and move on. This brings me to why we're here now. I have spoken to Evan, and we both agree that it's time for you, Dylan, Declan and Darci, to decide if you wish to have a relationship with your father too. The decision is entirely up to you. If you don't want that, then that's fine. Your father, as well as myself and Evan and your sisters, will respect that. No one is going to force you to do anything you don't want to do. He is coming over this afternoon though. If you wish to stay upstairs and not see or talk to him, that's fine."

My mum looks at all of us, mainly focusing on Darci and the boys who are trying to make sense of what she's just said. After a few minutes, she asks each of my siblings what they want to do.

"Dylan, how are you feeling?"

"I don't know. I didn't ever expect to be in this position. I'd be lying if I said I hadn't ever thought about it though. I mean, he's my dad. I may be 25, but I still need him. So, I guess I'd like to meet him and see what he has to say. Then I'll make a decision about what I want to do."

My mum turns to Declan.

"I know how close you are to Delilah and Dakota, so I know they've spoken to you openly about things. Have you made a decision about what you'd like to do?"

"I'm sorry we didn't tell you the truth, mum. But, yes, I'd like to see where things go with dad too. I don't want to hurt you, Evan, but I want a relationship with my real dad as well."

Everyone turns to Evan who hasn't said anything since we sat down. I wonder if he resents me for causing all of this: the ripple effect on my family. I didn't want to hurt him either but, at the same time, I've known for a long time that I want my father in my life. When I made that decision, nothing was going to stop me. Now that I have stopped to think, I've realised that we might have been unintentionally hurting someone who's done nothing but embrace and love us since day one.

"Please don't apologise. I knew going into a relationship with your mother that this day might come. I don't take it personally, I promise. I love you all as if you were my own children, but you're completely right: nothing compares to your real father. I respect your decisions and, no matter what happens, I'll be here for you all as long as I live."

I get up, walk over to Evan, lean over and hug him, desperate to show how much I appreciate everything he is doing for us. "

Thank you," I whisper to him as he hugs me back.

Everyone turns to Darci.

"Okay Darci, it's your turn. How do you feel?"

"Well, I don't remember him. The only person I've ever thought of as my dad is Evan. I don't know what to do. I don't know this man. He's a stranger to me."

"Honey, if you don't want a relationship with him, that's fine. But, Evan isn't going to be hurt if you do want to try and get to know your biological dad. In fact, I'm sure Evan will be more than happy to stay with you while you do it."

"Absolutely. I'd be more than happy to do that if it makes you more comfortable, Darci. You know I love you with all my heart, but it won't do any harm to get to know him. He could be like a friend to you if that's what you want. If not, just say the word."

"You won't be mad if I spend time with him?"

"Of course not. I want you to do what makes you happy, my love."

Darci relaxes after hearing Evan's comforting words. When she's ready, she tells us her decision.

"I want to meet him, only if Evan stays with me until I feel comfortable."

Evan agrees and, after my mum discusses what we should expect, the doorbell rings.

"Okay, here we go."

~

After my dad leaves, we spend some time talking about how the meeting went. Everyone reacted well to meeting my dad, especially Evan. The decision was made for each of us to begin a fresh, new relationship with our father. Darci is ecstatic about having two fathers now. She loves Evan, but she says nothing compares to having the chance to get to know her real dad, and Evan respects her decision. In fact, he respects all our decisions. We all noticed how much of an effort he made, which makes me love and appreciate him even more. He didn't owe my dad anything; he didn't have to do what he did, but he did it for us, and for my mum, and that's something I'll never forget.

After the discussion ends, we spend some time relaxing. My mum wants us to spend as much time together as we can before Dakota leaves, so we watch a few movies, and then we help our mum cook the food for Dakota's going-away dinner. At 7:00 p.m. all her friends and our family start to arrive. Within an hour, laughter fills the house. My mum has prepared a slideshow of photos of Dakota throughout the years, and when it finishes, she invites everyone to sit down at the table for dinner. Everyone talks about how excited they are for Dakota, and my mum tries to hold back her tears. The night seems to fly by. As everyone is chatting away, my mum taps a knife against her glass and gets up from the table to address Dakota.

"No one tells you when you have a child that eventually they'll leave. You know that one day they will, so you try to enjoy every moment of every day before they'll spread their wings and go out into the real world as they try to capture their dreams, no matter how big or small they are. I am immensely proud of all five of my children. You're all finding your own feet in the world, and you've all worked so hard to pursue lives that you can be proud of. Nothing makes me prouder than seeing you happy and seeing you find the courage and strength you need to pursue the things that make you happy. Dakota, you have always been someone I knew would do just that. Your dreams are calling out for you in the Big Apple. I know you're going to blow everyone away. You're stunning inside and out, and I am extremely proud of you. You are a beautiful person with a heart of gold, and I am so excited for your future, which is so bright. I know you're going to go far in life. I love you so much. Here's to you, and New York!"

My mum raises her glass as we all cheer for Dakota. It's the first time in weeks that I've seen the spark back in my sister's eyes. It's the very same spark that I thought she had lost, but now it has returned stronger than ever. I know that Dakota is ready for the next step in her journey and, just like my mum, I'm so proud and happy for her.

~

On Wednesday night, we head to the airport to say goodbye to my sister and James, who made a surprise decision to accompany Dakota on her new journey as a model. My uncles, aunties and cousins have already said goodbye to her, so it's James' mum, dad and sister, my siblings, Evan, my mum and my dad at the airport. It feels like a small army is saying goodbye to them. Evan is comforting my mum, who hasn't been able to stop crying since we arrived at the airport and my dad is standing with Darci as she cries too. After Dylan says his goodbyes to Dakota, Declan and I approach her.

"Don't tell the others, but I'm going to miss you two the most."

Declan and I laugh.

"We're going to miss you too. I'm so proud of you, Dakota. You're the kindest, most loving person I've ever known, and I know you're going to surprise yourself by doing so well in New York. I love you so much."

"Thank you. You have no idea how much that means to me. I love you so much. I'll call you as soon as I get there."

She hugs Declan once more and, when we're ready, we join our family and watch Dakota and James head for the plane. They wave at us once more as they vanish behind the gates. Just like that, they're heading for a brighter future.

~

Since Dakota's departure, four weeks have come and gone in the blink of an eye. My dad is working on building relationships with each of my siblings, and I have spent more time with him working on strengthening our relationship. He comes over for dinner every second Saturday, and he's getting along with Evan and my mum. To everyone's surprise, the three of them get along a lot better than we ever thought they would. When they got to know each other, they felt more comfortable. Now they spend more time together, so their relationship is growing stronger day by day, which makes our lives so much easier. Dakota and I no longer have to sneak around, and my siblings and I are finally getting what we always wanted: our dad back in our lives for good. Everything has worked out for the best, and now I'm about to be offered the chance of a lifetime: one that I can't pass up.

CHAPTER THIRTEEN
ONCE IN A LIFETIME

September comes and goes. Dakota is back in Perth, although not for very long. She's headed back to Sydney to pack up her apartment before moving back to Perth. On her trip to New York, she was offered more jobs than she could accept. She's decided to move back home to Perth permanently, and then fly between Perth, Sydney and New York. Her lifestyle has become hectic but, through it all, she's supported me and my dreams. I'll need my family's support more than ever soon, as my dreams are about to take me to the city where they say dreams come true: *Los Angeles, California.*

Over the last few months, my album has been selling quicker than I can keep up with. At the start of September, I filmed my first ever music video for *Wildfire*, and it went viral almost instantly. I was overwhelmed by the support I was getting, and I was surprised by how many people recognised me when I left my house. I was doing interviews left, right and centre, and I was being approached by companies to appear in ads and magazines. I can't believe this is happening and, despite having no idea what I'm doing, I love it. I'm lucky that I have Melody and my uncle, who have both been amazing in guiding me.

I'm lost in a world of my own thoughts when my laptop starts to beep, alerting me to an incoming Skype call from Melody. I hit the accept button as I sit down at my desk. I say hello to Melody, who tells me to brace myself for some news. I start thinking the worst, but nothing can prepare me for what she's going to tell me.

"Melody, what is it?"

"Sorry, I shouldn't have worried you. It's good news, I promise."

Thank God, I think to myself.

"Delilah, before I tell you this, I just want you to know how proud I am of you. You've really started to cement yourself into an industry that chews people up and spits them out, regardless of how talented they are. I know how hard you've had to work to get to where you are, and I know you've been through so much in your personal life. To see you juggle the two while keeping a smile on your face has been nothing short of inspiring. Not once have I heard you complain about how much you've had to give up to pursue your music career. You took a huge risk. You basically sacrificed everything in your life to commit to this, and it's paying off."

I smile as I listen to everything Melody is saying to me. My family and friends have all said something similar and, every time, it makes my heart sing. Sometimes I don't remind myself of how far I've come and how much I've given up to pursue something I've dreamt of since I was little. I've found so much happiness and passion in what I'm doing, and I know that I'm on the right path in life, even if I used to doubt that I'd ever be good enough to succeed in a business that is ridiculously competitive.

Through it all, I've remained true to myself, my beliefs, and who I am as a person. In the end, that's all that matters. I've had to learn how to keep my feet firmly on the ground. I've been bombarded with offers that I never dreamed of, and so many doors are opening for me. Sometimes I get caught up in this new lifestyle and let it go to my head: that is a habit I'm determined to break. I'm never rude or disrespectful to those around me, but sometimes I get caught up with being recognised, getting free things and getting the best of everything.

I have confided in my mum about coming to terms with this new life. There are only two things I want to change about myself and my life, and those two things are my confidence and my self-doubt. I always question if I really deserve all the opportunities that have come my way over the last few months. My negative voice always tells me that I don't deserve them, but I'm working on changing that. With the help of Angie, who I still see, I hope I'll be able to break out of this habit. My confidence has slowly begun to build, and I constantly remind myself that I am good enough, and I do deserve the best that life has to offer. I also know that, at any moment, this can all disappear. If it does, I need to be able to bounce back and be happy enough within myself and my life that it wouldn't drastically affect things.

Melody interrupts me. "Delilah? Are you okay?"

I'd almost forgotten she can see me, and I feel the heat rising to my cheeks as I nervously laugh.

"Sorry, I got distracted by what you were saying. Thank you, Melody. I know I thank you all the time, but I really wouldn't be in this position without you and my uncle. I'll be forever grateful to you both. You've made my dreams come true. If all of this ends right now, then I'd be fine with that. I mean, I don't want it to end, but if it does, I'll be content with what I've achieved."

"Well, it's funny you should say that. Delilah, your career isn't going to end anytime soon. In fact, it's only just beginning to take off. I have an opportunity for you – one that I feel you're ready for – but I expect you're going to be a bit taken aback by it."

My mind starts to race.

"Okay ... that sounds good. What is it?"

"Do you know who Taylor Bardot is?"

I recognise the name, and I'm instantly curious as to why Melody is asking me.

"Of course I do. She's one of the most well-known female managers in the music industry. She's massive in America. Why do you ask?"

"Well, I got a call from her this morning. She used to work with me here in Sydney. She's from here originally, but she was offered a job in LA about three years ago. She obviously couldn't pass it up, so she took the job and, you're right, now she's one of the most in-demand managers in this industry. Anyway, she called me after I sent your album to her. She said she'd already listened to it. From what she told me, there's quite a lot of buzz surrounding you in America. Your album is playing on almost every radio station, and the insider word is that people who are involved in the music industry there, mainly in Los Angeles, have been gathering all of the info they can on you before approaching your uncle and me to talk about getting you over there. When I say you're the next big thing, it's not just me saying it because I'm your manager. I'm saying it because it's true. Delilah, LA is calling for you. There's an opportunity to go there and meet up with some of the high-profile professionals in the music industry, Taylor included. She really wants to meet you, and she wants to work with you. So, if you're ready, I think it's time we send you to Los Angeles. I don't know if you know, but everyone who has a dream says the same thing about LA: it's the city where dreams come true. I know your dreams are already coming true, but Delilah, not many singer-songwriters get this kind of opportunity so early on in their career. Most of them don't *ever* get this kind of opportunity. I know it's overwhelming, but I think you should sit down and spend some time considering this. Give it a few days and, if it's something you want to do, then I'll contact Taylor and send her your info. She can contact you, and the two of you can work something out. It might be best if you have your uncle sit with you when you talk to her, but that's up to you. I've got to head to a meeting now, but call me if you want to talk. Otherwise, I'll speak to you in a few days."

I thank Melody and close my Skype account. I stare at my computer screen as my mind tries desperately to process every bit of information that Melody has just given me. *What the hell is going on? This cannot be real!* I don't know what to do, think, or say, so I just sit at my desk for thirty minutes as I replay the conversation over and over again. Taylor Bardot, *THE* Taylor Bardot, wants to talk to me? *ME?* I don't get it, I mean I get it in the sense that she obviously likes my music, but I never, ever, in a million years, expected something like this to happen. I thought it would take years for me to establish a career in Australia, let alone America. Now one of the most popular managers in the music industry wants to talk to *me* about going over to Los Angeles. This cannot be real.

~

I've spent the last forty-eight hours going back and forth on the multiple conversations I've had with my mum, Dakota, my uncle and Melody about what to do. I know it's time to take the next step in my career, but I'm terrified of talking to Taylor only to have her change her mind. It is overwhelming me to the point that I feel sick. I decide not to run from it though, and instead I embrace it. I embrace every single feeling, good and bad, and I decide that, in the end, there is no harm in talking to Taylor and seeing what she has to say.

On Thursday morning, I get up early and go for a quick run with Jessie. I shower and head over to my uncle's house, where we go into his office and prepare for our Skype call with Taylor. At 9:00 a.m. Perth time – which is 6:00 p.m. on Wednesday in Los Angeles – we get the call we've been waiting for. After accepting the call, Taylor pops up. She is even more stunning than I've seen in photos. She has long, straight, honey-blonde hair, hazel eyes and a warm smile, which greets us when she appears on our screen.

"Hi Delilah, Hi Derek. I'm so excited to meet the two of you! I'm Taylor. How are you?"

"Hi, Taylor. We're excited to meet you, too. We're good, thank you. How are you?"

"I'm great. I'm a huge fan of yours. Melody told me how much she's loved working with you. You're incredibly talented, and I would love the chance to talk to you about getting you over here to Los Angeles. There's a ton of different opportunities just waiting for you here. If you're ready, I'd love to get you here as soon as possible."

My uncle gently nudges me. "Honey, are you okay?"

"Yeah, sorry. Just a bit overwhelmed."

I turn my attention back to the computer screen as I gather my thoughts.

"I've never really thought about coming over to LA this early in my career, but if you think it's something I can do, then I'd really like to do it. But can my uncle come with me? He's one of my co-managers, and he's a huge part of my life, so I don't want to do this without him."

"Of course he can. I've discussed it with Melody. Unfortunately, she can't make it as she has other clients to manage. But, if your uncle is happy to accompany you, then we'd love to have him join you. Plus, it's good to come over with one of your co-managers. It makes things easier for you. You're probably going to be very overwhelmed when you get here. I won't beat around the bush: you're quite popular here already. Everyone loves you and your voice!"

Every time Taylor says something, I find myself engulfed by nervousness and excitement. It's a combination that has started to take over my whole body and not just my mind.

My uncle lightly nudges me, "Delilah, I would never pass up this opportunity. If you really feel ready to do this, then let's do it kiddo!"

I nod before my uncle continues. "Alright Taylor, we're in. Now, manager to manager, what can we expect from this trip? And what kind of time frame are we looking at for flying over and coming back to Perth?"

Taylor takes out a notepad and starts to read from her notes.

"Well, from the meetings I've had with fellow music industry professionals, we'd like Delilah to do some live shows here in LA. There's an opportunity to expand to other states but, for now, we'd like to solely focus on Los Angeles. This is where you'll build your brand. We've already looked into it, and a lot of your American fans are willing to travel to LA to see you play. We are thinking a few smaller shows, as well as some pubs and clubs, will help promote your music and yourself. You've got a strong support base here, and the demand for you to come here and play live is growing stronger every day. It's something I'd like to act on now."

Fans? That doesn't even sound right! My uncle and Taylor continue to discuss the plans for the trip, and we try to settle on a date.

"It's the 2nd of October now – well, in LA it is – and I'd like to get you out here by the 10th, which is next Thursday. I know it's quick but, like I've said, I'd like to get to work immediately. I think three weeks would be an appropriate time frame for you to achieve what your uncle and I would like you to accomplish. It seems like a long time, but it will go by so quickly. We need to make the most of your opportunities now. If all goes well, we may even be able to extend that time frame. How does that sound?"

I try to calm my breathing down. This is all happening way too quickly.

"Wait, is this really happening? I'm not dreaming, am I?" I say to myself, although I soon realise I've said it aloud.

"No kiddo, you're not dreaming. This is real life. I know it's a lot to take on right now. It is happening exceptionally quickly, but you've got the talent, and the support base. Like Taylor said, you've got to capitalise on these things now. Otherwise, they might slip away. I'm right by your side. You're not facing this alone, Delilah. We've got nothing to lose, so just say the word and I'll get it organised. If you really don't think you're ready though, then you need to be honest. No one's going to be mad at you, and only you can make this decision. We're simply presenting the options available to you. It's your call."

"No. We've worked too hard to pass up this opportunity. I don't want to be scared anymore. Let's do it. Let's go."

"Thatta girl! Okay, Taylor. We're in. What do we do from here?"

"Great! Well, I've got time now. I'm done for the day, workwise, so if you're ready we can organise flights? I'll organise your accommodation and your transportation. When you've picked out the time to fly, just let me know. My company will take care of that too."

I'm surprised by Taylor's offer.

"Wait, you're paying for all of this?"

Taylor laughs as she responds.

"Of course we are, Delilah. All you need to do is come over with your guitar and your voice. I'll take care of the rest."

Whoa, this just keeps getting more intense and exciting! My uncle continues talking to Taylor as he looks up flights. While I have time, I take my phone out and quickly text Cam.

Hey, what are you doing in about an hour? Fancy meeting me at the beach?

I hit send and within a minute Cam has responded.

I'll bring coffee. See you then.

I smile at my phone as my uncle gently nudges me again.

"Okay kiddo, everything's booked. We fly to Sydney on Wednesday afternoon, then we're on a flight to LA on Wednesday night. We will arrive on Thursday night, our time, but it will be Wednesday afternoon in LA. I know it's confusing, but we will adjust. Taylor will get everything else organised, so all we have to do is prepare for the long flight over."

I try to take everything on board.

"Thank you, for everything. I can't wait to meet you, and to work with you. I'm really excited for this trip."

"My pleasure. It was lovely to talk to you both. I'll send both of you an email with your accommodation details and an outline of the schedule for the three weeks when I get into the office tomorrow morning."

We thank Taylor again before ending the Skype call.

"I'm so proud of you, kiddo! I told you that one day the world would see your talent. Now the city of dreams is calling your name!"

"I know I've said it a million times, and I know I don't have to keep telling you, but I'm going to anyway: I really couldn't do this without you, I wouldn't be where I am without you. I can't imagine doing this without you. I know we're family, but you're also my best friend and I've always been so inspired by you. I'll never be able to thank you enough for everything you've done for me. You've given up so much to help me strive towards my dreams. I've accomplished things I didn't ever think would be possible. You helped me believe that I was worthy and that I could do this. *You* made me believe in myself, and I'll never forget that."

"Oh, Delilah, thank you. That means so much to me, but I should be the one thanking you. You've given me the greatest joy over the past 22 years. I know how hard things have been for you growing up, especially recently, but I'm so proud of the person that you've become. What you're creating is magic. Being a part of it is an honour. Okay, enough crying! You'd better go home and let your mum know what's going on."

"I'll let you know how it goes."

~

Forty-five minutes later, I'm sitting in my favourite spot at my favourite beach with one of my favourite people.

"So, that's everything that happened. I still can't believe this is happening to me," I say to Cam as I finish explaining my Skype call with Taylor.

"Wow, that's incredible. You deserve this, Delilah. Why do I get the feeling that you don't think you do?"

I exhale as I pick up some sand. I watch as it drops to the ground through my fingers.

"It's not that I don't think I deserve it. It's just ... I don't know how to say what I'm feeling without sounding stupid. I just feel this overwhelming fear of failing. I mean, what if I go there and nothing works out? What if no one turns up to my performances? What if I don't sell enough tickets to the shows? What if people hate my voice live? What if I risk everything to go to LA, and I fail? Then what?"

Cam takes a sip of his coffee.

"That's a lot of 'what ifs', Delilah. You can't live your life like that. Look how far you've come in the last year. Look at what you've achieved in such a short amount of time. You've pretty much gone and done the impossible. If you weren't good enough, these opportunities would never have found you. You didn't just get lucky. You've worked incredibly hard to achieve what you've achieved. You should be proud and excited for this next part. You need to embrace it. Otherwise, you'll never enjoy anything you do. I've seen the way you light up when you talk about music, and I've seen the way you light up when you sing. This is what you were born to do, and the world sees that. That's why they love you."

I pick up some more sand.

"You're right. I just can't stop overthinking things. I really am excited about this. I didn't think I would find what I've found on this journey, and I'm so thankful for every chance I've been given. I just need to learn to embrace everything without questioning if I can do it. I mean, I wouldn't have made it this far if I wasn't good enough."

I smile at Cam as he grabs my hand.

"Do you want to come with us?"

I mean it as a joke, but I suddenly feel stupid for asking a question that I don't mean. Cam and I have spent the last month working on our friendship, and we have made a natural transition back to how we used to be. We're practically a couple, but without the titles of boyfriend and girlfriend, and we're both ridiculously happy. Part of me wonders when we'll finally become an official couple again. We've discussed getting back together all month, but we both agreed that we would do it when the time is right. I just can't stop questioning when that time will be.

"I, ummm, I'd love to go, but I've got work. I couldn't get away with just a week's notice, and I couldn't be gone for three weeks. I'm sorry."

"Don't apologise. I was kidding. I mean, I would love it if you could go, but I know it's not realistic."

Cam finishes the rest of his coffee.

"Hey, don't stress. We can Skype every day, and I'm into emailing now, so whenever you feel overwhelmed or nervous over there, or even just happy, email me. It'll be like we're together without being with each other."

"I'd like that. Thank you."

We spend the next two hours sitting on the beach chatting, then I head home. I sit down with my family and Dakota continues to fill us in about her trip to New York. We make dinner together and look through her photos before I finally work up the courage to tell my family about my day, and how I'll be flying to Los Angeles in a week's time. To my surprise, my mum responds a lot better than I thought she would. After everyone congratulates me, I fill them in about what is expected of me, and I tell my family all about Taylor.

After almost an hour and a half of talking about my new adventure, my mum sits at her laptop and googles LA. She gets overly excited and starts writing down the names of all the places she thinks I should go while I'm there. I see the look of pride as she plays my album through the speakers in the lounge room; my songs fill the house and my mum hums along to each one. As she continues to search through the thousands of links she's found, I go outside to call my dad and tell him the news.

"Hi, Dad. I just wanted to call you to tell you about an exciting opportunity that I got today."

I spend thirty minutes on the phone with him. He congratulates me and we make plans to have lunch in a few days. After I get off the phone, I head back inside and sit with my mum. We look through photos of Los Angeles, and I feel nothing but excitement for what is happening in my life.

~

After spending the morning packing, my uncle and I are now at the airport ready to board our first flight to Sydney before heading to Los Angeles, California. Nothing can prepare me for this trip. I know that it's going to change my life in the best possible way, and I cannot wait to see what happens next.

Chapter Fourteen
City of Angels

I spend the first flight from Perth to Sydney thinking about every possible thing that could go wrong. When we get to Sydney, I sit in the international terminal and try to remind myself of how many things could actually go right. After arguing with myself for hours, I finally find enough strength to let go of all the negative thoughts. I decide to focus on all the exciting new things I'll get to experience. All my fears fade away, replaced by pure exhilaration.

Within an hour, my uncle and I are sitting in first class on our Qantas flight to Los Angeles. We were surprised by the first class tickets: something Taylor arranged for us. At first, we didn't know what was happening; we got onto the plane and handed the stewardess our tickets, but she handed them back to us.

"I'm sorry, your seats are no longer available. You've been upgraded to first class, courtesy of Miss Bardot. If you follow Gracie here, she will take you up to first class. Enjoy your flight, and welcome aboard. Good luck in LA, Delilah. Everyone on this flight wishes you the best of luck. We're right behind you."

I turned to my uncle and laughed nervously.

"First class, whoa!" he said with a grin.

I thanked the first stewardess, then Gracie, who works in first class, came down to get us.

"Hi, Miss Walker, Mr Walker, welcome aboard. Follow me, I'll take you to your seats."

We smiled at Gracie and followed her down the corridor to the middle of the plane. I was shocked that such a big space even fits on a plane! I've never sat in first class, let alone seen it in person. There are ten individual pods, each with a pillow and a blanket laid out on the seats. Gracie led us to the two seats.

"These are two of our best seats. They're at the front, so there's a little bit more room. It's a long flight, so Miss Bardot wants you to be as comfortable as possible."

My uncle let me sit in the pod closest to the window and he sat in the middle row. When we were seated, Gracie showed us what each pod has. There's space for us to put a foot rest up, we have our own individual TV screen with unlimited movies, and we even have a place to charge our phones. She handed us a menu, and told us the food and drink was available whenever we're ready.

"Enjoy your flight. Please let me know if there is anything I can do for either of you."

We thanked her and smiled back as she welcomed the other passengers into first class.

I look over at my uncle, who is looking through the menu.

"Is this really happening? I cannot believe everything that has come my, I mean *our* way, in the last week. It's insane!"

"It's really happening, kiddo, and you deserve it. This is going to be an amazing trip. I can feel it!"

Soon enough, it's time to take off. We buckle up and, within minutes, we're in the air flying away from the country where my dream started. As I watch

Australia disappear behind the clouds, I become insanely excited about the trip ahead of me. Everything suddenly becomes so real, and I'm being treated like a rock star. It feels nice to be praised and rewarded for all the hard work I've put in over the last year. It has been a rollercoaster ride and, despite all the hurt I've endured, I wouldn't change a single thing. If things hadn't happened the way they did, I would not be here: flying to a place that I've only ever dreamed of visiting. I truly believe that everything happens for a reason, and I know that this is all part of a plan to get me to where I've always dreamed of being. I smile and close the blind above the window. I turn the TV on and put my headphones in. I flick through the hundreds of movies, then notice there's a music option. It's a playlist of songs that have been popular over the last year, as well as classics from bands like Queen, Bon Jovi and Coldplay, among others. I notice my name on the playlist. I continue to look through and see that almost every single song from my album is on there. I look over at my uncle, who's noticed the same thing. He puts his thumbs up and puts his headphones in. I sit back in my chair and take a deep breath of air.

The plane ride passes a lot quicker than I'd imagined, mainly because I sleep for almost ten hours. Being in first class means there's more room to move, and relax, so you're able to lie down: definitely beneficial, considering I haven't slept very well over the few days. Almost three hours into the flight, I snuggle into my seat, pull the blanket up to my chest, pop my sleep mask on and quickly fall into a deep sleep. Nine and a half hours pass before my body decides it's time to wake up. I remove my sleep mask, take the blanket off my body and place it on the floor next to me. I get up and stretch my legs, noticing the rest of the first-class cabin is dark. Almost everyone in first class is asleep, except for a man who's sitting behind my uncle. He's reading a newspaper and sipping an orange juice. When he notices me, he offers me a friendly smile, which I return before sitting back down. I pull the menu out and start to read through the options when Gracie approaches me.

"Hi Delilah. Did you have a nice sleep? I was going to wake you earlier to see if you wanted anything to eat, but your uncle asked us to let you sleep."

I look over at my uncle, who's snoring quietly.

"I did, thank you. And thank you for not waking me. I needed that sleep."

"That's good. Is there anything I can get you? It's 9:35 a.m., so breakfast options are probably the best, although you're welcome to have anything you like. Would you like some time to look through the menu?"

"Yes please." Gracie leaves to tend to another passenger, who has just woken up. I sit in my chair and look at the clock as I try to process the time, and how quickly it has passed. We took off from Sydney at 9:00 p.m. on Wednesday night, so by the time we get to LA it will be 6:00 p.m., on Wednesday. Talk about confusing. Taylor had warned us about the time difference, and she told me to prepare for jet lag: something I did my research on so I knew what to expect. My uncle and I spent some time last Friday figuring out the best way to get our bodies used to the time difference as quickly as possible. That way we wouldn't lose too much time sleeping, or not sleeping. The tips included adapting to the new time difference before we arrived, which I tried to do. I didn't have much luck since there is a 15-hour time difference; my body didn't want to break the pattern we were already in. Other tips included trying to get fresh air, taking short naps when needed, and finally, just giving ourselves time. We know it is going to take time for our bodies and our minds to get used to the time difference, and that's something that we'll deal with after we land.

When I check the time again, I notice I've spent fifteen minutes staring at the menu without reading it. I finally settle on some blueberry pancakes and a banana smoothie. While I wait for my breakfast, I take out the booklet Taylor had emailed my uncle, which he had printed and handed to me when we met at the airport in Perth. I had tried not to look at it too much, mainly because it had overwhelmed me the second I opened it and saw all the things that Taylor has planned for me. Not only has she scheduled shows at pubs and bars, but she has somehow managed to find a concert hall in LA, where she said tickets have sold pretty quickly. On top of this, she has also managed to book spots on some of the biggest TV shows in America. I'm scheduled to appear on *Good Morning America* and *Live with Kelly*, via satellite – they are both based in New York – among others. To top it all off, I'm also scheduled to do photo shoots with a few American magazines and newspapers. I also have a ton of radio interviews and meetings booked, and all this is tightly packed into three weeks. I have a few days off here and there, which I've decided to use to explore LA, and possibly the surrounding areas. I try to continue reading the schedule as my food arrives, but then put the stack of pages back in my bag and decide not to focus on them anymore. Instead, I decide to take it one day at a time. That way I'll minimise how overwhelmed I'll feel by everything that has been planned for me.

~

After more than 24 hours of travelling, we finally arrive in Los Angeles. We step off the plane, collect our bags and head through customs. We are walking out into the terminal and towards the doors to find an Uber when we notice a man in a suit. He has an iPad in his hand, and it has our names on it. I look at my uncle who shrugs his shoulders and approaches the man. He introduces himself to us: his name is Archer and he works for the same company as Taylor. As he helps us with our bags, he tells us how he works with musicians who Taylor brings to LA. He has recently started to work with some of Taylor's more high profile clients too, who are already established in LA.

Archer takes us to our villa, which is located about fifteen minutes outside the city. He explains that Taylor wants us to feel at home without being in the city all the time.

"She basically said she wants the two of you to be able to come back here after a long day of work. This is like your refuge. Since you're not directly in the city, you won't get caught up in the LA lifestyle, or the nightlife, which is pretty exciting if you've never been here before."

As we pull up to the villa, I notice how big it is.

"Whoa," I say as I step out of the car.

"So, here it is. Taylor's company purchased this place for talent like yourself. There are four bedrooms, all with ensuites, a pool and a sauna, but the best part of this place is the view. There's a decking area which has a clear glass wall, and you've got stunning views of the city. If you look to the left side of the house, you'll see Runyon Canyon and the famous Hollywood sign."

We walk inside and Archer gives us a quick tour. He's right: there are stunning views from the left side, and from the decking area we have views of all of LA. I'm blown away by how beautiful this place is. Now that I'm here, I'm excited to get to work.

When we've finished looking around, we go into the lounge room where Archer hands us his business card. He tells us that he, along with another driver Asher, his brother, are on call while we're here. He tells us that the hours the two work are split, and they're listed on a sheet of paper on the dining room table. They're our private drivers for the next three weeks; depending on the time we have to call one of the two, then they will take us wherever we need to go. We thank him, and he leaves us in the villa. We look around again and, after choosing our bedrooms, we sit down in the lounge room and talk about what we're expecting from this trip. After half an hour, my uncle's international phone starts to ring. He answers it, tells me it's Taylor, and puts it on loudspeaker. Taylor welcomes us to LA, and tells us she will be over within the next thirty minutes to meet us.

Sure enough, exactly thirty minutes later, Taylor joins us in the lounge room. She runs through the schedule, and I ask her a ridiculous amount of questions. She tells us that there is a chance to extend the trip, but at this point she wants me to solely focus on trying to get as much as possible accomplished in three weeks. I'm regularly finding myself in a state of shock. This is something that you only ever dream about. I certainly didn't think something as amazing as this would ever happen to me. Yet, here I am: in the city where dreams come true. Or, in my case, the city where dreams continue to come true. Taylor tells me to relax and enjoy the rest of the day. She also tells me to enjoy tomorrow, which is my first scheduled day off, before we get into the first photo shoot and interview on Friday morning. Then, on Friday night I'll head over to one of the pubs Taylor has booked me in at. I'll perform a few of my songs, acoustic style, which I'm beyond excited about. For once, I'm not nervous about performing live. *Maybe it's the LA vibe that has caught on*, I think to myself. When we arrived, I noticed how upbeat and positive the people are. Everyone I have encountered so far has been so friendly, and a few people even recognised me. It's incredibly surreal: being in a place so far away from home, yet still being recognised. That's a feeling I'll never forget, or be able to describe.

After our conversation with Taylor ends, I quickly shower and hop into bed. As much as I long to sleep, my body has decided that isn't going to happen. I spend almost an hour tossing and turning before I give up. I get out of bed and head over to the sliding door that's facing the city. I walk out into the crisp air of LA's winter. I look out at the darkened sky and the bright lights in the distance, and decide this spot has quickly become my favourite part of the villa. It's now just after 8:30 p.m. and I'm lost in a world of my own, thinking about all the things I've been through, when there's a knock at the door. Before I have time to get to the door, Taylor is rushing in.

"Don't leave that door unlocked. Anyone could walk in!" she winks. "There's been a change of plan. You're going to fly to New York in a few hours. We managed to secure you a ticket and the car is ready to take you. You were meant to appear on two of the shows there via satellite, but *Good Morning America* wants you to perform *Wildfire* live tomorrow morning. I know it's late notice, but this is a huge opportunity for you. You need to take advantage of it.

Your uncle and I will both be coming with you, so don't stress. We will take care of everything. I contacted one of my stylists who's based in New York. She's moved some jobs around, and she's going to meet us in her New York apartment. It's close to Times Square, which is close to where *GMA* is filmed. She's going to put a few outfits together for you. When you're done with *GMA*, you'll go back to her apartment, get changed and then we will head to the studio to film for *Live with Kelly*."

My uncle has walked into the lounge room with a newspaper in his hand. He shrugs his shoulders. I hold my hands up in front of my body before I speak.

"Okay, stop ... just for a second, please. I knew this trip was going to be full on, and I am so grateful for all these opportunities, but doesn't anyone else think this has happened way too quickly? I mean, it just doesn't even feel real. How can things possibly be happening so fast? Plus, we literally just got here. I haven't even had time to unpack my stuff and now you want me to fly to New York? I'm exhausted. I can barely keep my eyes open. Not that it's making much difference because I can't sleep anyway."

Taylor sits down next to my uncle.

"I know, I'm so sorry. This doesn't usually happen, but they want you to perform. I remember you and your uncle saying you wanted to take every single opportunity that presented itself here. I know you've just flown around the world to be here, I know you're exhausted, but it's now or never. Their schedule for next week, and the weeks that follow, are already planned, so this is your only chance to be on *GMA*."

My uncle puts the newspaper down.

"This isn't about being in the right place at the right time, Delilah. You're getting these kinds of opportunities because you deserve them. You're talented and, yes, it has happened quickly and, no, most successful singer-songwriters don't have overnight success the way you have, but this world is full of surprises. It's time to embrace everything and not question if it's happening too quickly. You don't want it to end before you know it. You've got so many amazing opportunities, so we're going to take them, and make the most of them. There is something very special about you and the gift that you have. It's touching real people, and the world is ready for you. Let's show them what you're made of. That's why we're here, isn't it?"

I grit my teeth and let my hands fall to my sides.

"Yes, that's why we're here. What do I need to pack?"

Taylor looks relieved.

"Nothing ... wait, no, that's not right. Bring your guitar, a pair of pyjamas and your toiletries. That's all you'll need. We're only there for tonight. When you've finished filming tomorrow, we will be on the first flight back to LA. You've got a lot of work to do here too, so it's going to be a very quick trip."

I massage my temples and suddenly feel wide awake.

"What time do we leave?"

Taylor checks her phone.

"*Shit*. The plane's in an hour and a half. Grab your things as quickly as you can. We need to get to the airport within the next thirty minutes or we can't get on the flight."

227

Without saying another word or waiting for a reply, Taylor is off on her phone. I stand in the lounge room, frozen to the spot.

"Delilah? Did you not hear Taylor? Let's get a move on, quickly."

My uncle nudges me towards my room.

At 10:30 p.m. we're half an hour into our five-and-a-half-hour flight, heading to New York: another place I've never been before. I'm excited to be in the Big Apple, especially after hearing Dakota's stories, but I don't even have enough time to explore. This is going to be an incredibly quick trip, jam-packed with a ton of things to get done. *I'll just have to come back another time.* I try to calm my erratic breathing down.

Taylor told me we'll arrive in New York just before 3:30 a.m., and then I'll have to be up at 5:00 a.m. for hair and makeup before picking an outfit to wear. Then it's straight to the studio for my interview and performance. I have no idea how I'm going to make it through this day, although I tell myself I'll rely on caffeine and adrenalin. We're sitting in business class this time, which is smaller than first class but just as nice. Taylor looks beyond stressed. She's been flipping through pages of information ever since we took off and, despite not being able to access her phone, she's been typing away and reading highlighted bits of the documents she has with her. I'm sitting between her and my uncle who, unlike Taylor, looks relaxed. When he notices me looking at him, he smiles.

"Everything okay, love?"

"Yep. Just a little bit nervous. We haven't even been in LA for 24 hours and we're already on the move."

"I know. It's a bit crazy, but that's a part of the fun, hey?"

I close my eyes and take a few much-needed deep breaths. When I open my eyes, Taylor and my uncle are watching me closely. I don't ask them why they're looking at me; I just close my eyes and repeat this pattern of deep breathing until I feel calm. When I feel better, I open my eyes and notice that my uncle is still watching me.

"I promised Cam I'd do this when the time was right, and I feel like that time has come. Before we left Perth, Cam wrote a letter for you. He came around to the studio on Wednesday morning to drop it off. He made me promise not to give it to you right away, so I waited. Here."

He passes me an envelope with my name scribbled on the front.

"It's up to you when you read it, but I think you should do it now while you've got some time."

There's a row of empty seats, so I ask a stewardess if I can sit there for a few minutes. I get up and move before gently opening the envelope. I start to read the handwritten letter.

"Delilah,

I remember a fight we had when we were in high school. We were 16 and I went to apologise to you, but I couldn't get any words out, so I sat down and wrote my feelings out. It was the first time I did something like that, and ever since then I've found a way to tell you everything I'm feeling without feeling stupid. You never make me feel like that, it's just something I feel stupid for, I know, it's stupid.

Anyway, I wanted to write this letter for you while you're in America. I know you have moments when you don't believe you deserve all the good

229

things that have happened to you. Especially recently. I know everyone tells you that you do deserve them, but I also know you well enough to know that sometimes you just go along with what people say so you don't have to face this fear head on. It's okay to be scared, but Delilah you should never, ever believe that you don't deserve to reap the rewards of your success.

All your previous failed attempts and bad days have led you here, don't be afraid to embrace everything that comes your way. I really believe our lives are predetermined and even if we fall off the path we're on, we always find our way back to it. In saying that I also truly believe that our paths to success are written in the stars right from the start of our lives. Some people have success that's 'bigger' than another individual's success, but sometimes people like you have a gift that the world needs.

Sometimes there's a singer-songwriter who connects with the world more than they realise, and Delilah, you're one of those people. You've connected with so many people already. I looked up your videos on MusicNow, and the comments are incredible. Because of you, people who had all but given up hope have chosen to fight for a better life. You're motivating and inspiring people. Your gift is helping people find a sense of happiness that they thought they'd never have again. That's an amazing thing to achieve when you're only 22.

Your entire life has been building up to this moment. You're right where you're meant to be, fate has led you here, and you have to continue to let fate work its magic. It's taking you on this journey because you're meant to be doing this. It's destiny, baby! Whenever you feel like you can't do this, just remember what I told you, "you **can** do this." I am so proud of you, and I love you more than you'll ever know.

Cam."

I read the letter over and over and feel my emotions spilling over my body. I wish more than anything that I could call Cam and thank him. His words were just what I needed, and it's triggered something in me that I've been fighting to find. It's nothing bad for once; it's something good. I'm suddenly motivated and determined, more than I was before we arrived in America. I finally grasp the severity of this trip, and I know that it can lead to even more doors opening. Cam is right: it is my duty to take every single opportunity and grasp them while I can.

Despite feeling overcome with emotions about being whisked away to New York so quickly, I allow my mind to welcome this next step in my journey. Despite knowing how tired I'll be, I decide to throw every single piece of my heart and soul into these interviews and my performance. After all, I have so much to gain, and sometimes the risk is worth the reward. I want this more than anything I've ever wanted in my whole life. Cam has started a fire within me, and he's summed it up perfectly. I am right where I need to be, and I refuse to let these opportunities slip away without making the most of them. When I feel ready, I go back to my seat.

"He's a keeper, isn't he?"

"Yeah, he is," I say.

~

Another 24 hours has passed and we're back in Los Angeles. The trip to New York went by in the blink of an eye. Although it was a quick trip, I accomplished more than I thought was possible in such a short period. My interviews were very relaxed, and I enjoyed them. It was a new part that I haven't been exposed to: doing an interview where people can physically see me. I even found the live performance of *Wildfire* to be exhilarating. It made me feel alive, and it made my passion even stronger. I've truly been surprised by how much more my passion has grown. Every time I do something that focuses on my music career, I get this burning sensation that runs like fire throughout my body. While at first it scared me, I have embraced the feelings. The more my passion grows, the more I grow; the more I grow, the more I can love myself.

My first week in LA is packed with things to keep me occupied. Despite being so busy, I thrive on everything that I'm doing. I'm meeting lots of new people, and I'm able to promote my music and do what I do best: perform. My uncle and I have become even closer than before. We've kept in contact with Melody, who's been blown away by how well things are going. She's kept in contact with Taylor too, who's told her how many more opportunities I've had since arriving.

My first performance in a pub in the heart of LA went off without a hitch. The crowd was amazing, and the cheers I got at the end made me feel something I haven't felt before. It was indescribable. My urge to do it again is building, and now I'm determined to play as many live shows as I possibly can. It's everything I dreamed it would be.

CHAPTER FIFTEEN
LA LOVE

A week and a half into my trip, I find myself sitting in Taylor's office. I've been in and out of here since arriving. My uncle is sitting next to Taylor, and I can tell something is up. I feel too scared to say anything, so I just sit and wait for someone else to end the silence. Finally, my uncle speaks.

"Relax honey, don't be worried. I promise this is exciting."

Taylor takes over and tells me something I had not prepared myself to hear.

"Delilah, another opportunity has come up. I've spoken to my team, along with your uncle and Melody, and we believe now is the time for a change for you. Delilah, we want you to move to Los Angeles permanently."

I almost choke on the sip of water I've just put into my mouth. Has she really just said what I think she's said? *Move to Los Angeles?* I hadn't even thought about that!

"It's hard. Trust me, I know from experience. Moving from Australia was the single hardest thing I've ever had to to do. I didn't know anyone here, I had no family and no friends. When I first arrived, I was miserable, isolated and incredibly lonely, but I had to thrive on that. I had to constantly remind myself why I had left my home and moved here. That's when things changed for me. Eventually, I found my footing and everything else worked out. Now I'm extremely happy. But, through it all, I had a job that I was so passionate about, so going to work every day wasn't a chore. It kept me going, and it made me feel alive. I know that is what your music and your career has done for you. I know what sacrifices you've had to make to do this but, trust me, in the long run it's for the best. This is another sacrifice you'll have to make, but you belong here, Delilah. This is another prime opportunity for you, and it would be stupid to pass it up. Having said that, it's also a life-changing decision, one you shouldn't take lightly. So, while I highly recommend it, I also know what it takes to make that decision, and it's entirely up to you. Unlike me, you wouldn't be alone. You'll have my team and me, and if you decide to move here, we will support you and make your transition as easy as possible. I also want you to know that this isn't just a move across the world. It's the chance to start working on album number two, with me."

My heart is racing. I still can't believe what I'm hearing.

"Album number two? Taylor, are you saying that if I move, not only will you take me on as a client, but I'll also get the chance to write and record music for another album?"

"That's correct. I know it's a lot to take on. How do you feel?"

"I, uh, I don't know."

I turn to my uncle, suddenly worried about what would happen with him and Melody since they're my co-managers.

"What about you? We've been on this journey since the start, and I can't do this without you."

My uncle gets up from his chair and moves it next to me.

"Honey, what we've achieved together is nothing short of magic, and I will never forget this. But it's time for me to take a step back, and it's time for you to take a step forward. I will always love and support you, but my life is in Perth. My job is to help other musicians achieve success, and you'll be perfectly fine without me. I'll always be here, ready to tackle anything you face, but it's time for something new. Melody and I have done what we needed to do to get you here. Now it's time for you to continue without us. It's time for Taylor to take over. She can take you to a new level, and that is something you need to consider. You're so much more than this, Delilah. Don't bind yourself to Perth. It will always be home, but your life belongs here now. You can't pass this chance up. It won't happen again, believe me."

Deep down I know he's right, but I don't know if I'm ready for such a big change. I've encountered quite a few people in the music industry since being here, especially people who work with Taylor. They've all said the same thing: "If she's serious about establishing a career, she needs to move to Los Angeles. It's where all the opportunities are. LA is the place to be."

I try to make sense of this offer, again. It's happened so quickly and, like my whole career, things have moved quicker than I thought they would. I suddenly remember something Cam wrote in his letter to me: *Your entire life has been building up to this moment. You're right where you're meant to be, fate has led you here, and you have to continue to let fate work its magic.* I look back up at my uncle and Taylor.

"I need time to think, to really think. I don't think I can make this decision while I'm here."

~

Time goes so fast in Los Angeles. My uncle, Taylor and I have agreed not to extend my trip – not because there isn't anything else to accomplish; there is – but because right now I need to go back to Perth and assess my options. I now have to decide if I want to pack up my whole life and move to LA permanently, or if I want to stay in Perth and try to continue building my career there. It is a decision that I'm not taking lightly, but it's a decision that's about to be made even more difficult when the last person I expect to surprise me turns up at my door.

~

It's Monday morning, the last Monday that I'm in LA, and I'm enjoying the morning off. There is a knock at the door; because I'm not working today, I know it isn't Archer or Asher. I instantly wonder who it could be.

"Are you expecting anyone?" I ask my uncle, looking up from my book.

"No, are you?"

I immediately know something is up, so I pretend not to care.

"Nope. I'm going to shower. Can you get the door?"

"Oh, ummm, I'm really into this article. Can you do it?"

He looks back down at the newspaper that he's pretending to read. The way he is acting instantly gives up his act; I know he is behind this surprise. And what a surprise it is.

I put my book down and walk over to the door. I try to look through the small keyhole, but whoever is on the other side is covering it. I slowly open the door, and there they are. Cam and Dakota are standing at the door with a bunch of flowers in their hands.

"Surprise!" they say in unison.

"Oh my God! What are you guys doing here?"

"We wanted to surprise you. We've had this planned ever since you told us you were coming. I have to go to New York for work anyway, so I thought I'd surprise you on my way through."

After hugging me, Dakota approaches our uncle, hugs him, and then disappears for a tour around the villa. I wait for Cam to walk in. When he's inside, I close the door and face him.

"I spoke to Dakota a few hours after we talked at the beach. She was already coming here before going to New York, and I wanted to surprise you too. So, here we are."

"I'm so glad you're here. It's nice to actually see you face to face and not through a computer screen."

We kept in contact throughout my first two weeks here. We Skyped every day; when we couldn't speak to each other through our computer screens, we'd email. With the time difference, it was quite a challenge, but thankfully we found a way around it. It was the next best thing to being together. During my second week in LA, Cam sent me an email asking me a question I wasn't expecting:

I need you to be honest. Am I the one?

I replied with one sentence:

You don't even need to ask. You've always been the one.

He didn't respond after that, and part of me started to worry. That night we Skyped, so I asked him about it; we talked for almost four hours and, by the end of the conversation, we decided that we were ready to get back together, this time for good. We're getting a second chance at love, and not many people get that, so I know how lucky we are. It's funny how after all these years, I still get butterflies whenever I get an email, text, Skype call, visit, hug or kiss from Cam. It's like I'm seeing him for the first time. That's how I truly know this is the person I want to spend my life with.

I haven't told Cam, or anyone else for that matter, about the offer to move to Los Angeles permanently. I guess I've been avoiding it because I'm so scared of making such a drastic change. I still don't know what to do. Ever since the offer, my mind has worked overtime to process and assess all my options and all the changes and things I'd have to sacrifice if I picked up and moved to the other side of the world. I've always wondered if my career would one day bring me to America, but I hadn't really considered moving away from Perth. When I did, I always thought I'd move to Sydney, or maybe Melbourne.

I know what lies ahead of me if I take this risk. I mean, it's the biggest risk of my life. I know that if I take it, I'm going to be exposed to more opportunities than I'd ever get in Perth, but I don't know if I'm able to move so far away from my family. Maybe I need to talk to Dakota; she's done this before, she's packed up and moved away from us. Now she's flying in and out of places all the time, so she'd know how I feel. She'd know how to help me approach this life-changing decision.

"Delilah? Did you hear what I said?"

I realise I've completely zoned out in the middle of our conversation.

"Um, yeah I ... okay no. I'm sorry. I got lost in my thoughts."

"What's up? You get like this when something's bothering you. Talk to me."

His words are comforting, and I find myself wanting to blurt everything out, but I don't feel comfortable discussing it yet. Until I feel like I'm comfortable enough to talk about it, I'll keep it to myself.

"I'll tell you later, I promise. It's nothing bad. This trip has just been so overwhelming. I can't tell you how many times I've used that word: overwhelming. But I don't know how else to describe it. It has been exciting ... and tiring ... but mostly exciting."

I grab his hand and show him around the villa. When we reach the deck, we sit down and look out at the view. After a few minutes of silence, Cam tells me something I wasn't expecting to hear.

"I quit my job."

"You what? Why?"

"I just needed a change. I also managed to finish my degree, so I'm about to graduate a semester earlier. It just felt like the right time to change things up, so that's what I'm doing, and that's why I'm here. Delilah, your career is taking off, and this is a train that will not slow down anytime soon. Regardless of where you're based, my job as your boyfriend is to be there for you. So, wherever you go in the world, I'll be right by your side, ready to support you unconditionally. If you want me to, that is?"

"Of course I do! Nothing would make me happier. The winds are changing. I feel it. This trip has opened my eyes to how much more there is out there for me. Everything is about to change for the better, and I'm done with my fears. I'm ready for everything that life is going to throw at me, good or bad. Having you by my side, well, that's something I'm happy to have."

I feel the urge to tell Cam about the move. The timing feels right. Maybe by talking about it with Cam, I'll be able to process it easier too. Maybe it will help me make the decision that's best for me.

"Alright, spill it. I know you're dying to tell me something. It's written all over your face. You keep doing this weird eye twitching thing, which you do every time you have something big to tell me."

He walks over to the glass barrier that runs on the lining of the deck, leans against it and looks at me again.

"I have an eye twitch? Oh great!" I say, laughing as I massage the spots around my eyes, hoping the twitch goes away.

"Yes, you do. It's cute, so don't worry. Anyway, what's up?"

"Cute isn't the word I'd use."

I get up and stand next to him, looking out at the view.

"Taylor asked me to consider moving here full time. She sat down and told me about all the opportunities that are waiting for me here. She said I could start preparing my second album, and she wants me to continue doing live shows here. She wants me to keep building up this support network of friends ... she calls them *fans*, but that's still so surreal to me, so I call them *friends*."

Ever since I started performing here, I've continued to gather a pretty large following. The support I'm getting from people around LA has been nothing short of amazing. I know I wouldn't be succeeding like this if people weren't connecting to my music. Knowing that I'm giving people the same sense of happiness and comfort that music gives me makes me the happiest version of myself. There's nothing in this world that will ever take this feeling away. I know how lucky I am, and I just want to continue giving people what I've given myself.

"But?"

"But ... I don't know what to do. I know deep down what the right choice is. It's pretty obvious to see there's more for me here. All the doors that are opening for me are here. But by leaving Perth, I leave everything I love behind, I leave everyone I love behind. That scares me. I don't know if I'm ready to face a life here, by myself. But, at the same time, I want to continue on this path. I want to continue doing what I love. My heart is pulling me here to Los Angeles, but my head is screaming at me to stay in Perth."

"This is an amazing opportunity, babe. Seriously, who would have thought this would come out of a short trip like this? And there's still a week to go! In the end, you have to make the best decision, for you. Don't worry about leaving your family and friends behind. They're going to support you regardless of where you are based. Remember what your mum always said to you about following your heart?"

"Yes. She told us that you must always listen to your heart, even when your head tells you something different. Your heart will always want what you really want, and your head will tell you to do the opposite because it's scared. You must never give in to the fear. She told us that every night when we were growing up."

I hear my mum's voice as I repeat her words in my head over and over again. I wish I could speak to her more than ever; I'd love her advice on what to do, although I know what she'd say. She'd say the same thing as Cam, my uncle, and Taylor have all said. As much as I long to tell my mum and talk to her about it right now, I know that I have to tell her face to face. I've promised myself that I'm not going to make any final decisions while I'm in LA. I'm going to wait until I'm back in Perth, when I have time to sit and think clearly without worrying about what time I need to be up for an interview, or how I can get from the villa to Santa Monica.

"You know I'll move anywhere in the world with you. If this is what you want, then let's do it, together."

I turn my back on the view of LA and face the villa.

"I know you would, and I appreciate that more than you'll ever know. I think I need to just focus on the rest of this trip and then deal with all of this once I get home. I need to talk to my mum and see what she thinks, and then I need to be honest about what I think is best for me."

~

My last week in Los Angeles goes by way too quickly. We've been in LA for three weeks and one day; we had some scheduling issues and the trip got pushed back an extra few days, but now it's Friday night, and there's only two days left until we fly back to Perth, and right now I'm in the dressing room of the famous El Rey Theatre.

At 11:00 this morning Cam, Taylor, my uncle and I headed into the theatre space, where I spent fifteen minutes sitting in the middle of the room crying. I wasn't crying because I was sad; I was crying because I'm ridiculously happy. I can't believe I've come this far. Now I am about to play my first ever solo live show, in a theatre, in Los Angeles, with an actual audience of people who are coming to watch me. It just didn't seem possible. The minute I stepped into the venue and looked around, I burst into tears. I'm still in shock over how much has happened on this trip, and I am so grateful to even be in this position. Knowing I get to perform my whole album for people of all ages, from all walks of life, makes me so excited. I cannot wait to connect with the audience. After my performance, I'll have the opportunity to meet some of the fans – or as I call them 'friends' – who are staying back to meet me.

It's now 6:30 p.m. so I have half an hour until I head to the stage. I spend some time warming up, then sit down and talk to the band who are local musicians from LA. They tell me that they work with Taylor, and they often provide backing music for the artists signed to the company. Taylor introduced me to the three musicians: two guys, one who plays the guitar and the other one who plays the drums, and a girl, who plays another guitar and sings in the background. They tell me they've spent the last two weeks learning my songs, and they're excited to

244

perform with me tonight. I'm blown away by having an actual band play with me. Originally, I was meant to play acoustically by myself, but Taylor said she wanted me to have a band too. As I'm talking to the band, there's a knock at the door; Taylor walks in and sits in front of us.

"Okay, so we're just about ready to go. I don't want to give too much away. I want it to be a surprise, but this is going to be an amazing night for you, Delilah. This is the culmination of not only a year's worth of work, but it also brings your electrifying three-week trip together. What you've accomplished in this time frame is amazing, and I am so proud of you. So, let's focus on this moment right now. Forget everything else. Walk onto that stage with pride and do what you do best. You're going to blow everyone away!"

I hug her before she leaves me with the band. We have a final moment to pump ourselves up before we head towards the stage. When the band is in position, Mike, the drummer, gives me the thumbs up, signalling that it's time for me to hit the stage. As I walk on the stage, Taylor introduces me.

"Ladies and gentleman, boys and girls ... the reason we're all here tonight: please welcome the lovely Aussie with a heart of gold and a voice to match, Delilah Walker!"

I half expect to walk out and see the venue empty but, to my surprise, it's packed. In fact, there are still people trying to get in. When the stage lights hit me there's a roar of claps and cheers. I'm overcome with emotions, and I have to stop myself from crying happy tears again. As I look out over the crowd, I notice Cam, my uncle, Taylor and Dakota, who are standing near the front of the stage, beaming with pride. I'm surprised to see Dakota; she left for

New York on Wednesday. I didn't expect her to be here tonight, but she is, and I am thankful to see her face in the sea of people. As I smile at the crowd, for the first time in my life I feel stage fright. Knowing there are people who have travelled here, who have taken the night off, who have given up their time, to watch me sing live has hit me. My heart feels like it's about to burst through my chest. The negative voice that tells me I can't do this keeps screaming at me, and I feel like I'm on the verge of a panic attack. I almost run off the stage, but Cam's voice pops into my head. *"Take a deep breath. Turn around if you have to. This is exciting, so allow yourself to be excited and enjoy it. You can do this."*

It's what he said to me when I performed live for the first time at Darci's 16th birthday party. I didn't come this far just to give up. I close my eyes and squeeze them, allowing the darkness to consume me as I keep repeating the mantra that I've used every time I've had to sing. *"It's okay; you can do this."*

When I'm ready, I open my eyes. I look at my family, who look worried. I try to offer them a comforting smile, then begin to talk.

"Hi. I just wanted to quickly thank you all for coming here tonight to listen to me sing. If you know the songs, please sing along. This song is called *Wildfire*."

The crowd erupts into another fit of cheers and claps as the band and I begin to play. This moment is beyond surreal. As I sing, I watch this crowd of people, brought together by music, sing along with such happiness. I can't even explain how that feels. Seeing people I don't know singing my songs gives me the greatest joy I've ever experienced, and I feel like nothing can ever top this feeling.

After the performance, I spend time meeting all sorts of people. I take so many photos and sign so many autographs that my hand hurts. While I do feel overwhelmed, I am so happy to be in this position. Things just keep getting better for me, and I'm on a path that is leading me to the most amazing destination.

~

As we watch the sunrise on Saturday morning, Cam turns to me.

"Let's go for a walk," he says.

Something about him seems different. For a moment I think we're going to part ways again. Oh, how wrong I am.

"Right now? We just woke up. I was looking forward to just staying in bed and relaxing."

I feel guilty as I see the disappointment on Cam's face.

"Give me a second. I've just got to go and check something."

Cam jumps out of bed and runs into the lounge room. I sit up in the bed and listen to the muffled voices.

"Your uncle is going to get some breakfast, then we will go for a walk."

I rest against my elbows and watch Cam. Something about him seems off, and he looks nervous. I wonder what it is that has made him feel this way.

At 10:00 a.m. I'm showered and dressed, waiting by the door as Cam is talking to my uncle again. I try to listen to their conversation, but they're whispering. I can't make out anything they're saying. I am trying to move closer when my phone vibrates, which makes me jump. I look at the screen and a text from Archer pops up.

I'm here. Ready when you are.

"Ready?" Cam asks when he reaches me.

"Yep. Archer just got here. What were you two whispering about?"

Cam opens the door, and I wave at my uncle before the door closes. When we reach the car, Cam opens that door for me too.

"We were just talking about the flight back, I didn't know if I had the same time as you, so I just wanted to confirm."

I raise my eyebrows.

"You're a terrible liar, Cameron Collins."

As we pull away from the villa, I keep my eyes on Cam. I notice his hand is sweaty and his knee is shaking.

"Where are we going? I thought we were going for a walk?"

Something's bothering him, and I don't know what it is. I figure it's best to approach him calmly, rather than hassling him.

"We are. We're just driving to the spot first. Sorry. I know I'm being secretive but, trust me, it'll be worth it."

After almost forty minutes in the car, we finally pull up at a beach. I instantly recognise it: we're in Santa Monica, and I can spot the Santa Monica pier in the distance.

"What are we doing here?"

"I thought we could spend the day here. I know you've wanted to come here during this trip, but your schedule's been pretty demanding. Today we have all day to stay here and explore."

We thank Archer, who tells us he'll be close by when we need him. We start to walk around, stopping in shops and looking at restaurants before settling on one for lunch. We spend the entire day walking across the beach and exploring this beautiful place before making our way towards the pier: a place that I've wanted to visit ever since I was little.

The sun is disappearing behind the clouds as the day comes to an end. I notice there are dark rain clouds rolling in, the breeze has picked up and most of the people on the pier are beginning to head back to their cars or find shelter. Cam's still walking towards the end of the pier. There's a look in his eyes that I've never seen before; despite the rain beginning to fall from the sky, he doesn't stop until he's where he wants to be.

"What are we doing? It's freezing, and it's raining."

I put my hands in front of my eyes, trying to shelter them from the drops of water. Cam shakes his whole body before he draws a deep breath.

"I've had a lot of time to think, especially over the last two weeks. I know we're young, but this is something I've wanted to do for a long, long time. Please don't say anything. I need to get this out now. Otherwise, I might never do it."

The butterflies have returned to my stomach; this time they're fluttering around stronger than ever before.

"I've said it before, but I just want to reiterate how much of a mistake I made ending things with you earlier this year. It was the dumbest thing I've ever done, and it's my biggest regret, but I believe it happened for a reason. We went our separate ways, and we tried to find love with two different people, but it didn't work out. I know it's because we've always been destined to be together. I mean, if I'm honest, we've been destined to be together since long before we were even born. Over the last few weeks everything has suddenly worked out. The stars have aligned and I've had an experience like no other. I know what I want from life."

The rain has started to get heavier, creating a grey glow around us. Thankfully, the lights from the pier are still on, making the grey glow a little less intense.

"I quit my job, I got on a flight, and I came to you, because this is where I belong: with you, wherever that may be. I don't care where this journey takes you. I'll be by your side every step of the way. Delilah, you've changed my life for the better, and I love you more than I'll ever be able to tell you. I want to spend the rest of our lives trying to show you just how much you mean to me. You've helped me become a person I'm proud to be, you've given me the greatest joy and happiness, and you've given me the best life I could ever want. I knew from the moment we first kissed when we were sixteen that you were the one. So, now I have a question to ask you. Delilah Jade Walker, will you marry me?"

The rain is hammering down on us, and I'm past the point of being freezing, but I don't care. Nothing else matters. Here and now, with Cam, that's all that matters. I look down at him as the rain falls over him and the ring box he's holding.

"Yes! Yes, of course I'll marry you."

I help him up, planting a kiss on his lips as he puts the stunning ring on my finger. We're both drenched and cold, but we just stand there looking into each other's eyes, feeling nothing but an overwhelming sense of love and happiness.

When we're ready, we head back to the car. Archer is waiting with towels and fresh clothes for us, which Cam had packed before we left. We head back to the villa, where my uncle is waiting for us. I show him the ring, and he congratulates us before we sit at the table for dinner.

~

The rest of the night is indescribable. I can't stop smiling. As we get ready to leave LA behind, I replay everything that has happened during the last three weeks. This trip has blown all my expectations out of the water. I'm heading back to Perth as a different person — a better person because of this trip. I'm happier now than I've ever been. Now I just have to go back to where it all began and make the final big decision about my life. The future has arrived, and it's time for everything to change: this time, in the best possible way.

Chapter Sixteen
Time to Shine

After my duties in LA officially wrapped up, my uncle and I discussed delaying our flights for another week. He suggested staying for another seven days so we could look around LA more. We haven't been able to do too much exploring over the last three weeks as I've been so busy. At first, I was hesitant; part of me just wanted to get back to Perth and take a few days to let the last three weeks catch up to me. However, after Taylor said she could get our flights changed, I agreed to another week in LA.

My uncle, Cam and I spend another week in the villa. We explore the places I'll be spending most of my time if I end up moving here. Archer and Asher have kindly offered to drive us around so I can get used to the city, which is incredibly helpful. They both know so much about LA, so they answer all my questions. They show me pretty much every place in California, which makes me fall in love with the idea of moving here even more. I appreciate how much time they're giving up to help me, and it makes the process of considering all my options a lot easier. It's been comforting to explore LA and California. It's something I wanted to do during the first three weeks but, with my demanding schedule, I wasn't able to venture out too far.

By the end of the week, I have been in LA for a solid month. I've achieved so much, I've grown so much, and my happiness has exploded. The more I think about it, the more I'm drawn to the idea of moving away from Perth. I always remember how people describe LA as the city of dreams. People think it's not true, but it is. I've seen so many artists in LA, and all of them have the same goal: to make their dreams come true. I know not everyone is as lucky as me, and that makes me appreciate how successful I've been. I'm so thankful that I get to live my dreams. I just wish everyone got to experience this feeling. Everyone deserves to be this happy and, while I know that sometimes that's just not possible, I always try my best to encourage anyone who has a dream to fight for it. If I can help inspire people to chase their dreams and fight for them through my music, then that's something that I will proudly do.

~

In the middle of the week, Dakota comes back to LA after wrapping up another successful trip to New York. She's been booking more jobs than she ever thought she would. We spend a much-needed day together before she heads back to Perth. It's nice to sit down and sip coffee as we catch up on the last month of our lives.

"We did it, sis. We're both living our dreams! How crazy is that?"

"Yeah, it's pretty crazy ... and surreal ... and amazing and every other positive word in the English language...or any language."

Dakota and I have become even closer over the last few months. Having someone who understands what I'm going through helps me come to terms with leaving my family behind. Dakota has done just that; we're both away from our family now, and we're both pursuing dreams that require a lot of sacrifices. So, having each other to lean on helps. I decide to tell Dakota about the chance to move to LA permanently. I tell her about all the pros and cons, and I tell her how I keep going back and forth on my decision.

"Delilah, you have to do what's best for you. What is your heart telling you to do?"

"Honestly? My heart is telling me it's time for a change. Being here has opened my eyes up to so much. Yes, I'm scared to leave Perth. But if I let my fears stop me, I'll never leave Perth again. There's so much more for me here, and it just feels right."

I let the words I've just said sink in. I've been fighting myself over this decision ever since it was presented to me. I promised myself not to make any kind of decision while I'm still here, but the more time I spend in LA, the more I warm up to the possibility of a new life here.

"You've got your answer then. Trust me, Delilah, it's difficult to move away from home, especially when you miss out on things like birthdays, Easter and Christmas, but it's worth it. You can't put a price on your dreams, and I've seen you come alive in the last few months. You've fought so hard for everything you've got, and the look in your eyes whenever you perform or write music is breathtaking. It is certainly inspiring. Don't be scared to make such a drastic change. It'll be worth it."

I know she's been through something similar. When she decided to become a model, a number of people told her she'd never succeed. She didn't let that stop her; she kept trying and, eventually, she booked a job. The rest is history. She wakes up happy every day. She knows she's got a job that she loves, she's so passionate about what she does, and it shows. I know that by taking this chance, I'll continue to have the same sense of happiness. Dakota is right: there isn't a price I can put on my dreams.

Dakota and I spend the rest of the afternoon in the heart of LA, where we walk up and down Sunset Boulevard. We explore the hall of fame and shop up a storm before we head back to the villa. Dakota was meant to fly back on Wednesday, but Taylor has come through again. She's somehow managed to get Dakota on the same flight as us. I don't know how Taylor does it; she is wonder woman when it comes to organising things without any stress. Over the last few days I've also been able to spend more time with Taylor. I've gotten to know her on a more personal level, and I've opened up to her about everything I'm feeling.

I know deep down that I'm going to leave Perth; discussing it with Taylor helps me begin to make the transition from living in Australia to living in America. She has lots of books from when she moved, which she lets me borrow, and she's told me I can call her whenever I want, if any more questions pop into my head. I appreciate how much Taylor has done for me over the last month; she has gone above and beyond for me, and I'll never forget that. She is one of the most inspiring, hard-working women I've had the pleasure of knowing, and I am excited to start the next chapter of my journey with her.

Before we head to the airport on Thursday – one week into November and four weeks after arriving – we stop by Taylor's office to say goodbye. While we're there, she offers the villa to me until I find a place of my own.

"We own this one and another two. So, when you move here, we can offer you the one you stayed in rent free until you're on your own two feet. I really do know what it's like to come here and feel scared and overwhelmed, so if this is what I can do to make the transition easier, then I'm happy to do it."

Cam and I both thank her; we appreciate the offer, and we both know that her offer will help take some of the stress off. Not only am I packing up my life and moving, but Cam is doing the same. While I have a ridiculous amount of anxiety about telling my mum, I also have anxiety about how Anna will react to her son moving to the other side of the world too; although, it's something of a relief to know Anna has my mum and they'll be able to go through this transition together. They'll be able to support each other and they'll be able to discuss things openly. Cam and I both ask Taylor a ton of questions before we leave. After making sure we have everything we need, we thank her again and head to the airport.

While waiting for the flight back to Australia, Cam, my uncle, Dakota and I discuss everything that's happened over the last month. We're in first class again and, as soon as we take off, I fall asleep. When we land back in Perth on Saturday, we're greeted by my family and Cam's family. Cam and I are too excited to wait, so we announce that we're engaged straightaway. When I show everyone the ring, the excitement picks up again. My mum starts crying and hugging Anna; Cam and I look at each other and smile.

We head back to our house and, after a brief chat with everyone, I retreat to my room where I quickly fall asleep again. I wake up on Saturday afternoon and prepare to get my body back into a routine. Jet lag is beginning to hit, and I know it'll be a few days, if not longer, before I'm back into the swing of things.

I have some time off now, which I decide to use to get myself back into a routine before going through my room and figuring out what to take when I move. Which reminds me: I have to sit down and tell mum my final decision. I have my heart set on moving to LA. But, now that I'm back in Perth, I feel my decision slowly changing. I'm finding myself wanting to stay, but I have to keep reminding myself of why I wanted to move to begin with.

~

After spending a week getting back into my routine, I come to a final decision. I, Delilah Jade Walker, have officially decided to pack up my life and move to Los Angeles, California. It's a decision I haven't taken lightly. In fact, I have spent most of the last week changing my mind more times than I can count. I've spent countless hours with Dakota, my uncle and Cam, venting to them about how frustrated I've become trying to decide. But, after allowing myself the time that I needed, I have settled on a final decision. Now it's time to sit down with my mum and tell her about my plan.

A week after I arrive home, I sit in the lounge room of my house looking around. There are photos of my siblings and I as we've grown up spread across the walls. We look so happy in each photo. I think that's the best thing about having four siblings: I was never bored. As we've grown up, our bonds with each other have continued to thrive, and now we're closer than ever. I know how lucky I am to have such a strong connection with my family members; I know not everyone gets this kind of family, and that's what makes my decision so difficult. I know that leaving Perth means leaving my family behind. Although I know they're always going to be here for me, knowing I won't see them every day scares me. In the end, I know the time is right. I know that my family just want me to be happy, and I know that my decision will lead to just that.

As my mind wanders, my mum walks in and sits down next to me without me noticing.

"Daydreaming again?"

"Mum, there's something I need to talk to you about."

"Why do I get the feeling you're going to tell me life-changing news? I know something is up, and I know it's not the engagement. It's something else. I can feel it."

"I don't know how to say it, but you know the LA trip changed everything. I was presented with an amazing opportunity, and..."

"You're moving there, aren't you?"

"Yes, I am."

"I've noticed you've been trying to hide something since you've been back, and your uncle is a terrible liar. He left your new contract on the table when I went over a few days ago."

"I suppose that's a good thing that he's not a good liar, but I guess we should discuss the obvious. Why didn't you say something earlier?"

I've suddenly been hit by the monumental decision I've made; seeing my mum look so scared makes this decision even more difficult.

"Because I wanted you to tell me when you were ready."

"Honestly, I've been anxious and stressed about telling you. It makes this real. I mean, it makes it feel real. The whole trip was so surreal. I thought everything that happened was a dream. This is one of the best things that has ever happened to me, and I've never been so scared and excited before. I know this is the right decision though, mum. I can feel it. This is the next step for me. Leaving my home and leaving you will suck, but the time is right and it's time to make the most of these opportunities that are coming my way."

"Honey, I've always known that you and Dakota would chase your dreams to the ends of this earth. I knew long ago that the two of you would have dreams that would take you out of Perth, and away from home, from me. It has taken years for me to come to terms with that, but all I've ever wanted for you and your siblings is happiness. If that takes you away from here then, as hard as it will be, I will support you. I knew the minute you left that you'd come home a changed person. I know how hard you've worked, and now is your time. So, go for it, my beautiful girl."

I try to respond, but my mum gets up.

"I want to show you something."

She walks over to the wall by the TV, takes a DVD off the shelf and places it in the DVD player. A few seconds later, vision of me singing when I was little pops up onto the screen.

"I had some of our old VCRs converted. I don't know if you remember me filming these, but you were always so confident singing in front of me. I knew from the moment you sang for the very first time ... I know you're scared, but it's okay, Delilah. You've come so far, and your talent is changing lives. People believe in you. If they didn't, they wouldn't take these risks with you. Your family supports you, your friends support you, and I know you're learning to support yourself. So, give this everything you've got. If it's not right, or you're not happy in a year's time, you can always come home. But you're never going to know if you let your fear stop you. I know you've already made the decision to move, so stop questioning if it's the right thing to do. Life is about taking chances and, my darling girl, this is what you've been destined to do ever since you could talk."

She kisses my forehead and leaves the room. I look up at the television and watch the old footage of me singing. I'm beaming with confidence and I look happy. I know my mum's right: this is the one thing that makes me feel complete. Without it, I wouldn't have survived 22 years of living. As much as this decision has torn me in half, I know that moving away from Perth is the best thing I can do. With the decision made, I am determined to enjoy my last few months in Perth with Cam, our families, and our friends.

~

Two weeks after getting back to Perth, Cam and I sit down to discuss our wedding. We both agree that we want to get married before we move to the States, and we both want a small, intimate wedding, which includes our family and our closest friends. Most of them will be in our wedding party anyway. We don't want a big wedding; we just want to spend our special day with the people who have been with us from the beginning, the people who have supported and loved us unconditionally, and the people who mean the most to us. We spend another two weeks organising it and, with the help of our mums, we manage to get everything planned and sorted for a New Year's Eve celebration. We want to end the year on a high, and we want the new year to begin the exact same way.

Now that everything's sorted, Cam and I decide to have our engagement party. Beforehand, we spend the day with the people we want to ask to be in our wedding party. Cam spends the day at his house with Gavin, Lucas, Dylan, Declan and Marc, who he's going to ask to be his best man. I spend the day at my uncle's house with Darci, Nia, Rosie, Hadi and Dakota, who I'm going to ask to be my maid of honour. At first, I didn't know how to ask them. I wanted to do something special so, after thinking about it, I got gift boxes for each girl. In each box there's a card asking them to be in my bridal party, along with a framed photo of each girl with me. I put a candle with each girl's name on it, and I put some chocolates and rose petals in. As I wait for them to arrive, I look around my uncle's backyard. I think about how much things have changed in the last few years, and how much I've grown. My family have been to hell and back, especially recently, but things have taken a turn for the better. We're finally on a path to happiness. My friendship with my two best friends is stronger than ever, and my love for Cam is indescribable.

I watch the clouds float through the sky, taking slow, deep breaths and allowing the sunshine to wash over me. I feel so proud of myself for what I've achieved over the last year of my life. I've been faced with some of the most difficult situations I've ever been in. At times I didn't think I was strong enough to make it through, but I've come out of the other side in a much better place, and I've learnt never to doubt myself. I've learnt to believe in myself in a way that I've never done before. Now I feel my belief and strength within myself growing stronger every day.

As I continue to watch the clouds, I hear cars pulling into the driveway. I turn around and watch as Hadi and Rosie get out of Rosie's car, then my sisters and Nia hop out of my mum's car. My mum quickly waves at me before she heads inside. I wave back as I wait for the girls to reach me. We sit down at the table my uncle has set up for us. We start to talk about the wedding, and I tell the girls about the final date that Cam and I have agreed on. I tell them how everything's planned, and I tell them how we're planning on having a small, intimate wedding. As we continue to discuss the details, I hand them their boxes and I explain what they are.

"You girls are my best friends, you're my family, and I can't think of anyone else I'd want standing by my side as I marry the love of my life. I want you to open your boxes and read the cards I wrote for you."

When each girl has read the card and looked through the box, they get up and hug me, all excitedly agreeing to be in my bridal party. As we enjoy lunch, Dakota pulls me aside.

"Are you sure you want me as your maid of honour?"

"Of course! You've always been there for me, through thick and thin. You mean so much to me, Dakota. You didn't give up on me when I gave up on myself. You kept me going, and you helped me fight for my dreams when I thought they were impossible. There's no one else I want as my maid of honour. I mean that with the utmost respect to the other girls ... but Dakota, nothing compares to our bond."

"Nothing would make me happier than being by your side then!"

"Good! Because I wouldn't have taken no for an answer."

We sit back at the table and discuss the wedding again, this time making plans for the bridal party. I feel nothing but happiness and love coming from the people who will be proudly standing by my side when I say 'I do'.

~

As the sun begins to set, the girls head inside for dinner. Cam's family and groomsmen will be joining my family and my bridal party for our engagement party. Before I head inside, I stand by my uncle's pond and focus my attention on the stars as they begin to brighten the darkened sky. I find myself thinking about how thankful I am to be in such a good place. My mum and Evan, along with my dad, have been working with Mandy to regain some form of relationship, and it's done wonders for them. My mum is slowly learning to trust my dad again, and she's become more accepting of him being in our lives. My brothers and sisters are also working with Mandy and my dad, and they're getting to know the person I knew was always there. My dad is finally in a much happier place, and he's learning to forgive himself and start over. He's got a job, and he's working on bettering himself every day. That makes me so proud. I never thought this would happen, but my family finally feels complete again. I'm lost in my thoughts when my uncle joins me.

"Everything okay, love?"

"Yeah. Just thinking. Thank you for letting us have the engagement party here."

"Anything for you."

I look at the water in the pond and take a deep breath.

"I ... um ... I have something I want to ask you. It's no secret that you've consistently been here for me and my siblings, and it's no secret that we're so appreciative of what you've done for us. I'm so grateful that I have such a strong bond with you, so I was thinking ... there's no one that I want more to walk me down the aisle than you. Would you mind doing that for me?"

"Delilah, I would be honoured. But what about your dad? You're finally on good terms with him, and so is your mum. Won't he be hurt if you don't ask him?"

"Honestly? I don't think he will be hurt. He knows how close we are, and he knows how much you have stepped up to the plate to be there for us. You've been by my side for 22 years, so you're the only person I want by my side on the happiest day of my life."

"Speak to your dad first. If he's happy to let me do it, then you know I'll be right there with you, kiddo."

My uncle and I walk inside to join all my family and friends. As soon as I spot my dad, I pull him to the side.

"I asked uncle Derek to walk me down the aisle tonight. I don't mean to hurt you. I just want him to be there with me. If things were different, obviously, I'd want it to be you, but ..."

"Delilah, you don't need to explain it to me. I understand your decision, and I respect it. He stood up and did what I couldn't do at the time. If he's the one you want by your side, then you have my blessing. Just being able to be there to see you get married is something I will treasure."

"Thank you. I'm glad you're going to be there. I never thought we'd be in this place, but it's meant to be."

I enjoy the rest of the night. My dad tells my uncle he has his blessing to walk me down the aisle and, after my uncle accepts my offer, I'm able to feel a weight lift off my shoulders. Both Cam and I are surrounded by so much love and, despite having a small, intimate wedding, I know it'll be the best day of our lives. I cannot wait to become Mrs Delilah Collins.

~

The morning after the engagement party has come with a cost. I drank way too much champagne, and now I have another classic Walker hangover, complete with booming headache. After breakfast of two hash browns and a large iced coffee – the only breakfast that has ever helped my hangover – Cam insists we go for a walk along the beach. According to him, the fresh air is just what I need. We're fifteen minutes into our walk when Cam gets a call from Marc. He needs help moving his stuff from his parents' home into his new apartment, so Cam apologises, kisses my cheek and leaves me on the beach.

I sit on the sand and enjoy the warm sun as it kisses my skin. To my surprise, the fresh air and the sunshine are doing wonders for my hangover, and I start to feel better. I'm watching the gentle breeze picking up loose sand when I notice a familiar person waving at me. I stand up as Ryan approaches me.

"Hi stranger."

"Hi! How are you?" I ask.

"I'm good. I'm actually better than good. I'm great! How are you?"

We sit down.

"I'm good, thank you. That's wonderful. What's been going on?"

"Well, since I saw you last, I've spent time with Angie. I worked through all my issues and fears, and I've continued to repair my relationship with my family. We're in a good place now, and I'm happier than ever. Things have worked out for the best, and I feel like I owe you a heartfelt thank you. Everything really was meant to work out this way, and I just want to thank you, for everything. You came into my life at the perfect time, and I'll never forget what you did for me. Without you, I'd still be in a terrible place. In fact, I don't even know if I'd be here. My life really didn't have any meaning, I'd lost all my friendships and my family, but you changed all of that. Delilah, you saved my life, and I'm not just saying that. Because of you, I've turned my life around, and I'll never forget that. I've been dating someone too. She's amazing, and I really love her. We're moving to England in six months. My parents wanted a fresh start somewhere else and we have family there, so it just feels right."

I can see just how happy he is; he's clearly in a much better place, and I'm glad I was able to help him get there.

"That's amazing, Ryan! I'm so happy for you. You really deserve to be happy. You're a beautiful person, and I loved getting to know you. I know things didn't work out with us, but I think we both needed each other during a difficult period in our lives. You helped me as much as I helped you."

"I agree. So, what's been going on with you? I listened to your album. It's amazing, Delilah!"

"Thank you. I really appreciate that. Cam and I are engaged, and we're moving to Los Angeles in the new year. Things have been much better since we got back together, and I'm really excited about spending the rest of my life with him. My dad and I are getting to know each other, and my mum and Evan are doing the same. I've moved over to a new record label. So, everything in my life has been pretty amazing!"

Ryan and I chat for another hour.

"I'm glad I got to see you again. I just, I really wanted you to know how much I appreciate everything that we went through. Maybe our paths will cross again one day. But, if not, good luck with everything. I hope you get everything you want from life. You deserve nothing but the best."

"I'm really glad I got to see you too, Ryan, and I feel the same. You deserve nothing but the best too, and I'm thrilled that you're in a better place. Good luck with the move."

I walk back to my car and feel relieved. I've been thinking about Ryan recently, so it's almost like we were meant to see each other again. Knowing he's in a better place makes me feel a sense of peace. It's nice to see him getting the best out of life, and I'm lucky enough to be in the same place.

~

Everything is now moving forward. Cam and I are set to move to LA on the 6th January. We will spend a month and a half getting into our new routine before I continue promoting my first album. We're hoping it will lead to concerts around the United States. Taylor has begun to line things up for me, and my popularity is continuing to grow. I know I'm on the verge of so many more amazing things, and I cannot wait to move. But first, I have another big commitment to fulfil in Perth, and it's one I can't wait to face.

CHAPTER SEVENTEEN
THE MOTIVATOR

December has begun, so I'm now four weeks away from my wedding and five weeks away from my move to LA. Cam and I have been running around getting everything organised, and now we're ready to take a few weeks off and do nothing but enjoy spending time with family and friends.

I'm woken up bright and early on the first Monday of December. I roll over and reach for my phone, noticing my uncle's name pop up on the screen as I answer his call.

"Hello?"

"Sorry, did I wake you?"

"Yes, but it's fine. I need to get up anyway. What's up?"

"I've had a ridiculous amount of offers come in for you ever since we've been back. Obviously, I've graciously rejected them all since we agreed you were going to use the next two months spending quality time with your family and friends before the big move ... but ... I received an email on Friday afternoon. I've been questioning what to do but, after reading it again this morning, I believe you should consider this offer. I've forwarded it to you. Carefully go over it and give me a call once you're ready."

We continue talking for another ten minutes before I hang up. I wonder what the email says. I get up from my bed, head over to my desk, turn my laptop on and wait as it loads.

"Good morning Miss Walker.

My name is Lesley Bloom, and I work at Bloomfield Axis. We work with young adults aged between 15 and 25 who have troubled pasts. Many of our clients are struggling to find their passion due to past or present circumstances. We work with these people yearly, on aspects such as developing their confidence, as well as helping them deal with their past or current situations. We do two intakes twice a year: one in January, and one in July. Our July group have been working hard to get to a better place in their lives, and this is why I am reaching out to you.

Towards the six-month mark of our treatment programs, we like to invite people who we believe can be influential to come in and talk to them about their story. It is with great pleasure that I extend an invite to you to attend our talk to this group of young adults on Monday 9th December at 11:00 a.m. Many of the girls in our group look up to you, and they would be over the moon if you were free to talk to them. We want it to be a surprise, so only the staff know I'm contacting you. We're going on Christmas break after Friday 13th, so it would be an amazing way to end the halfway mark of the program.

This is an important event, and our group of students would be delighted if you could attend and speak to them. Many of them have personally told me that you are their role model, and I can say with pride that your music has helped them. I understand how busy you are, and I know there is a slim chance you will be available, but if you find yourself free, please consider joining us. I know it would mean the world to the students. If you can make it, please feel free to send me an email with the best way to contact you, and I'll be in touch. I hope to hear from you soon.

Yours sincerely,

Lesley Bloom
Owner/ Coordinator at Bloomfield Axis."

I re-read the email three times. I never thought people who didn't know me would look up to me. Heck, I didn't even think people who knew me would look up to me. But, by the looks of it, it's happening, and that's an incredible honour. As I read the email for the fourth time, Cam walks into my room.
"Morning. You're up early."
"Yeah, my uncle called me. He wanted me to read this email. Here."
I pick my laptop up and hand it to Cam. He read it before looking at me.

"Wow, that's incredible! Are you going to do it?"

"I really don't know. I'm good at singing in front of people, but I'm not so good at public speaking. I don't see myself as someone who is a role model."

"Babe, I know it's scary, but this is an amazing opportunity for you. Remember when you didn't think you could sing in front of people? Look at you now. You do it with ease. And of course you're someone who is a role model! Lots of people look up to you, including me. You're brave, fearless, funny, confident, and you have the most beautiful personality. You always put other people's needs before yours, and you do things for people even if it makes you feel uncomfortable. You are everything that I try to be, and I'm not just saying that. Delilah, if you allow it to happen, you can inspire people all around the world. This place is giving you the chance to help others who see what we all see. You can do something good with your platform."

It always feels weird when people compliment me, even when it's someone like Cam or my mum. Maybe instead of questioning it, I should just go with it. This is the perfect way to give back to people who have supported me, so I decide to do it.

I call my uncle and spend another fifteen minutes on the phone with him. He lets me know that he will contact Lesley and organise everything, then he will fill me in. He tells me to start focusing on my speech, which I instantly worry about. I voice my concerns to my uncle, who comforts me.

"Don't overthink it, honey. Just write honestly about your experiences. Talk about how you made the transition into music, and focus on how you learnt to believe in yourself, even when you were faced with tragedy. It will come to you. Don't beat yourself up if it takes a few days to get it all sorted."

"Okay, thank you. I'll get started today. Let me know when you've spoken to Lesley."

"Will do. Speak soon. Love you."

"Love you, too."

~

After spending most of the morning with Cam and my family, I decide to head over to my dad's house to invite him to my talk. When I arrive at my dad's, I immediately notice how different his house looks. The grass is no longer brown, there's a new front door, the windows are clean, and the curtains have been replaced. The house finally looks like someone lives there, and it shows just how far my dad, and my family as a whole, has come. I've seen my dad become the person I remember before his mum died: the funny, loving person that I admired more than anything in the world. He no longer looks angry or tired. He looks happy, he's always smiling, and he now takes pride in how he looks. He's opened himself up to his most vulnerable self, and it's paying off.

I knock on the door and, after my father calls out, I let myself into the house. I notice the whisky and cigarette smell is gone; the house now smells of vanilla, it's a pleasant change. The rooms are all clean and the windows are open, allowing the sunshine to brighten the rooms. The cold, distant feeling I used to get from being in my dad's house is gone; now I feel welcomed and relaxed.

"Wow, the place looks amazing. It almost looks brand new."

"Yeah, Anthony helped me fix it up. I felt like it needed an upgrade. How are you?"

"Good. I got asked to do a talk next week at a place that works with young adults who are going through some difficult things. I was scared at first, and most of me didn't want to do it, but I spoke to uncle Derek and Cam. They encouraged me to do it, so I'm going to. That's why I'm here. I want to invite you to hear my speech."

"I'd love to. I actually spoke to your mum about it earlier. I'm looking forward to it."

Did I just hear that correctly?

"Wait, when did you talk to her?"

"This morning. I called Evan to chat and then I spoke to your mum after."

"That's a big step. I'm really proud of you, dad. I didn't think we'd ever get to this place."

"Me neither, sweetheart. But you fought for me, and I'm very appreciative of that. You've given me my life back, and I am so lucky to have a second chance. I never thought I'd be in this position, but it makes me very happy that you, your siblings, your mother and Evan have accepted me back into your lives. I'm the happiest I've ever been."

Knowing my family is united and stronger than ever is the best feeling.

"So, how are the moving plans going?" he asks.

I've spoken to my dad multiple times since being back from LA. We've had lunch, and he's over for dinner once a week, so I've been able to communicate with him and keep him in the loop in regards to my life changes. At first, he wasn't keen on me moving, especially since we've only recently patched things up. But, after we had spoken about it, he understood why I had made the decision to move away. He, like my mum, was happy and relieved to hear that Cam is moving with me. I know they found comfort in knowing I wasn't moving to the other side of the world by myself.

My dad and I spend the next hour and a half chatting and going through old family photos from when I was young and, of course, before he left. Before too long, I head home and sit down to get my speech onto paper. The days are passing by quicker than ever, and I know time isn't on my side. But, once I get going, the words flow through my hand and onto the paper. Soon I have the perfect speech.

~

Before I know it, Monday has arrived, and I am standing in the hallway waiting to go into the room to deliver my speech. My family and friends are already in the room, and I carefully listen as Lesley begins to tell the group about who their special presenter is. The minute she mentions my name, I hear applause and lots of talking. The volume begins to rise as Lesley tries to calm down the excitement. After another few minutes, she introduces me and I walk into the room. I'm greeted by a group of 12 young adults, who are all smiling and looking at me with excitement in their eyes.

"Hello. I'm Delilah, and I'm honoured to be here to talk to you today. I've faced some pretty tough times in the last year. But, without going through what I went through, I wouldn't be where I am now. I got to a point where I had all but given up on myself. I was desperate for the pain to stop. I made a mistake and nearly died, but I was given a second chance. I took it with both hands and made peace with my past so I could move forward with my life.

I've always wanted to a singer-songwriter, but I always doubted that I would be good enough, or that I had enough talent to succeed. I was so passionate about music, and it got to the point where I either decided to go for it or just let it be a forgotten dream. My family and my boyfriend encouraged me to go for it. With the support of them and my friends, I took the first steps on the most magical journey. I'm so happy now, and I hope you all know that you can achieve anything you want to achieve.

It's difficult to believe in yourself, especially when you doubt your inner strength, but trust me when I tell you that you can do anything you set your mind to. It takes a lot of sacrifices, and it takes a lot of self-belief. But, once you believe you can do it, nothing can stop you. While part of it was luck, most of it was because I worked hard. I had a vision of what I wanted to achieve and where I wanted to end up, and that's what I had to keep thinking of when I had moments when I didn't think I could continue. If you focus on yourself, if you focus on your life, everything clse will fall into place

People will tell you that you're not going to be able to do it. People will tell you that you're not worthy as a person because of things you've gone through, or things you've done, and people will try to make you believe that you are a failure. But, let me tell you something that took me years to learn: you must not let anyone else define who you are and what you are capable of achieving.

People will always find a way to tear you down to make themselves feel better, but being brave is about standing up and saying no when someone tries to tell you that you're not capable of making your dreams come true. You are. It doesn't matter where you've come from, or what you've been through. You can always fight for your dreams. If the world turns its back on you, fight harder. I know first-hand that nothing worth having comes easy. But, when you achieve the impossible, you learn who you really are. That's when your life will change for the better. Forever. Thank you."

As I finish my speech, everyone stands and applauds me. I look around the room, and I feel so grateful to have this opportunity. As I scan the room I make eye contact with one of the girls sitting in the second row. She looks familiar, but I can't pinpoint where I know her from. I head into the group to talk to the people who are patiently waiting for me. As I end a conversation with two girls, I'm approached by an older woman.

"Hi, Delilah. My name is Mary. My daughter, Emery, is a huge fan of yours. She's been battling depression and anxiety after being bullied at school. She recently graduated, and she's now looking at going to uni to be a teacher. Your music has been the one constant positive thing in her life. She always talks about how she listens to your songs when she has a bad day. She's been following you and looked to you as her inspiration to keep fighting. I just wanted to personally thank you. Without you and your music, I really don't think my daughter would have chosen to keep fighting."

A tear drops from Mary's eyes as she talks about her daughter and the struggles they have both faced. The impact of how people look up to me hits me, and it's such an honour. I hug Mary and try my best to comfort her.

"You don't have to thank me. It's an absolute honour to offer that kind of support to your daughter. It's the support and love from people like your daughter that keeps me going. I'm so glad to hear she's kept on fighting, and I'm so happy she's going on to uni. That's an amazing achievement."

Mary calls Emery over to me. I spend ten minutes talking to her, answering all her questions and chatting to her about her battle and her dreams. She tells me she met me in Boom Clap one day; that's when I remember meeting her. She was with her sister, who is also a fan of mine. They were really excited to meet me; in fact, if it wasn't for them, I would never have known that Dakota uploaded the first video of me singing. After talking to Emery, I take a photo with her and give her my email address. I ask her to keep in contact with me, and tell her that if she's ever in LA, I'd love to meet up.

After I've finished socialising with the group and Lesley, I head to lunch with my family and friends. We reflect on the talk and how amazing it was for everyone. They're so proud of me. We've all come so far and, for the first time, my family is united as one: stronger and happier than ever. Little do I know that everything is about to come crashing down.

CHAPTER EIGHTEEN
SAYING GOODBYE

It's Thursday morning, three days after my talk at Bloomfield Axis. I'm at Cam's house, going through his things; we're trying to sort out what we're going to take and what we're going to leave behind. Anna walks into the room, and I notice her eyes are puffy. She looks terrible. She reluctantly hands me the phone, and I notice her hands are shaking.

"Hello?"

"Delilah, it's me," my mum says. "I tried calling you, but your phone is off. I can't believe I'm even saying this, but I need you to meet me at the hospital. Uncle Derek ... uncle Derek had a heart attack. The doctor has informed us that he's not going to survive. We need to say goodbye."

The minute I hear the words come out of my mum's mouth, I drop the phone onto the floor. The back piece of the phone falls off and shatters, but Anna quickly picks it up. It's still working, so she talks to my mum. Cam grabs me as I fall to the floor. He keeps asking me what's wrong, but I can't speak. I just start screaming and crying. *This can't be happening. No! This cannot be happening!*

Ten minutes later I'm still in Cam's arms, crying uncontrollably. I can't get the words out of my mouth every time Cam asks me what is wrong. So, after nodding my head when Anna asks, she lets him know what's happened. He tightens his grip around me as Anna tells him the news. He kisses my forehead and holds me closer to his chest. When I'm feeling strong enough, Cam helps me to stand up. I walk to Anna's car in silence with Cam closely behind me. We get into the back seat of the car, and Anna begins to drive to the hospital. Both her and Cam try to talk to me, but all I hear is muffled voices. I'm in shock, and I have no idea how to process what I've been told. I've never thought about facing the world without my uncle in it. I mean, I know death is a part of life, but I really can't imagine the world without him. He's so selfless. He's caring, loyal, and loving. Without him, I certainly wouldn't be where I am today. He has been a huge part of my upbringing, and to lose him this close to the wedding, heck to lose him at all, is breaking me in the worst way.

When we get to the hospital, I jump out of the car and run as fast as I can.

"Dclilah. Wait, please!" Cam yells at me.

I just keep running. I run straight through the waiting room, and straight past my family, who are sitting outside my uncle's room. I push the door open and walk into the room. I'm immediately swamped by memories of both mine and Cam's time in hospital. I feel shivers go down my spine when I hear all the machines beeping. I look towards the bed and, to my utter shock, my uncle is awake.

"What? Mum ... Mum said I had to come and say goodbye?"

Tears stream down my face. I walk over to my uncle, who looks weak. I sit down next to him and hold his hands.

"I had a heart attack. I don't know how it happened, but I'm back."

I continue to cry, putting my head down on the bed. My uncle tries his best to comfort me.

"I'm not going anywhere, I promise."

"Good. I don't want to face this world without you. I love you."

"I love you too, kiddo."

~

I open my eyes to see people running around the room. The machines are beeping, and a nurse is gently picking me up out of the chair.

"Delilah, honey I'm sorry. You need to wait outside."

Before I can open my mouth to ask what's wrong, she's opening the door for me.

"What the hell?" I say as I spot my mum and Anna.

"Delilah, come here sweetheart."

"No, mum. Why did I just get kicked out?"

"He's gone into cardiac arrest. His heart isn't able to keep up. The heart attack, it ... it's ... Delilah, he's not going to make it. Aunty Kelly and the boys have decided to take him off the life support machine."

I push my mum off me.

"No! You're lying! I was just talking to him. He was awake, and he was talking to me. He can't be gone."

"Delilah, I'm so sorry. You fell asleep and then he did too. He was fine for the first hour, but in the second hour he took a turn for the worst. I asked the doctors to leave you. You needed to be with him, but there's nothing they can do. The nurse has told us that when they're ready, we will be able to say goodbye."

Cam appears at the end of the hallway with the rest of my siblings. They slowly approach us. Dakota tries to hug me, but being around everyone is too overwhelming. I push past everyone and walk back towards the entrance of the hospital. I walk through the sliding doors and find a quiet spot; I stand and pray for a miracle with every bit of my being. The more I stand there and think, the worse it gets. I finally allow myself to believe that this is the end of my uncle's life. I feel pain that I've never felt before, and it's taking over my whole body. I'm in utter shock, and I have no idea how to process the fact that in a few minutes I'm going to have to go back into the hospital room and say goodbye to my hero.

I close my eyes and take some deep breaths until I feel brave enough to face the inevitable. I slowly open my eyes and, when I can muster up the strength, I walk back inside and head to my uncle's room. I notice my mum isn't sitting with the rest of my family. I approach my siblings, Cam and Anna, and sit next to Dakota.

"Where's mum?" I whisper to her.

"She's saying goodbye. We've all said our goodbyes. You're the last one. Aunt Kelly, Cooper and Thomas went to get a coffee, but when they get back, mum wants to give them time to themselves."

I squeeze Dakota's hand, unable to find any words. I just continue to take deep breaths as I wait for my mum to come out of the room.

Another five minutes go by before my mum slowly opens the door and looks at me.

"It's your turn, honey. Take all the time you need."

Her eyes are red and puffy, and she looks exhausted. I get up from my seat and open the door. I look at my uncle's near-lifeless body. I don't know what to say, and part of me doesn't want to say goodbye, but I know that if I don't take this chance now, I'll live to regret it forever.

I grab his cold hands. I know that even though he's on life support, he's all but gone. I begin to talk to him anyway.

"I didn't think this day would ever come, especially this early. A few hours ago, you promised me you weren't going anywhere. Now you're leaving this world behind. I don't know what to say, or where to begin. Thank you. Thank you for loving me, and accepting me, and for being the father I needed when my real dad couldn't be there for me. You gave up so much of your life for me, and for my siblings. You never gave up on me, even when I gave up on myself. I know how lucky I am to have Hadi and Rosie as my best friends, but you were my best friend too. I was more than your niece, and you were more than my uncle. I promise to keep going for you, because I know that's what you'd do for me. I know that's what you'd want me to do. I'll love you forever, and I'll never forget you. Goodbye, uncle Derek. I'll see you in another life."

I get up from the chair and kiss his forehead before walking to the door. As I open it, I spot my aunt Kelly and my two cousins. My aunt reaches for my hand and stops me.

"Delilah, I know this will be as hard for you as it is for all of us, and I know this is asking a lot, but I spoke to the boys and we want you with us when we turn the life support machine off."

I look at my cousins who offer me comforting smiles. I'm barely coping with this tremendous loss,

283

so I can only imagine how horrible it must be for the three of them.

At first I want to say no, but I think of all the things my uncle did for me, and I know this is the least I can do for him, his wife and his two children. I nod at them before following them back into the room. We stand there and say one final goodbye before the doctor enters the room. When we're ready, my aunt gives the final nod. Within a matter of moments, the machine stops beeping and everything goes quiet.

~

Eight days after my uncle's passing, my family and my uncle's friends and work colleagues arrive at his funeral, ready to say one final goodbye. During the week, my aunt asked me to prepare a speech. Since my uncle and I were so close, she thought it would only be fitting if I say something on the day we bury him. I reluctantly agreed, and over the last eight days, I've struggled to sum up my memories of him.

As the funeral starts, we listen to his favourite songs as his coffin is brought into the room. I take my seat next to my two cousins and my aunt. When it's time, my aunt introduces me, and I stand in front of the large gathering of people. I look around the room and take in everyone's faces. We all look the same: lost for words as we grieve for someone who was taken far too soon. I clear my throat then begin to read from my piece of paper.

"I can't tell you how many times I've tried to write something down, how many pieces of paper I've been through, or how many tears I've shed while trying to sum my uncle up. The truth is, I don't think you *can* sum him up, because he was such an incredible person. We were all so blessed to have known such a strong, fearless and loving person. It's never an easy thing to say goodbye to someone you love, and maybe I, like many of you here today, will never get over the loss of him. But I certainly know that I'm a better person because of him. I am brave, I am strong, and I am living my dreams because of him. Without his love and encouragement, I'd still be trying to decide if I am worthy of capturing my dreams.

My uncle taught me so much, but the thing he tried his best to teach me was to forgive those who hurt you, love everyone with every ounce of your being, and open yourself up to the wonderful things that this world has to offer. And that's what I'll remember when I think of him. I'll remember his infectious smile and his big heart. He loved every person who he came across. I ask of all of you to keep him alive through the memories you share of him, and to keep him in your heart for as long as you live. He will be alive in our hearts, and for that we should be forever grateful. Rest in peace, uncle Derek. I'll never forget you, and I'll love you with every single beat of my heart until I take my final breath. Fly away, sweet angel. Fly away and be free."

After I finish my speech, I sit back down and squeeze my aunt's hand. She smiles at me and we continue to listen to my mum and my aunt Debbie talking about their brother. We then listen to a few more speeches before it's time to bury him. Each member of my family drops a red rose on his coffin before it's lowered into the ground. The crowd of people begin to filter out to the carpark, and soon it's just me standing there. I look down at his grave and blow him a kiss. It takes every ounce of strength to walk away from him but, when I do, I make a decision to leave Perth. I don't care about getting married, and I don't care about facing all this pain anymore. I end up doing the only thing I know what to do when I get scared, I run away.

~

I stand in the kitchen of the LA villa and stare at the empty wine, vodka and whisky bottles that line the breakfast bar. I have a headache from the alcohol I consumed yesterday, but I try to distract myself by looking at the calendar that's hanging on the wall. It's now five days after the funeral and two weeks before the wedding, which feels like the most pointless thing. I focus my attention back on the view of LA as I try to clear my mind.

After the funeral, I began to go through different stages of grief, kicking off with denial. I knew my uncle was gone, and I had obviously said goodbye. But, as the days began to fade away after his death, I noticed I no longer wanted to believe he was gone. I kept calling him and leaving messages on his voicemail. I was begging him to call me back, but of course he didn't. Everything felt like it was such an effort, but at the same time, life felt meaningless and paralysing.

When the denial started to wear off, I became angry. I was angry at the world for taking him before we were ready to lose him. I was angry at myself because I felt like I needed to spend more time with him, or tell him that I loved him more. I tried to remind myself that I had done all of that, but it didn't make any difference.

After being angry, I started bargaining. I desperately tried everything to convince myself that this was all just a nightmare. I even prayed and asked to trade places. In a selfish way, I didn't want to face life without my uncle. Of course, that didn't work either, so I became depressed.

I felt the worst feelings I'd ever encountered, and I lost all my will to do anything. I couldn't sleep, I couldn't eat, and I couldn't concentrate on anything. I couldn't even talk to Cam. I completely shut him out. I refused to talk to him, and I refused to answer any calls from my family and friends back in Perth. I thought that after going through these four stages, I'd be able to accept what happened and make peace with everything. But, as time went on, I just couldn't do that.

I decide to take a nap, although I can't fall asleep. I hear Cam come home from the shops and I can faintly hear him talking to someone. I get up from the bed, put my ear close to the door and listen to his conversation.

"I'm worried about her, mum. She's drinking all day and night. She's not going to the meetings she sets up with Taylor, and she's pushing me away. When she's not drinking, she's sleeping. She slept for two days straight, mum. I don't know what to do anymore. I know she's grieving, but everything I do seems to make things worse. I'm the one person who's here for her. I left my life behind in Perth to be here with her, and I don't regret that for a second, but what am I meant to do when she doesn't even look at me, let alone talk to me? The wedding is fast approaching and, at this point, I don't even know if that's going ahead anymore."

I creep through the door and walk down the driveway. I hear Cam open the window.

"Delilah? Where are you going?"

I shrug my shoulders and, without thinking, I start running. My body is screaming at me to stop as the rain begins to fall, but I ignore it. I just keep going. Eventually, I realise I have no idea where I am. I stop in the middle of a street, sit on the kerb and pull my phone out. I call Cam and, fifteen minutes later, I see his car come around the corner. I hop into the passenger side and avoid looking at him. He drives back to the villa in silence. When we reach the front door, Cam slams it shut behind him.

"I know you're grieving, I know you feel lost, and I know you're hurt, but dammit Delilah, I'm the one person you should feel comfortable with. You won't talk to me, let alone cry with me. I know I wasn't related to him, but I was close to him too. I'm grieving just as much as you are."

"This isn't a pissing competition, Cam. He was *my* uncle. He was like my father, and now he's gone. What do you want me to say? I can't express how I'm feeling. I feel dead inside. I know I shouldn't be drinking, especially after what happened last time I was hurt and I tried to numb it with alcohol. But it's all I can do right now. I'm not strong enough to find the words I need to voice how I feel. He was everything to me, and now I'll never see him again."

Cam lowers his voice.

"Running away from your problems won't make them go away."

"I'm not running, Cam. I'm grieving. This is worse than when we broke up. My whole world has crumbled around me, and I have no idea how to move forward now. I'm out of answers, I don't know how to come back from this."

I walk back to the room, slam the door, and put my head in my hands. The door opens slowly and

Cam sits next to me on the bed. He gently rubs my back before speaking.

"I'm sorry. I know you're hurting, and I know you're scared, but you need to focus on your music. I know the timing is shit, but it'll help you get through this."

"I know, but I don't care anymore. It doesn't seem to matter now. Without him here, nothing seems worth any effort, especially my career."

"He wouldn't want you to end your career like this, Delilah. He fought so hard with you to make all of this happen. He wouldn't want you to throw it all away. I know you feel lost, but he was there for you for 22 years. He loved you like you were his own. If you no longer want to do this for you, then do it for him. He wanted nothing more than for you to succeed. He was so proud of you and, no matter what happens from here on out, he'll be with you."

I start to cry as Cam talks to me but, for the first time in weeks, I don't feel the pain in my tears that I've felt since uncle Derek passed away. Cam continues to talk as he gets a tissue for me.

"When I spoke to him about surprising you here, he was on board with the idea right from the start. I wrote you a letter, and it motivated him to do the same. Before we left LA, he gave it to me. He told me to do what I had asked of him: to give it to you when the time was right. I think you need this more than anything, and I think the timing is right. I love you, Delilah. I may not feel the same level of grief, but I'm here for you. We're going to get through this together, and I'm not going anywhere."

Cam hands me an envelope, kisses my forehead and leaves me alone. I rip the envelope open and take out a piece of paper. The minute I see my uncle's handwriting, I hug it to my chest. It makes me feel close to him and, while I'm scared to read what he's written, I know it'll help ease my pain.

"Delilah,

I'm not planning on dying anytime soon, but should something happen to me, I want to make sure you have this letter. I know you will struggle to deal with another loss in your life. I hope this letter helps you cope should my time come to an end.

You are the kindest person I've ever known. You have a heart of gold, and you have more talent than anyone I've ever known. I hope you know just how proud I am of you and what you've achieved. I always knew you were destined for something phenomenal, and that's what we've created. If I die, I want you to continue with your music career. It is what you were born to do, and you must fight for it with every single ounce of your soul. Don't let this journey go to waste. You've worked so hard, so please don't give up.

I know you always wanted your father growing up, and I know I never took his place, but I want to thank you for letting me be a father figure to you. I never looked at you as my niece, you were always so much more, and you will forever hold a special place in my heart. I am so proud of you for helping your father get back to a better place. I know he will never leave you again, but I know you still fear that he will. Make sure you work with him to help him stay in our family, because it's where he belongs. You are the light of my life, and no matter where you go, or what you do, I will always be with you. I'll be your guardian angel, and although I won't physically be there, you can always talk to me, and I promise you I will listen.

I love you, my superstar.

Uncle Derek."

After reading the letter, I finally make peace with the fact that he is gone for good. As hard as it is, I accept that he is in a better place. It takes all my strength but, when I'm ready, I walk back out to Cam and hug him.

"Let's go home and get married," I say as he hugs me back.

Chapter Nineteen
The End of the Beginning

After a long trip back to Perth, Cam and I arrive to our families waiting for us. Although we're all still trying to come to terms with the loss of a family member, we decide to honour him at the wedding. I know he wouldn't want me to cancel what's meant to be the happiest day of my life.

Cam and I spend the next few days finalising the details of our wedding. When everything is sorted, we go for a walk and sit under a tree. I look at the ring on my finger. I still can't believe how quickly we're getting married, but it feels right.

"I know it's a touchy subject, but what are you going to do about walking down the aisle? Are you going to ask your dad? Or do you just want to walk down by yourself? We should probably get it sorted since the wedding is coming up."

I hadn't allowed myself time to think about what I'm going to do. I've been avoiding these questions, but I know that I must face them now. Otherwise, I never will.

"I'm going to ask my dad. I thought about not having anyone do it, because it didn't feel right knowing my uncle can't be there to do it. But, I know he would want me to embrace this day, and asking my dad is the right thing to do."

"That sounds good to me. Your uncle will be there in spirit, you know that, right?"

"Yeah, I know."

Cam and I spend another hour under the tree before he drops me off at my mum's house. When we pull into the driveway, I notice an unfamiliar car in the driveway.

"Whose car is that?" Cam asks.

I shrug my shoulders and unbuckle my seat belt.

"I have no idea. I'll see you tomorrow?"

"Yep. I love you."

"I love you, too."

I get out of his car and wave at him as he backs out of the driveway. As he pulls away from the house, I walk towards the front door. I can hear laughter filtering through the house. I head down the hallway until I reach the kitchen, where I spot my dad.

"Hey kiddo … are you okay?"

I feel the colour drain from my face and my body suddenly tenses up. "Yeah, sorry. Uncle Derek used to call me kiddo. I haven't been called that since he …"

"I'm so sorry. How are you holding up?"

"You don't have to apologise. I'm okay. Some days are better than others, but I'm just taking each day as it comes."

My dad releases me and, after hugging my mum and Evan, I sit down with them.

My dad has been amazing ever since we lost my uncle. He has stayed in our guest room, and cooked breakfast, lunch and dinner. He's done anything he could to make this whole thing a little bit easier for us. When I ran away to LA, he comforted my mum and helped her get through the long days that followed. He's been a pillar of strength for all of us when we didn't know how to keep moving forward, and I'm very grateful for that. Something snaps me out of my thoughts, and I look quickly between my parents and my stepdad.

"Who's pregnant?" I ask sarcastically.

The room goes quiet and my mum's cheeks flush with pink. She clears her throat and Evan gently grabs her hands. After a comforting smile from him and a gentle nod from my dad, she looks at me.

"We didn't plan this, to be honest. I didn't think it would happen … but I'm pregnant."

I blink a few times then hop off my bar stool at the breakfast bar.

"That's amazing, mum. Congratulations! I'm really happy for you, and you too, Evan."

"Other than your dad, you're the only person who knows about our exciting news. We know you're preparing for your wedding, but your mum and I have talked about it, and we want to know if you'll be the godmother?"

"Oh my gosh! Yes, I would be honoured. Do you know who you want as the godfather?"

"That would be me," my dad says.

I'm stunned by his response. I knew he was forming a special bond with my mum and Evan, but I never thought they'd get to such a comfortable place where they'd ask him to be the godfather of their child. I smile at my dad, who is beaming with pride.

"I think you're the perfect choice, dad."

I kiss his cheek before sitting back down.

After drinking my cup of tea, I look over at my dad.

"Hey dad, there's … there's something I want to ask you. I've been avoiding coming to terms with uncle Derek not being at my wedding, but I have to accept it. I don't want you to feel like this is a second-best offer, but if you're happy to do it, I'd really love it if you could walk me down the aisle?"

"Honey, I know how much you wish your uncle was here. I'm not upset that you asked him first because you two shared an indescribable bond, and nothing will replace that. But I'd be honoured to be by your side. Let's do it for uncle Derek. He'll still be there with you, nothing will change that."

I hand him a tissue before drying my own eyes off. He gets up from his bar stool and tightly hugs me before he whispers, "I love you, and I'm so proud of you."

My dad tells us about his new girlfriend, who he met in his support group, and we discuss the wedding. This day has been full of surprises, but my family is moving onto the next chapter of our lives. For the first time in a long time, I feel happy.

~

The days come and go so fast and, before I know it, my wedding day has arrived. I wake up at 6:00 a.m. to my phone buzzing. I grab it off my bedside table and see I've received a text from Cam.

Good morning Miss Walker. I just got back from my morning run. I had to try to calm myself down, I've never been this excited before! Today's the day you become my wife. I can't wait to see you. See you soon (almost) Mrs Collins. I love you.

I smile at the screen and re-read Cam's message before replying.

It's already the happiest day of my life. I can't wait to become Mrs Collins. I love you, Mr Collins.

I hit send, roll out of bed, and quickly shower before heading downstairs. My mum and sisters are already up when I walk into the kitchen. The sweet smells of tea, coffee, orange juice, berries and pancakes fill the air.

"Good morning, sunshine!" Dakota says with a bright smile when she spots me walking in.

"Good morning."

I place a pancake on my plate, put some fresh berries on top, fill my mug with coffee and add a dash of milk.

"How do you feel?"

"I'm good. I'm excited. I just hope the rain holds off."

I look out of the window at the thick, grey clouds. I know the rain is threatening to fall at any moment. I still have to get ready, so I hope it passes before we head to the church.

After breakfast, my father, Hadi, Rosie, Anna, Nia, the makeup artists, and hairdressers arrive. We spend the next few hours listening to music and chatting away as we get ready. When our hair and makeup is done, my bridesmaids get changed. The girls walk into the lounge room, and I'm blown away by how stunning they look in their lace, lilac dresses. The curled hair and flawless makeup compliments each girl, but what makes me the happiest is how happy they look. I'm so excited to marry the man of my dreams, and having these five beautiful girls by my side makes me even more excited.

After approving the final looks, my mum, Anna and I head to the guest room down the hall. They help me get into my sweetheart-neckline, lace, mermaid dress. When I'm ready, I turn around to face my mum and Anna, and see they are both holding back tears. My mum calls my dad to the room.

"You look ... beautiful, Delilah," my dad proudly says.

After taking photos with my bridal party, my parents, and Anna, we head outside; two limousines are waiting for us. My mum, Anna and my bridal party get into the first limo, and my dad and I get into the second one and head towards the church. We arrive and my dad helps me out of the car. I gently place my right arm through his left arm, and we walk towards the entrance of the church.

"The clouds have parted, the rain has stopped, and there's a rainbow right above us. I think your uncle is here."

I look up at the sky and smile.

"I think you're right."

Cam starts crying when he sees me, which makes me cry too. When we reach him, he shakes my dad's hand. I kiss my dad's cheek, and then I take Cam's hand.

"You look stunning."

"And you look very handsome."

When we read the vows, there isn't a dry eye anywhere. Cam goes first.

"Destiny is a funny thing. Growing up, you don't believe in it, but then you meet your soul mate, and everything becomes clear. You realise just how real destiny is. Delilah, we've been destined for this day all our lives. Nothing makes me as happy as you do. You're fearless, strong, and talented. You're loving, selfless, and fiercely loyal. Delilah, I promise I'll support you through your worst days and your best days, and I'll love you through them too. To me, you are perfect. You're the first thing I think about when I wake up, and you're the last thing I think about before I go to sleep. You're my favourite hello, and my worst goodbye. It's you, Delilah. It's always been you. Seeing you smile makes me the happiest man in the world. As long as I'm breathing, you'll never be alone. I promise you'll never question if you're good enough, beautiful enough, or talented enough. You'll never question if you are wanted, and you'll never question if you are loved. You are my life, my heart, and all the stars in my sky. I can't wait to spend the rest of my life loving you as my best friend and my wife. I love you, more than you'll ever know."

I'm blown away. Hearing all his beautiful words has made me fall in love with him all over again. And now, it's my turn to express how I feel.

"Love is far from predictable but, with you, it's magical. I've never felt so safe and loved, and I've never felt as happy as I am when I'm with you. I love you more than words can ever express. When you meet *the one*, they say you know. Well, Cam, I think I knew when I was 7, even though I couldn't stand the sight of you. I knew when we were 16 and we went on our first date. And now, at 22, when you've helped me get through the toughest time of my life. I lost someone I was exceptionally close to, and you never gave up on me, even when I'd given up on myself. You're the best thing that has ever happened to me, and I'm a better person because of you. The look in your eyes when you look at me makes my heart skip a beat, and I still get butterflies when I'm around you. Knowing I get to stand by your side as your wife makes me feel so content, and I'm thankful to be able to love you. I'm the luckiest girl in the world because you love me, and I get the privilege of loving you wholeheartedly for the rest of our lives. I love you."

Cam wipes tears from his eyes, along with our guests. Soon after saying our vows, the priest announces us as Mr and Mrs Collins.

After more photos, Cam and I hop into our limo and head to my uncle's house, where we're having our reception. At first, I loved the idea, but after my uncle passed away I didn't want to be around the place. It felt too raw, too soon, but after talking to Cam I agreed to having it there. In a way, it's our way of being close to my uncle. This is a day I desperately wanted to share with him.

"You know, nothing feels really different ... except one thing that I didn't think was possible."

I look at Cam, "What?"

"I love you more. I didn't think it was possible for my love to get any stronger, but it has. I'm the happiest I've ever been."

The whole day and night is extraordinary and, to my surprise, I feel a sense of closeness to my uncle. There are tables covered in confetti and flowers. Champagne glasses and fairy lights are everywhere, and there are pictures of Cam and me on display. Our family and friends have been dancing and singing ever since we got to the house, and Cam and I were touched when Marc and Dakota said a few words for us.

The smells of burning candles, perfume, cologne, food and drinks fade away as I step outside and look up to the sky. The rain has been pouring all night but, when I step out into the fresh air, the clouds part and the stars begin to shine. I notice one bright star right above me, and I know it's my uncle. Suddenly, out of nowhere, a butterfly flies in front of me. I put my hand out and it rests in my palm, flaps its colourful wings, then flies off. Not only did he bless my life when he was alive, but now he's blessing my life by being my guardian angel. For the first time since his death I feel like I'm going to be okay.

One year later...

Cam and I have spent the most magical day at the beach in Hawaii. We didn't end up having a honeymoon because we moved to LA straight after the wedding, so we decided to take some time off to celebrate Christmas, New Year, and our one-year wedding anniversary.

We've been in tropical paradise for two days now: exploring the beautiful island, snorkelling with the marine life and walking along the warm white sand.

After a quick swim in the crystal-clear water, Cam and I head back to our hotel. After unlocking the door and walking into the room, I hear whispers floating through the air. I walk further into the room, and spot my family standing in the lounge room. My mum is standing next to Evan, who is holding my giggling baby sister Delanie in his arms. My brothers and sisters are standing next to Evan, and they're all smiling back at me.

Since moving to LA, Cam and I haven't been able to see our loved ones as much as we'd like. In the first six months, I toured around the world. I finished my tour in Australia, so I spent a week in Perth before going back to LA. For the last six months I've been busy working on my second album, so thankfully I've had a fairly good distraction from the homesickness that soon began to consume me. During that time, Cam's family and some of our friends flew over to see us. My siblings have been over a few times in the last year, but I haven't seen my mum in over six months. She was heavily pregnant with Lani when I toured, and after that she couldn't fly, so we had to make do with emailing and FaceTiming. I'm over the moon to be able to hug my mum in person and hold my baby sister in my arms.

"What are you guys doing here?" I say to my mum.

She smiles at Cam before looking back at me to answer my question.

"Your husband called us after the two of you planned this trip. He wanted to surprise you, and so did we. We decided to join you here to celebrate all the wonderful things that have been going on."

~

After my family check into their rooms, we head down to the beach. My mum and sisters didn't want to wait until tomorrow to see just how breathtaking it is, so we spend a few hours swimming and walking along the sand before heading to dinner.

Cam has made a booking at an outdoor restaurant; when we arrive, I spot my dad and Cam's family. We enjoy our dinner while catching up with each other. We talk about how quickly the last year has gone, and we suggest things to do over the next five days. We talk about what we can do for Christmas and New Year. We talk about taking a family holiday at the same time every year, which everyone excitedly agrees to. As everyone continues to chat, I look up at the night sky and watch the stars.

Despite all the wonderful things that are happening around me, I can't seem to stop telling myself that my uncle should be here to enjoy these moments with us. I know he's where he's meant to be now, but it's time like this that I wish he were still here. I have to remind myself how lucky I am. Cam and I are united as one, and our families have done the same thing. We're surrounded by so much love, and I realise something very important: life is difficult, especially when an unexpected death comes your way, but family and love will get you through the toughest days. That is something I will be thankful for, and that's certainly what I am: *thankful*.

~

Our time in Hawaii is perfect. We fill our days with swimming, snorkelling, exploring, and relaxing. Before we know it, New Year's Eve has arrived. Cam and I spend the day relaxing at the spa before joining our families for dinner. After eating, we head to the hill that looks over the beach. We join the crowds to celebrate the end of one year and the beginning of another. We find a spot on the hill and sit down. Darci and Nia run around with the other teenagers, my siblings and Cam's brothers chat away with our dads, and my mum and Anna play with Lani. I look at Cam and smile, thinking about how much he has given up to be with me. Just like me, Cam went through a period where he was homesick, and he found it difficult to find a job but, with time, we both settled into our new lives. Now, he's working as a sports journalist, and we're living in our own home in the Hollywood Hills.

I turn my attention back to my family. My mum and Evan are happier than ever. She still runs the yoga studio with aunt Debbie, but she spends most of her days at home with Evan as they raise Lani, who's the happiest baby I've ever seen. My dad is still with his girlfriend, and he's been working on himself. He's got a new house, and he's healthier than ever. He's close to my mum and Evan; he often babysits Lani, and he's continuing to work on his relationships with my siblings. Dakota is still modelling, and her career is booming. She still splits her time between America and Australia, and she has been enjoying time being single after her and James decided to break up. At first, she was devastated, but with time she learnt to live her life for her and now she's happier than ever. Darci recently graduated from high school, and she has decided to take a gap year to travel around Europe with Nia and two of their other friends. Dylan started his own real estate company, and he is learning to balance his time between work, his social life, and seeing his girlfriend. Declan still lives with Dylan, he's nearly completed his sports science degree, and he still loves playing soccer. William still works at his insurance agency, Anna's still a primary school teacher, and Gavin and Lucas still have an incredibly busy physiotherapy business; in fact, they're talking about expanding and opening more studios. Everyone is on a path that's leading them to success and happiness, and it brings such joy to my life to be surrounded by such amazing people.

As the New Year approaches, I rest my head on Cam's shoulder as fireworks light up the sky. Everyone is smiling, laughing, and enjoying this moment. We hug as the New Year begins, and we all beam with happiness. We're living our dreams, we're happy and, most importantly, we have each other: that is priceless. This is what I've always dreamed of, and I know things can only get better from here. I cannot wait to see what the future has in store for us.

ACKNOWLEDGEMENTS

To the most important people in my life: my parent, brothers and grandparents, thank you for supporting me throughout this whole process. I love you all more than you'll ever know.

To Georgina Gregory, my amazing editor! I couldn't have done this without you. This novel is just as much yours as it is mine. Thank you for pushing me to be the best author I can be.

To Dani, from Orlando Media. You never cease to surprise me with your talent. Thank you for creating a cover from a million different ideas.

To Karen, thank you for helping me achieve the goals I set for myself and for encouraging me to keep going when I desperately wanted to quit. I'm releasing the novel because of you.

To my friends, in particular Dani, Jess, Bobbi, and Rhi for reading this book before I let it out into the world. Your excitement for the second instalment made all the long nights of writing and editing worth it. You're the best friends I could ever ask for.

To Dr. Singh and Talya, who both went above and beyond their duty of care to continue to help me get through the darkest days of my life. Your reassurance and constant care for me has never gone unnoticed, thank you for saving my life.

And finally, to my guardian angel, Rolly. This if for you. I miss you and think of you every single day. I hope you're proud.

AUTHOR'S NOTE

As quickly as Delilah's journey started, it has now come to an end. Delilah, her journey and all of those who surround her have proudly been created by me, and in saying that, they have all become a part of my life and I'm truly sad to see this journey end.

I am proud of where this story not only took Delilah, but also where it took me. From writing these two novels I have opened myself up to a world that has changed my life forever.

I want to take the time to thank all of you, the reviewers and the readers, who took time out of your day to read about Delilah and her crazy journey. Because of you, I am able to live my dreams and I'll never be able to thank you enough for that. I have so much love for you. Keep reading and supporting your favourite authors, it's you beautiful people that make all of this worth it. Without you, authors are nothing.

This hasn't just been a journey for all of the characters you've met throughout two novels, but it's been a journey for me, too. I'm learning more about myself and the joy that is writing, and I cannot wait to continue to share my stories with the world.

Here's to the next chapter! Happy reading and much love.

THE KAI EARDLEY FUND

Kai, a 20-year-old East Fremantle boy with a lot to live for, ended his life in July 2016 after struggling with anxiety and depression. Kai's suicide changed his family's lives forever. He was studying at Notre Dame, and struggling with the demands of growing up. The family's mission is to create a positive change for the mental health of the youth of today. The Fremantle Foundation allows the Eardley family to effectively give back to the local community and to be involved with how funds raised are disbursed.

THE MISSION:

Out of tragedy, comes an opportunity for change. The aim of The Kai Eardley Fund is to create positive change for the mental health of our youth and to honour the life of Kai Eardley.

Suicide is now the biggest killer of men aged between 19 and 45. Twelve men are lost to suicide every day. Our hope is to reduce this number. Having lost Kai, we will always wonder what we could have done differently and our only conclusion is that there is little else we could have done in July last year when Kai reached crisis point. We wish there had been some early intervention available before he reached that point of no return.

I (Claire - Kai's mum) believe a peer-based program available to young men, which helps to erase the tough macho stigma associated with our Australian male culture, and provides them with some skills to navigate mental illness and crises they will inevitably

CPSIA information can be obtained
at www.ICGtesting.com
Printed in the USA
BVHW04s1639170418
513519BV00024B/39/P

9 780648 249702

About Meagan Dux

Meagan Dux is a twenty-something author from Australia. She graduated from Murdoch University with a Bachelor of Arts degree, where she majored in Theatre and Drama in 2017. During her time at university, Meagan was an actor and stage manager. When not writing novels or working on future projects, Meagan can often be found drinking copious amounts of coffee, reading, writing, taking photos of the sunset, and spending time with her beloved Labrador, Marley. She resides in Western Australia.

Meagan loves to connect with her readers. You can connect with her via her social media channels:
Facebook: www.facebook.com/authormeagandux
Instagram: www.instagram.com/authormeagandux
Twitter: www.twitter.com/meagandux
Snapchat: authormeagandux

Be sure to stop by her website for extra content:
www.meagandux.com

endure in life, is an important piece of education that is not available in our education curriculum today.

We know that young girls also take their lives and we have not forgotten them. As this Foundation grows, and we roll out the suicide prevention program in WA, we intend to expand our work to address the gaps in the education of girls in this area. The more support we get, the more boys and girls we can support.

MEAGAN'S MISSION:

Meagan has now joined forces with *The Kai Eardley Fund* in a bid to raise money for their amazing cause. After Meagan nearly lost her life to depression she's determined to help other people who are struggling.

If you've read Meagan's novels, you can recommend them to your friends and they can capitalise on the book deal Meagan has available. For $40 you get both Delilah novels signed with free shipping, with *HALF* of each sale being donated to The KEF. This offer also extends to the first Delilah novel (*The Rise of Delilah*). More items will be added to Meagan's store to help raise much needed funds. These items are only available through Meagan's website (www.meagandux.com)

The Kai Eardley Fund has already raised close to $150,000, but we need to come together and fight for better mental health systems now before we lose even more beautiful people like Kai. Be sure to check out *The Kai Eardley Fund* at:

www.kai-fella.com.au